DOUG

A SHARP SPEAR POINT

Also by Douglas Owen

A Spear in Flight
Inside My Mind: Volume I

Edited by Douglas Owen and
Vivian DelChamps

A Sharp Spear Point
The Second Book of the Spear Series

Copyright © 2014 Douglas Owen
All rights reserved

978-0-9880864-8-7

Published by Science Fiction and Fantasy Publications

This is a work of fiction. Names, characters, places, and incidents are products of the author's imagination or are used fictitiously and are not to be construed as real. Any resemblance to actual events, locales, organizations, or persons, living or dead, is entirely coincidental.

A Sharp Spear Point / Douglas Owen – 1st Edition

0 9 8 7 6 5 4 3 2 1

This book is dedicated to my family and friends for not complaining about the amount of time I spend writing instead of paying attention to them. My wife, for putting up with the non-stop typing, my parents for understanding how distant I can be during the creation phase, my brother and his wife for their support while I squirrel away time. Last but not least, to my aunts, uncles, and cousins for being supportive in my efforts in getting the stories out that ping pong between my ears. I love you all and could not ask for better people in my life.

Prologue

The head rolled across the cold stone floor and stopped at the feet of a Hobs. The acolyte backed away, eyes wide with terror; the decapitated head stared up at nothing, the fire of torches reflecting in its lifeless gaze.

The Queen of the Hobs dropped the bloodied sword at the foot of the dais, climbed the steps to her throne and sat. The bones that made up her mighty perch were cold, but she didn't want the royal vizier to see her discomfort. She jutted her pointed chin and watched the entire court hold their breath. Over fifty Hobs lifted their heads to watch her as guards dragged the decapitated body of the senior Seer away.

"Leave it!" the queen growled when a guard bent to pick up the head. The Hobs guard straightened and followed the body to the end of the long hall. Their footfalls echoed in the silence of the vaulted chamber.

With narrowed eyes, the queen scanned the occupants of the hall and screamed, "Where is Danton?"

Her voice took a lifetime to dissipate. She imagined the blood chilling in the bodies of those present.

Another Seer, trained in the arcane arts and dressed in rough spun linen dyed a deep red, tentatively stepped forward. Sweat glistened on his forehead in the torchlight as his gnarled hand reached out in supplication to his queen.

"My Queen," he said, voice trembling. "Danton has left. He took many of our soldiers and marched to the surface with the goal to find more human children. He wanted to restock our kitchen lauders and build you a larger throne with the bones of our enemies."

She traced the arm of her seat of power, stroking a skull. One finger circled the eyehole, scratching the edge with a long, sharp nail. Dirt came away, revealing bleached white underneath. The queen swallowed, imagining the taste of the succulent meat of human children as she tore it off the bones.

"Human children," the queen murmured. "I could do with more children. I hunger, and their flesh will allow me to birth babies for our clan."

One of her offspring ran up to the side of the throne from the group behind her. She reached out and ruffled the infant's hair, her nose catching the scent of released gas.

"You foul creature," said the queen. "Get yourself back with the others." She watched the child run back to the others. A smile crept across her face, but disappeared in a flash.

The queen turned back to her court, the madness of loneliness overtaking her mind once again. She snapped, "So, where is he now? I see no new human children for me to feast upon. My babies hunger for flesh." Her gaze touched each of the faces before her and a smile lit the corner of her mouth. She looked back at the Seer. "When will he return?"

The Seer swallowed once again. She could see the man's mind racing as he thought of an answer. His hand smoothed the hairs on the back of his head.

Voice cracking under the strain, the Seer said, "The time of his return is not known to us, my Queen."

She straightened her back. The popping of vertebrae resonated in the vast hall. "Unknown? Unknown! You say his return is unknown?" Silence filled the hall.

A clearing throat broke through the silence. The shuffling of feet whispered as the group parted and cleared a space around the speaker. One lone acolyte, standing in the back, looked up. She motioned him forward. He dragged his feet toward the front of the group with part of a disembodied arm clutched in his hand. Blood dripped to the floor.

"What is this?" The queen leaned forward.

"I-I-It's part of a Spear, my Queen."

The Seer grabbed the arm of the acolyte, pulling him aside. "Where did you get that?"

The acolyte cowered under the grasp. "We killed one."

"How?"

"Several of us came—"

The Seer grabbed the forearm off the acolyte and hissed at him. The smaller Hobs slunk back, disappearing into the crowd of onlookers.

"My Queen," the Seer said, walking forward a few paces. "We can find out where Danton is."

"How?" asked the Queen.

The Seer reached into his robes and withdrew a long dagger with a curved blade. The edge glistened in the torch light, one edge sharp, and the other serrated.

The queen's guards moved forward, faces obscured by helmets, drew swords. They stopped on either side of the queen.

"Hold," the Queen said.

The Seer froze.

The queen pushed the two guards aside, and motioned for the Seer to continue.

The Seer pushed the point into the flesh of the severed arm, slicing through skin. He drew the blade down the line of the bone, stopping suddenly.

Removing the blade, the Seer dug his fingers into the laceration. His fingers searched. The Hobs frowned. The queen sat back, yawning.

"I have it!" The Seer held up a small silver disk. He kicked aside the remnants of the arm and looked about. "Bring a map!"

"Bring the map," called the queen. The glint of the disk piqued her interest.

The sound of feet slapping stone echoed through the hall as six Hobs brought a large, rolled up canvas. Once again the onlookers parted, allowing the Hobs' tapestry to be laid on the floor and unrolled. The enormous map of the Realm lay before their feet.

"My Queen," the Seer said. "Do you have anything of Danton's? Some hair ... blood perhaps?" His eyes went to the children behind, but he shook his head.

"You want one of my children?" the queen asked.

"No, they are not purely of his blood."

The queen could feel the weight of the charm she wore around her neck. A gift from him, Danton, many years ago. Inside, sealed with spells and incantations, three drops of his blood. One to represent him, one to represent her, and one to represent the brood of children they had reared over the last three hundred years. It was not a decision she wanted to make. It was the only thing besides the children that reminded her of him.

She tore the small vial off from around her neck and held it out. "Take it."

The Seer perspired as he accepted the vial from his queen. Over his shoulder he hissed, "Mortar."

An acolyte raced to the side and picked up a mortar and pestle. He ran back, his breath racing through a body not used to exercise.

Once the tools were in the Seer's possession, he took the disk and vial, placing them in the mortar. He rolled a piece of paper and lit it using a torch.

The queen's spine arched as the sound of the crystal vial shattering rang in the air. A tear rolled down her cheek. If they did not find him after this he would be lost to her forever.

Nodding with satisfaction, the Seer stood back and held a burning tallow over the mortar. His voice shook as he said ancient words of power. "Balla-tan-dra. Fro da'tand re. Har ma 'la pan re. Locota pa Danton. Fro da tand Danton. Kallara pa tand Danton!"

The fire licked at the mortar. The blood burst into flames.

A glint of silver sailed through the air and landed on the map. The Seer walked to where the disc landed and examined it. His mouth widened into a smile as he read the markings on the map.

"He is at the Town of Lands!" The smile on his face fell into despair. "The disc is split, my Queen. It's not a good omen. I fear for him."

The queen grabbed the sword from her guard and jumped from the podium. She moved fast for her age, and the Seer did not see the blow that took off his head.

"He will live!" the queen screamed and she climbed back to her throne, returning the blade and looked at her court. "I want Danton brought back to me alive!"

The thunder of running feet filled the audience chamber.

A SHARP SPEAR POINT

-1-

Bethany's feet pounded against the hard ground as she ran towards the city of Salman. Her horse had only survived six hours at a fast gallop, and she had been running now for two days. The grass grated against the bottom of her shoes as she made way across the plain, head down, a singular purpose in her mind. Warn the others.

They had told her it would be best for her to travel to Salman first, and bypass the Town of Land. She believed they were right.

All she wanted to do was stop and sleep. But she pushed on, slowing only to sip water or chew on dried beef. Her stomach ached and her throat burned. Cramping pain lanced up from her feet, and her legs screamed at her.

She remembered three days ago, when Shail told her to go.

"You'll return to Salman, and report to the Spears what we have seen. The horse will travel fast, but for less than a day. You will need to run." Shail stood in front of her, cloak pulled tightly around his shoulders to ward off the cold of the night.

Bethany stared at him, arms crossed. "I can fight just as well as the others."

"Yes, you can. But this is not about fighting. You are the lightest and will be able to get farther on the horse than the others.

You also run faster, and can cover the long distance in less time." He gripped her shoulder, but she shrugged it off.

"Bethany, you are the one who will save the Realm. If they don't know about this invasion ... We'll try to hold them with surprise attacks at night. They won't know how many or who is attacking them. But you have the most important job, bringing the Spears."

"Yes, Master Shail." Bethany stared at the ground.

"Look at me."

Bethany met Shail's gaze.

"You will bring a contingent of Spears back. We need to quell this invasion before it reaches the towns, or even one of the main cities."

Thomasyn finished strapping the last hastily made bow to a tree and angled it skyward. Twenty three of them pointed toward the Hobs encampment. Twine stretched out to twigs that held back the strings. Another rope reached between the grips.

"I can do this," he had said to Master Shail. "I'll string the bows together and run the horse. The arrows will take them by surprise, and I can disappear before they know what's happened."

Shail studied him. A smile lit the corner of his mouth, and he reached out, handing over the rope. "Only you would think of such a plan. Very well. We'll make some bows fast and use them to confuse the enemy."

Thomasy smiled, proud of his plan. A plan worthy of a Spear seasoned in battle. The sun was still an hour away, and he wanted to surprise the Hobs as they woke for their morning meal.

He waited.

Jon lay on his stomach with Masters Shail and Garion. The three watched as the sun crested the top of the forest and waited for life to show in the Hob's camp.

A SHARP SPEAR POINT

"I'm hungry," Jon said.

"You're always hungry," Shail said.

"We've been up for hours, and I haven't had anything but water." He smelled the grass in front of him, and wondered why it was so short. Reaching out a hand he plucked a blade and put it in his mouth.

"It's tuff grass. Not very good, but if you eat enough of it you'll fill your stomach." A chuckle escaped Master Garion's lips. "They say if you eat enough of it you'll grow hooves like the cows. They make water where they eat, you know."

Jon spat out the grass and wiped his tongue against his cloak. "You could have told me that sooner."

"And miss the look on your face? Never." Master Garion inched forward. "Thomasyn should be ready to—" Arrows filled the sky at the other end of the Hobs' camp. "He's done it."

"Do we attack now?" Jon's hand reached for his sword. He desperately wanted to kill the Hobs. Why should Thomasyn have all the fun? Why should he get the first kills? No, they would not count. He really didn't kill them, just shot arrows in the sky without aiming them. A coward's way of fighting.

"No, we have to wait for chaos to ensue. Let the arrows do their job and we can take out some of them. Just kill the stragglers and retreat. Attack and run, nothing more. Do not be a hero, Jon. This is a stalling tactic only." Shail's hand landed on Jon's shoulder, but the young Spear shrugged it off.

"Well, the sun is starting to rise," Jon looked toward the horizon. "When will these Hobs wake?"

"Look, over there," Garion pointed to one of the tents on the outskirts. "Some have fallen already, and they're waking the others to investigate."

The flap billowed aside, and a short, mottled green Hobs walked out and stretched. With one long scraggly finger he plugged the left side of his nose and blew. Mucus strewed on the ground and he did the same to the other side. He looked up as another creature opened the tent beside his.

"Ag, ya snorted out the crap again."

Ag leered at Ta and spat at the ground. "Most of the troops are getting up now. Danton wants to break camp early to start the march."

"We've run out of meat in this area. We'll have to take the town before they warn others. Surprise the Realm when we show up."

Ag scratched his groin. "Maybe we'll find some children." He smacked his lips.

"Ya, and soon it will be—" His eyes looked toward the forest as a shadow blanketed the sky.

"What ya looking at, Ta?" Ag turned to see what had his friend's attention, and an arrow pierced his eye.

The screams raced across the field. They pushed themselves to their feet to see Jon already running soundlessly toward the encampment, short spear in one hand and sword in the other.

"We'd better catch up to him, or he'll kill all of them before we get a chance to join the fight." Shail drew his sword and pulled a short spear off his back. He grunted as he stood. "I'm getting too old. One of these days I'll not be able to run."

"That kid will be the death of us. I think he has the blood lust in him." Garion pulled out his weapons as well.

"I would say let him go, but I'm sure there'll be more Hobs than even he can handle. Ready?"

They chased after Jon as fast as they could. The boy sliced with his sword. The edge opened the first straggling Hobs' throat. He threw his short spear. It took another Hobs in the belly. The creature fell backward grasping at the spear as blood gurgled from its mouth.

Thomasyn raced his horse toward the house. Twenty three bows danced on the rope behind them as the animal galloped. They raced toward the home ransacked by the Hobs army two days prior.

He reined in, and tied the horse to the hitch so it could eat and drink.

"One attack down," he said with a chuckle. "Serves Danton right for trying to invade our home."

"Gaaaaa!" A scream to his right.

Thomasyn drew his sword and spun. Blade held high, his body in a crouching stance, Thomasyn scanned for the Hobs. The creature ran toward him with its blade drawn. The glint of red smeared across the edge of the serrated weapon.

If the Hobs rushed, he would expose himself, so Thomasyn bided his time. The young man relied on his training, drilled into him since early childhood when he was a Spear in Flight.

He recognized an untrained fighter when he saw one. The creature held his arm too high, ran too erect, and did not protect his belly.

Thomasyn twisted. The creature brought down his sword but all it cut through was empty air. He wrenched his wrist, bringing the sword in front of him. The sharp edge of the blade sliced across his attacker's bare belly.

The Hobs folded and fell, intestines spilling out like a purple snake.

Thomasyn stayed crouched, eyes scanning the buildings around him, searching for a companion. Satisfied he was alone once again, he quickly wiped the blade before sheathing it and standing straight. "Did you have any friends here? Or did you just think they missed something after the last of us humans were eaten?" His foot prodded the creature, and a pungent odor made his nose wrinkle. "You stink, friend."

He searched the body, only to find a few small blades of bone and stones of different colors. He examined one, and noticed the face of a Hobs cut into it. "You have currency? The coins of the Hobs? Interesting."

Thomasyn put the rock coins into a pocket of his cloak, turned and started to coil the rope.

Shail called out to the others, "We're done here. Retreat and double around!"

"Just one more," Jon gasped as he spun. The sword whistled through the air and bit into the neck of another Hobs.

"Jon! Now!" Garion ran toward the hill, glancing over his shoulder. The main army gathered again, knowing they had been duped into running toward the forest. The support for the troops had stayed back. Armorers, smiths and cooks, only a few of them survived the sneak attack.

Hobs blood ran deep red, almost purple across the grass. The bodies of the creatures paid tribute to the ability of the Spears and the training they went through to become defenders of the Realm.

"Down!"

They all hit the ground, prone and ready to explode into action at a moment's notice.

They waited.

Bethany stumbled. Her feet squished against the soles of her shoes, and pain sprang up through her legs. Four days, running for four days, and she needed to stop to wrap her feet, rest for an hour or two and start running once more.

She had taken the time earlier that day to strip berries from a spicebush, and put them into one of her water bags. The essence from the berries would soothe her aching feet.

Her foot twisted, and she fell forward, rolled and stopped. With heavy eyes she put her hands on the ground, pushed off and fell back on her rear. She could no longer run.

Exhausted, hungry, and desperately wanting to bathe, she pulled off her shoes. She took blood cloths from her pack, soaked them in the Spicebush berry tea, and wrapped her feet. The soothing coolness slowly untied the muscles of her calves.

Sleep claimed her.

"I killed over twenty of them," Jon said, cleaning his sword. "I think this needs sharpening; it didn't go through the neck of the last one very well."

Thomasyn looked at his friend, his clutch mate. He did not like the glint of lust in Jon's eyes as he recounted the attack. "I wonder how Bethany is doing. It's been three days."

Jon looked up. "She's probably already in Salman by now. Remember that sweets shop when we were kids? When Chail gave us all two silver butts to spend as we wanted? The one with the hot pies and the plump old woman, she gave us those… I forget, but they were good."

Thomasyn smiled. "Blueberry and heartberry squares."

"That's it. I forgot." Jon licked his lips. "It would be so nice to have one of those right now. Bethany's probably enjoying one, along with a good bath. She always likes a good, hot bath after a long run."

Thomasyn nodded. "As we all do."

"No, not all of us. Remember Tannis? He hated bathing. I swear it was torture being in the same room as him." Jon looked up. "You have a stone?"

"Here." Thomasyn tossed a honing stone to Jon. "Are you okay?"

Jon ran the stone along the edge of the blade, caring for his weapon as if it was a part of him. "Yes, perfectly fine. I just wanted to serve them justice for what they did. I saw fingers in the stew pot we dumped. They eat us, you know. Humans, that is. Why would anyone want to eat humans when there's all sorts of animals around us?"

"I wish I could tell you, Jon. I honestly wish I could tell you."

Bethany's head bobbed, and her eyes opened slowly. She squinted as the mid-day sun almost blinded her. A foul blast of hot air hit her face as a dog whimpered and licked her.

"Uhg," she said.

"You're awake, good. It's time to change the bandages." The voice, calm and soft, made her look up to the man seated above her. "Whoa." He chittered, and the horse pulling the cart slowed, eventually stopping. "Let's see."

Bethany sat up, her muscles complaining with every movement. "Who are you?"

The man turned and pulled back a greyish hood with patchwork covering it. His thin hair hung long behind his neck, tied with a strip of leather. "My name is not important. You're a Spear, and fresh from your clutch from the looks of you. Fourteen? Yes, and strong. How long had you been running?"

"Three days. Need to get to Salman. It's…" She noticed the scarring on his hands, the sureness of his smile, and the poultice hanging around his neck. "You're a Wooder."

"No longer. I was allowed to step down, and I've just been trading between Salman and Capital."

"How far away from Salman are we?" Bethany pulled up a foot and started to remove the bandages.

"Less than a day, but the better question is how far away from the Capital are we? And I would tell you two days."

Bethany thought of Chail and Tess. The last time she saw them was fewer than two weeks ago, and they expected her to be at the Teeth in two months.

The ex-Wooder was in front of her now, and with swift hands he had taken the bandages off her feet. "Nicely healing. The wrap you used was good; it helped the skin bind back together again. The rest was, well, something I did."

Her eyes grew as she noticed unspotted skin where broken blisters had been abundant. "You have great skill."

"Just lucky. You had some of what I needed on you."

"I need to get to Salman. Now."

"Then we best get going." He stood, reached and picked up her boots. "You'll need these."

Bethany took her boots and smiled. "Thank you."

Thomasyn clung to a tree branch over the biggest tent in the Hobs encampment, listening. Shail told him to climb the tree for Hobs, being underground dwellers, do not look skyward.

"What! You didn't find anything?" The human voice was angry, cutting through the tent and into the surrounding area. It sounded human to Thomasyn, but with a guttural noise he couldn't quite place.

"Supreme Commander, my King. They disappeared as if phantoms of the night." The high pitched whine of a Hobs' voice was barely discernible, as if the creature mumbled his acquiescence.

"I'm not looking for excuses, Pin, I'm looking for results. First, you cannot control the troops when we take the small home, then they scatter like mad elephants toward an unknown attacker hidden in the woods, and now you can't make them find the tracks of who attacked us! Do you know what would happen if you told our Queen the same news?"

There was the sound of a thud, like that of a body hitting the ground. "No, Supreme Commander, Danton, my friend. We have fought together for years. I-I have shown you the secrets of the blood, and how to prolong your mortal life beyond that of a mere human, and the flesh that contains your soul."

"And for that I am eternally grateful."

"Are you feeling the bite of age again?" The Hobs' tone changed, taking on that of one talking to a pet.

The man seemed to soften slightly, "I am feeling my age again. Man was not meant to live four hundred years. The time weighs heavy on my shoulders. It has been a long time since we completed the ceremony."

Pin's voice softened even more. "Let me help, yet again."

Thomasyn didn't hear anything for a short time, and then the clanging of metal reached his ears. He strained to hear what happened next, but failed. He waited for what seemed like an eternity, until Pin's muttering floated into the air.

Thomasyn heard the sound of muttering, punctuated with Pin's name as well as Danton's. He could not make out any of the other words, and he imagined some type of spell being incanted.

A hissing sound of water hitting coals drifted up to him, tinged with sulfur. The burning of eggs became the next odor, followed by a scream from Pin and burning flesh.

"Now, drink, and relish in youth," Pin said, his breath coming in gasps.

Thomasyn heard something light fall to the ground and a gurgling sound followed. Danton coughed, screamed, and cried.

"Danton, you are fighting it again. Embrace the change. Allow it to encompass you, mold you, and reshape you from the harsh reality to the new." A slight laugh escaped from someone. "I am your friend. You need me, as I need you. Protect, shield, and we will be inseparable."

Thomasyn listened, enthralled by what he could imagine was happening. A small group of Hobs gathered at the front of the tent, smiling their wicked smiles.

The flap opened, and Pin exited holding the hand of a young human boy. The clothes hung loose on the human's shoulders, and light brown, hair dishevelled and long, draped down to his shoulders. Though the face was young, Thomasyn recognized it. He did not know how such powerful magic could be cast.

"Behold! Danton has yet again been reborn to us in youth. His strength will lead us through the Realm and to the throne of Capital itself!"

The group of Hobs nodded, and clanged their swords against their sheaths. Pin held up his hand to stem the rejoicing.

"We will take the Realm for our Queen. And our King, Danton, will present her with a hundred children to rebuild her throne and suck the marrow from their bones. She will shower us with meat, and the humans will be our bounty," Pin said, looking towards the young Danton at his side.

"I will lead you." Danton spoke clearly now, full of strength and determination. "We will conquer this land. The Hobs will be the masters of the Realm!"

Thomasyn noticed that most of the Hobs had joined the throng, and their cheers rang out through the clearing. They clapped, hollered, and raised their arms in supplication to Danton.

"I need to talk to the others," Thomasyn mumbled to himself, and he worked his way to the trunk of the tree, the bark scrapping against his legs and stomach.

"So why is a Spear trying to make her way to Salman?"

Bethany looked at the man who called himself Brand. "I was told to."

Brand nodded and coughed. "Need more training, do ya?"

Her voice cut the air between them with the sharp retort. "No."

"You misunderstand, little one. I went through life as a Wooder. Loneliness was our companion through the Realm as we searched for children to become Spears. We healed, searched and helped. The people would feed us, shelter us if we needed, but few would know us. I crave to talk with others, find out what they are like, and enjoy their company." He clucked the horse on, keeping it from slowing. His body erupted in a coughing fit.

"But, the Wooders, they spend time together, don't they?"

"No, not really. We usually travel together for a short time, but when you stop looking for that one child who will be… special, your life seems empty. Which is why I travel from town to town, trading what I can to survive." The ex-Wooder coughed. "I know I'm not long in this world, but at least I can say one of my finds did become special."

Bethany looked at him. "What do you mean?"

Brand took out a cloth and blew his nose. The sound was rattling, chunky. He sighed, opened the cloth and looked at it, shaking his head. "We better hurry."

"Why?"

"As I said, I'm not long in this world. Soon, I will be at the feet of the Five."

"How do you know?" Bethany fidgeted in her seat, legs swinging under her. "I mean, we usually don't know when we will die."

Brand looked at what came out of his nose once more time. "I do." He crumpled up the cloth, and threw it into the back of the cart. Bethany caught a glimpse of the bundle. Spots of red littered the exterior.

"But enough of me. What is this special reason you have for traveling back to Capital?" His grin belied the seriousness of his situation, and Bethany noticed a little trickle of blood at the corner of his mouth.

"Who was the special one you found?" Bethany took a small rag from the inside of her cloak, reached up and wiped the blood off his face.

"Oh, sorry. I usually get it all, but recently more of me is escaping through the lungs. I named him Chail. He was a monster of a child when I found him. Wrinkly and wailing like a banshee. But when he gripped my finger, the power in those little arms told me he was special."

When Bethany didn't say anything he looked over. "Are you okay?"

"You said Chail was the name of the boy you found?" Her mouth hung open.

"Yes. When a Wooder finds a child they name them, unless the mother is still alive and names them first." His face softened. "Do you know him?"

"He trained me. He... I consider him my father." Her thoughts turned to the last time she saw Master Chail, how proud he was of the three of them.

"I brought him to Capital, and he was indoctrinated into the life of a Spear. I followed his journey. I'm proud of his accomplishments..." He coughed, and the fit racked his body. It took him several seconds to recover. "I may have been wrong."

"I don't understand. I thought you were proud of his accomplishments?" She rubbed the old man's back, attempting to comfort him.

"It's not that. I am— proud of him. I have found out he's been very helpful to the Realm. He—" He coughed again. With a face reddening from the effort, his breath rattled into his lungs. "I wish I had children. If I had, I would have wished them to be like him."

Bethany hugged the man, and he leaned into her arms, basking in the love she gave him. As she released him, she could see the glint of a tear in his eye. "Any child would be proud to have you as a father. A Wooder, healing all they come across. I know if I had a father, either Chail or you would be my dream."

Brand cried, and it flowed like rivers down his face. "Thank you. That was very nice of you." He coughed again, and this time the energy behind it was weak, and without force. Gargling noises rattled his lungs, and his breathing was shallow. "I... Use the horse, and the cart, for whatever you need." Again, the coughing continued and phlegm covered his hand along with blood.

His gasps disturbed her. Bethany held him as his lungs tried to expel the fluid in them, and then he was still, leaning on her heavily. She knew what had happened, and she prayed to the Five for the safe passage of his soul to their care.

"We draw them away from the camp and light it on fire," Thomasyn said, looking at the other three.

Jon was the first to respond, his voice dripping with sarcasm. "And how are we going to draw them away?"

"Jon," Garion said, his eyes half closed as his gaze turned to the young Spear. He inclined his head slightly. "Listen first before passing judgement on any plan. You'll never know when someone can give you the best information."

"Right," Jon said, shaking his head. He rolled his eyes. "We can all think the best about anything, but when it comes to protecting, they all look to the best fighter. Someone like me."

Shail shook his head. "Let's wait for Thomasyn to give us the whole plan."

Thomasyn bowed his head to Master Shail before continuing. "One of us takes the horse and rides to the top of the hill here." He pointed at the ground where he had drawn a small map. "The main force of Hobs is here." He put a few of the Hobs stones on the ground. "Scream, yell, or get their attention any way possible. As they charge, the decoy will move down into the vale, drawing them away from the camp. Once they're over the hill, the other three will run into the camp and fire the tents."

"Really? That's it?" Jon stood up and walked a few paces away. "By the Gods, really?"

"Jon," Shail said. "Come back here."

Jon stopped, turned, and stood arms akimbo. His brow furrowed and a pout formed on his mouth. "What?"

"This is a good plan. The longer we keep the Hobs from marching on the town the better for the town. Bethany needs time to reach Salman in order to call the Spears. If we don't buy her time, the town will be overrun and many people will die." Shail stood and approached the young man. He reached out his hand and placed it on Jon's shoulder. "We will survive this day, and the others to come. It's a good thing Hobs are not very intelligent, and Thomasyn tells us Danton is under the control of one Hobs who is keeping him young, even after the centuries would have turned him to dust. Thomasyn, you said one of them fed him something?"

"Yes," Thomasyn said. "He recited something with both their names in it."

"Could it be?" Garion said. "The Hobs have truly created a shaman of such power?"

Thomasyn stared at the Spear. "A shaman?"

"Yes," Garion said. "A shaman. One who can twist the power of magic to their own control. There's not been a Hobs so powerful in thousands of years. And now, on the brink of a Hobs invasion, one has found the power."

"But what does it mean?" asked Thomasyn.

"If we can kill the mage, we may be able to take away the charm that rejuvenated Danton. He'll change immediately to the true age he is. Over 400 years old."

"So, who will ride the horse?" Jon asked.

"I was hoping you would, Jon," said Thomasyn.

"What? And let you have all the fun?" Jon laughed. "Why would I do that?"

Jon sat atop the horse and looked down at the Hobs' encampment. He let out a quiet curse and waited for the sun to drop near the horizon.

"Me. They picked me to be the decoy. I wanted to burn those evil monsters." He leaned forward and lifted his bottom off the saddle. Gas escaped him. He laughed. "Smell that, Hobs? It is the stink of a Spear ready to kill all of you."

The horse pawed at the ground, stretched its neck and chewed at the bit.

"Stop it, White. We'll start moving soon." He stroked the horse's neck as he sat back on the saddle. Jon looked towards the sun and decided it was about time. The rays of the orb were set low enough to be in the Hobs' eyes. "I guess now is as good a time as any."

Jon drew his sword. With a flick of his wrist, the young Spear turned the horse and held up his weapon. He inhaled and let out an unintelligible scream at the top of his lungs. The Hobs at the edge of the camp turned, and let out an alarm to warn the others. Soon the whole camp looked towards him. Jon made the horse rear as he let out another scream of defiance.

"Here I am," he yelled. "Come get me you dirty, sniveling cowards."

The Hobs rallied, pulled swords out to fight, and donned armour to protect themselves

"There is only one! Kill him!" cried a Hobs, as he drew his sword and ran toward Jon.

Jon waited. He wanted them to get close enough to see their eyes, feel their breath, hear the sound of their footsteps within a heartbeat of him. The horse whinnied, eyes showing white toward the approaching horde.

He counted twenty seconds, and knew it was time. Jon turned the horse and spurred it. The animal bolted down the valley, moving momentarily out of the horde's sight. Pulling back on the reins, Jon stopped at the bottom of the vale, and turned to face the charging creatures. He drew his sword again.

"Here, you slow sons of an ugly one. Your Queen is horrible, and none of you can kill me." Jon grinned. He had them following him as planned, but he wanted to kill at least one. He considered letting them catch up to him, striking a few down and galloping away before they could touch him.

He sheathed his sword and waited. The desire to do something overpowered him. Jon wanted to take them down as only he knew he could. "I am always in the shadow. Thomasyn is the one with the plans. They always listen to Thomasyn."

He spurred the horse once again, and galloped to the top of the next hill.

"They're following him! It's working!" Thomasyn slapped Shail on the back.

"Don't celebrate yet, Thomasyn. There're still a lot of them in the camp. Let's hope the blood lust of the Hobs drives them before common sense takes over." The man stood and walked to Garion. He whispered, "I'm concerned for Jon. He is letting the killing get to him. We need to make sure it doesn't take hold of him."

Garion nodded. "Yes, he's getting kill-happy. Do we know how many times he killed before being released from training?"

"Chail said five criminals during training, and two while out with a Wooder. The two were justified, holding a small town in terror and grief." Shail shook his head. "I grow concerned he took too many too early in life, making souls of men worth nothing to him."

"It's the worst thing that could happen, a Spear with no sense of value for human life. We'll have to find a way of changing that. Pull him back to the path of a Spear."

The horse reared as the Hobs closed the distance between them. Jon let them approach closer than before. He could almost feel their rancid breath against his cheek, hear the blood lust in their snarls. The heat of his blood pounded through his heart.

Jon slapped the reins and galloped the horse over the next hill just as a hand reached for the horse's tail.

"They're almost far enough for me to start doubling back. They'll never make it back in time."

Thomasyn stormed into the camp. A rough bundle of sticks made the torch he carried in his hand. It blazed in the cloudy near-dark. Smoke filled the air and raked at his throat. Two shadowed figures followed him, blades drawn. The young Spear stopped at a tent and pushed his torch into the dry cloth. The shelter caught fire, and the flames licked at the sky.

"Hurry! There are stragglers nearby." Garion passed Thomasyn, and the young Spear's sword flicked out taking the head off an unsuspecting Hobs who had stayed behind to guard the camp. The head rolled to the side, tongue lolling out, body falling in the other direction.

Thomasyn hurried past Garion, pushing his torch into another tent. Shail ran past him this time, killing another Hobs as he did. Hobs dashed about the camp. Screams reached out in the night. One by one the tents went up in flames, and one by one the disorganized Hobs fell on the blades of the Spears.

Thomasyn saw Pin's headdress first as the Hobs exited Danton's tent and screamed. "Hobs! To me!"

The remaining Hobs in the camp gather around Pin and encircle the shaman in a protective barrier. They turned and faced the Spears, rough swords in hand.

"Move as one! Slowly. Act as a unit. Protect our leader!"

Thomasyn stopped and threw the torch toward the approaching Hobs. The Spears backed up and started their retreat.

"There's too many of them," Garion said.

"Just keep moving. They'll hold a good distance from us to protect Danton. They don't know how many we are," Shail said.

"I can try to out flank them. Come in from behind to split their attention," Thomasyn said. "It's a good chance—"

"No," Shail said. "We stay together through this. I don't know if we can keep them at bay another day. Get ready to run."

Jon's sword whistled as it sliced through the air, cutting through the neck of the closest Hobs. He spurred the horse, and it jumped forward, kicking another Hobs as hooves dug into the ground.

"Another one killed!" he screamed. A laugh escaped his lips at the sight of another body falling. After a hundred yards he stopped the horse and licked the blood from his blade. It was warm, tingling and inviting. "Another kill that Thomasyn will never match." His blood boiled in his veins, and his laugh exploded from his throat.

The sun was set, and clouds obscured the moon's beams, keeping the path in near darkness, but he pushed on.

"How many are following us?" Shail asked, as he tried to look over his shoulder at the pursuing Hobs. His breath came faster.

"Too many," Garion said.

Thomasyn spun and ran backwards, trying to count the horde following them. "I count twenty three—No, twenty five." He spun again and easily caught up with the other two. "Is there any way we can better the odds?"

"Not easily." Shail's voice rasped in the air. "By the Gods they're fast. I can't keep up this pace very much longer."

Thomasyn looked at Shail, realizing for the first time just how old the man was. "We can spear a few of them before they overtake us."

Garion glanced behind him. "I don't think so. They'll be upon us soon if we slow our pace. Shail, can you keep up?"

"Do I have a choice?"

With speed and deftness, Thomasyn reached out his right hand and took two short throwing spears from Shail's back strap. The young man stopped, turned, and took out the throwing bone. A swift movement sent one of the spears sailing through the air. It struck the lead Hobs in the belly, felling the creature. Thomasyn sent a second throwing spear a similar trajectory. The weapon pierced the chest of the Hobs beside the fallen one. Thomasyn spun and sprinted in order to catch up with the other two.

"Twenty three."

"That was foolish," Shail said, gasping. "Did it slow the rest?"

"Barely," Garion said, as he looked back. "But they're not overtaking us now."

"Do you think Bethany's made it to Salman yet?" Thomasyn glanced back, gauging the distance between him and the pursuing Hobs.

"It would have taken her three days to get there, a day to gather the Spears and a forced march back. We need six days." Shail slowed, and Thomasyn kept pace with him. "She's only been gone four days."

Thomasyn grabbed two more spears from Shail's pack. Seconds later he caught back up to the two men. "Twenty one. Can you take five each?"

"I don't know," Garion said.

"Probably," Shail said, his voice strained.

"Turn, charge with throwing spears, take out two each and spike one when we clash. Nine will be down quick, leaving just twelve. Good plan?" Thomasyn asked.

They glanced quickly at Thomasyn and nodded.

The three took out throwing spears, setting one into throwing bones, readied themselves and said, "Now!" at the same time.

Six Hobs fell under the Spear's bombardment, and the remaining charged forward. Garion pushed his remaining spear into the belly of the first Hobs he clashed with, striking the back of the Hobs head with the bone. Shail took one down as well, and as he turned, threw his bone at another, opening the head of the creature.

Thomasyn took two out, slashed a third with the shaft of the spear and sliced open the skull of another. He moved with fluidity. His sword was brandished in his hand. One Hobs head violently twisted to the side, and a gash opened up from ear to opposite cheek. He spun. Danced to the side. Thomasyn took another Hobs arm off. The creature screamed and clutched at the stump. Recovering from the strike, Thomasyn seized an opportunity. The sword sliced the calf off a Hobs who was preparing to deliver a blow to Shail. The monster fell to one knee.

Tumbling, Thomasyn recovered, and pushed the tip of his sword through the neck of his last Hobs, allowing it to gurgle on its life blood.

Thomasyn stood and surveyed the scene before him. Garion, pulling his sword from the belly of a Hobs, staggered as he stood.

Shail knelt on one knee and struggled to speak between gasps. "Where am I going to clean my sword?" He grunted, and stood up. Blood dripped from a wound on his arm. "Damned thing got lucky."

"Are you all right, Master Shail?" Thomasyn came to the man's side, pulling a small length of cloth from beneath his cloak. "Let me clean that before their blood infects you."

Garion walked over to the two and sheathed his sword. "We can't stay here. Jon should be back at the hut by now."

Thomasyn looked over to Garion as the man furrowed his brow.

"Yes, we need to get moving, now." Shail looked around.

"This way," Thomasyn said, moving towards the northwest.

Jon looked before him, counting the fires in the enemy's camp. "Seven. Hardly worth the risk."

He spurred the horse.

"I've killed a dozen of them. All they can do is light a few fires."

"I thought it was the Hobs' blood that drove Danton mad." Thomasyn leaned against the fence. The horizon glowed a golden red as light brighten the morning, chasing away the full moon. Dew peppered the grass, and a chill made their breaths show in the air.

"It was, but it also seems this Pin may have had something to do with it as well." Shail had both hands on the fence.

Garion watched the sun as it made the long journey from under the side of the world. "Their blood is poisonous, and can kill a normal person in a few hours, if you're lucky."

"Jon's here," Thomasyn said, pushing away from the fence.

Jon walked his horse to the small farm. The others watched in silence as the young Spear took his time to reach them.

"Why doesn't he just ride the horse over to us?" Garion said.

"It's the way Jon is. You don't rush him; you just have to put up with him," Thomasyn laughed.

And wait they did. Jon took his time. When he was within speaking distance, Thomasyn called out.

"Jon, can you move a little faster?"

"Yes. Got any food?" Jon called back.

"No, but we can start a fire; did you bring anything with you?" Shail asked.

Jon held up three rabbits, freshly killed.

"Nothing like a good meal after a fight," Jon said, pulling the leg off a rabbit on the spit.

"Did you kill any of them?" Shail asked.

"A couple."

"You were supposed to just make them follow you," Shail said.

"They were losing their bloodlust. I had to wait for them to reach me and fuel their passion for killing." Jon took another bite and chewed. "Anyway, they're only Hobs."

"Only Hobs? You don't learn much about them in training but they are sentient creatures," Garion said. "Yes, they look different than us. Yes, they pray to different gods than us. And yes, we aren't able to breed with them. Hobs have a queen, and she is the only one who can breed. Hobs have no gender until the age of five, and unless fed their royal food, they are male. The queen is the only female of a clan.

"When the queen is ready," Garion continued, "the others battle for the right to mate with her. It's the same as bees, except the hive is made up of males and only one female. But they have a soul."

Jon snorted. "Do they really just give up?"

Garion looked thoughtfully into the fire. "I guess they do. The Queen can give birth to hundreds of children after one successful mating. Like animals, the queen Hobs only seem to need to mate once a decade. They show no interest in it, unlike people…"

Thomasyn giggled. "Humans seem to want to couple every chance they get."

"They sure do." Shail smiled.

Bethany sat on the bench seat of the wagon, reins in hands. The scraggly dog, whom Brand called Buzzard, lay beside his master's body in the wagon's bed. She had taken the time to wrap Brand in his cloak and place him in the back of the wagon so he could have a proper interment at Salman. The horse, old and tired, could not be coaxed beyond a simple trot.

She passed the farms and came to the inner gates of the city. The bridge was down, as it always was in peacetime. Two guards stood on either side. One yawned.

Moving the cart to the side, Bethany stopped, and climbed out. She made her way to the first guard.

"I need to have the Spears gathered," she said, her voice not fluctuating, but commanding.

One guard waved his hand at the wagon. "You can't leave the cart there."

"My name is Bethany, and I'm a Spear."

"You're a Spear? Aren't you a little small for a Spear?" The guards laughed.

Bethany pulled the guard's sword out of its scabbard, presenting the point under the chin of the man. "Maybe this will clear your understanding of a Spear's training." She tapped his chin. "Now, there is a body in the cart, an ex-Wooder called Brand. Deliver him to the Wooders, and tell me where to find the Spears!" With a flourish she reversed the grip on the sword and shoved it into the guard's scabbard.

Regan unrolled the map on the table and looked at Bethany. "Where?" He spread his weathered hands over the map.

"The Town of Lands. We stopped off there and traveled for less than a day with the horses. There was a hut, or home with a farm." Her finger tapped the map. "Right about here."

"And how big was the horde?"

"We counted over 200 tents. Four or five in a tent."

"Big enough." Regan sighed. "I'll send a messenger bird to Capital, and gather up the Spears. We have fifty stationed here, and they can be ready in a moment."

"Forced march?" Bethany asked.

"Forced march."

"Capital is twelve hours away at full gallop."

Regan nodded, his long grey hair falling over his forehead.

"I'll need a horse. And I'll run the rest of the way."

Regan half smiled and shook his head. "I see the way you're walking. How long did you run before you met the Wooder?"

"Two days." Bethany turned and walked to the door. "I've got another hundred leagues to travel."

"Bethany," Regan said. She stopped. "You can't save the Realm all by yourself. I'll send a bird to the small town half-way, fifty leagues. They'll have a fresh horse for you."

"Thank you, Master Regan. I have four friends who desperately need the support."

"I'll get the Spears gathered immediately, and meet them as soon as possible."

Bethany walked out the door, heading for the stables. "I hope you're right. There's a lot of Hobs."

-2-

Foam ran from the horse's mouth as Bethany pushed the beast forward at a gallop. Her legs sweated from the heat produced by her mount, and she knew the horse would not last very much longer. She could see the small town ahead of her, and she focused on reaching it before the animal died from exhaustion.

The horse slowed to a walk, and no matter what kind of coaxing Bethany did, it would not return to a gallop. Heaving breath in and out of its body until, finally, its legs gave out; the horse fell forward in the field and died.

Bethany was up on her feet and running toward the town. Her goal, the man standing at the outskirts holding the bridle of a horse meant to take her to the largest city of the Realm called Capital.

With no formalities, she mounted the horse, and rode off following the beaten path. *I need to hurry,* was all she could think of as she started to push the horse beyond its physical limits.

She rode.

The last of the trees whipped past, and her feet screamed from the pounding they were going through. She ignored the pain and continued to run. She felt another blister burst. The released fluid squished in her shoe.

An hour ago the horse had died, leaving her two leagues from Capital. So Bethany ran.

The high walls of Capital, majestic, solid, unyielding, stood before her, only one league away.

With her body screaming for rest and food, Bethany drove herself forward to the one place she could truly call home, the barracks of the Spears within the walls of the largest city of the Realm. Memories of her time training with the others came unbidden to her mind. She remembered Thomasyn and her fighting their first criminals in the arena of the training ground. How he had opened up a man's stomach to release his innards, and how she had sliced open the neck of hers.

As she approached the gates to the city, people separated, allowing her to pass. Her cloak announced she was a Spear, and a Spear running and looking as exhausted as she must be on a mission. She moved through the throng of people, past the gates and the two guards standing there. One nodded. She passed the spot where Bosco and his people tried to kidnap two of the young boy Spears when they were only five. There was a commemoration to how two children, grabbed by the kidnappers, had been saved by the group of children and their trainer. In the exact spot where Chail had killed the man, the memorial was erected to remind those who would dare touch a child, especially a Spear in Flight.

The large doors to the training area loomed before her, inviting entry to the place. The trainers moulded children into protectors or healers inside, but never both. For a millennium, newborn children who survived their parents, if found in time, trained here like she had. They trained her on how to ignore pain, avoid ambush, blend into the background, and disappear.

The most important training they received was the ability to fight, but in this case it was not what she relied on. She relied on those who taught her how to run. She remembered the running they did while they were young. The long jogs around the training grounds, the cross country marathons that lasted for days on end, Master Chail leading them from one town to another.

"Bethany!"

She spun, searching for the woman she loved. The one woman she could call mother. "Nanny Tess," she gasped, seeing the woman who raised her.

Tess ran towards Bethany and hugged her. "You were supposed to be on your way to the Teeth by now."

"I need to speak to Master Chail." She let go and started to make her way into the main barracks of the training area.

"He's not in the barracks. He's overseeing the new Spears in Flight. They promoted him to overseer of the whole training facility."

"Where?"

Bethany stared into Tess's eyes. "I'll take you to him," the woman said.

Chail's head whirled from the unbelievable amount of administration before him. With one finger stretched out he pushed a sheet of paper aside only to reveal another piece. He dropped his head into his hands, not wanting to look at the three other piles to the left.

The door burst opened into his office. As he saw Bethany entered followed by his wife, Tess. The pencil dropped, and his eyes widened. He lifted his tired body from the chair as quickly as he could.

"Bethany! What are you doing here?"

"Master Chail! There's a Hobs invasion. Outside the Town of Lands."

Tess gasped.

"A Hobs' invasion?" Chail asked. "How…Are the others still there?"

"Yes, Master Shail sent me to warn you. Master Garion, Thomasyn, and Jon are trying to delay the attacks. There are hundreds of them. We need to call the Spears for protection." Bethany slumped forward on the desk. Tess gripped her hands on the girl's shoulders.

"You're exhausted. You need rest, food." She tried to guide the young Spear towards a seat.

"Tess, call a Wooder," Chail ordered, motioning to Bethany's feet. He could see the weeping from the stains on the wrapped leather shoes.

"Oh! I'll get one right away." She dashed from the room.

"How many?" Chail asked. *It doesn't make sense. Why now? Why invade? What are they looking at getting out of this?*

"Seven score a hundred."

"Who else knows?"

"Regan, from Salman. He's called the Spears in his town to do a forced march to help protect the city."

"Did you run all the way from Salman to here?" Chail motioned to her feet, and the blood that colored her shoes.

"No, I had two horses from Salman to here. The last two leagues I had to run. It was the run from Town of Lands to Salman that did this. If I hadn't found Brand…"

At the sound of the Wooder's name, Chail brightened. "How is Brand?"

"He died in my arms before we got to Salman. He said he was proud of you, and what you've accomplished."

Chail looked blankly at her. Finally, the information hit him. His mind whirled. Brand was dead. The one who found him all those years ago, the man who followed him and helped him. Dead. His body fell back into his chair. "He's dead? Why? How?"

"He was coughing, and his lungs filled. There was nothing I could do to help him."

The door opened, and Tess entered with a Wooder following. The man stooped down and removed Bethany's shoes. "She needs to have these taken care of immediately." He looked up at Bethany. "You'll be off these for a few days."

Bethany stood, winced, and sat back down again. "I still have to show you the—"

"Chail!" Con entered the room. "A message from Salman. There's a..." His body rolled from the run, and his voice trailed off as he took in the scene. His eyes widened at the sight of Bethany. His mouth hung open.

"Yes, Con, Bethany is the one who has supplied the news. It's strange that she made it here before the bird."

"It was my apprentice. The one you wanted me to train. He's... He didn't see the bird in the window." Con closed his mouth and snapped out of his surprise. "I thought you were assigned to the Teeth?"

Chail stood. "Con! Go get the others. All Spears in Flight from age eight up. We'll meet in the briefing room immediately."

They stood around a large table as King Savoy entered the room. His face was not clean shaven as it usually was, but bristly. The man's sunken eyes glared out in the middle of dark circles. His thin frame was more emaciated than before.

"Majesty," Chail said. "I didn't expect you to be here. They told me—"

"Told you what, Chail? That I was weak?" He coughed. "I'm the King, and I will take part in all decisions concerning the Realm."

"There is no disrespect here, Majesty, only concern." Con took a deep breath. "You're unwell. You need to rest in order to gain your strength."

Savoy looked about the room. His eyes met all of the trainers present and rested on Tallia, trainer of the eight-year-olds. She returned his glare with unflinching light blue eyes. Bendon, trainer of the nine-year-olds, looked away with obvious concern. Core, the trainer of the ten-year-olds, leaned against the wall. His dark, sad eyes darted between everyone, never falling on the King.

"Anyone?" the king asked. He looked at Nory, current trainer of the twelve year olds. Blonde hair braided to the side framed her light complexion; she anchored her stare on him. Sil, the one woman he always looked to for support when it came to the Spears, let her grey hair cover her eyes as she shook her head.

"No, not this time, Sir," Sil said. "You're my King, and I love you, but I will not watch as you push yourself beyond the ability to heal. Didn't the Wooders tell you to rest?"

"And if they did?" His voice wavered a little, filled with gargling sounds.

"Then you should be resting, your Majesty. Not worrying yourself with a possible invasion when all your people have the issue well in hand. Please, Sir, go back to the castle and rest. We'll have Con keep you updated," Chail said.

Savoy sighed, and pushed away from the table. "Don't do anything without informing me."

"I can tell you right now," Chail said. "We'll be marching the Spears out to meet the enemy. How long we'll wait is all we need to decide."

Savoy stopped at the door. "Use the reserves. Call them up. Quell the Hobs, Chail. Don't leave any of the bastards alive." Savoy left the war council.

Con sat with the council and discussed the best way to proceed. All agreed a forced march would be the best mode of travel, but the worst for fighting.

Another bird arrived from Salman. It carried a message that Con delivered to Chail, who read it carefully, and then put aside. Con had read the message: it told of the Spears gathering, and now one hundred of the protectors along with militia would march to the town the next morning. They estimated three days before reaching the Town of Lands.

Chail instructed Con to send a bird in response, telling them of their plans to gather the Spears in Flight along with the militia from Capital. Their march would take more than a day longer to reach the goal. They would meet up in the town, thus joining as a unified fighting force.

When Con went to the king to convey the news, Savoy suggested using the Seers to message the Spears traveling close to the Town of Lands.

"Have them send a dream. Not all will understand, but if they do, it will compel them to gather at the town, and offer what protection they can from the advancing army." Savoy's breath wheezed through his throat.

"Yes, my King." Con stood, and was about to walk away.

Savoy motioned to him. "Con, I'm sorry."

"Sire?"

"I... I didn't trust you."

Con bowed. "It is the king's prerogative."

"No. It's not the way for a king to act. You've shown nothing but patience and understanding. They don't know. No one knows. The reason I ordered more children be harvested for Spears. It was a dream, sent to me by the Gods. The dream showed of an impending invasion, years ago. It's why we're training so hard." Savoy coughed, his throat rebelling against his words.

"You don't need to ask for forgiveness, Sire. You're the king, and what you say is law." Con started to move away.

"Con, give a dying man a little chance to meet the Five clear of conscious, will you."

He stopped again, looking over his shoulder. "You're not dying. It's a cold, a…something. You'll fight it off and be on your feet in no time. The Gods would not be so cruel as to take you away from us on the brink of an invasion. No, please Sire, rest." Con smiled, and walked out the room.

Bethany stared at her bound feet and sighed. Tess fussed over the girl's clothes, folding and picking. She had made her strip and clean up, and wear a smock while her own clothes were washed by the only woman she could call mother.

Now, several hours later, Bethany was cleaned, pampered and fed. Her mood had turned sour. And all she wanted to do was march with the Spears to help her friends.

"I want to help," she said.

"You can help by getting better. You're no help to anyone when you can't walk, let alone run." Tess turned to the girl. "Bethany, you're one of the strongest girls I know. Stronger than I am, or Chail."

"I'm not stronger than Master Chail."

"Actually, you are. Look at you, sitting there and arguing with me. You're trying to make me agree that you should be marching with the rest of the Spears. You want to make your way back to the Town of Lands. You're injured, and you have to heal."

Tess sighed. "I love you. I've loved all three of you since the first moment you were put in my arms those many years ago. If I could stop the suffering you're going through I would. But I am just a glorified wet nurse. You'll forget about me in a couple of years."

"I'll never forget you." Tears welled up in Bethany's eyes. "I never knew my mother. I don't even know where in the Realm I was born." She wiped the tear. "You're the only mother I've known."

Tess didn't turn; she just stood there looking down at the last of the clothes she was folding. Bethany's heart hammered in her chest. She knew Tess loved her, but was the love enough to accept her unconditionally?

"Nanny Tess, mother, I can call you that, can't I?"

A small tear ran down Tess's cheek. Her lower lip trembled.

"You're the only one I could talk to. You're the one I went to when the bleeding started. You're the one who bandaged my sprained ankle when I was nine. Master Chail is my father, and you are my mother. You nourished me when I was small. You held my hand when I was sick. You hugged me when I cried. Now," she said, standing up and walking towards the woman and hugging her from behind. "Now I can tell you I love you. And I will never forget you, no matter where they send me."

There was a knock on the door. Tess grabbed Bethany's hands and squeezed, then gently let them drop. She moved and wiped at her eyes before turning to the girl and kissing her on the forehead.

"I love you, as well." Tess looked up at the door. "Come."

Chail entered. His forehead wrinkled and he gazed elsewhere. His eyes fell on Bethany.

"I need you to come with me." He held out his hand.

"She's in no shape to walk around, Chail," Tess said, stepping in front of the child.

"She needs to come with me. The council wants to speak to her before allowing the use of the Seers."

"It's all right, Tess. I can still walk," Bethany said, moving around the woman. She ignored the pain lancing from the souls of her feet. "What do they need?"

"They need you to tell them what you told me. Danton is marching on the Realm."

She nodded and left the room with Chail.

Seven men looked at her from across the small room. Chail had told her their names, but she deemed them unimportant, for this was the only time she had met them. It would probably be the last.

Slowly she recounted the meeting of the Hobs outside the Town of Lands, and the chaos found in their wake. Some nodded, others shook their heads in disbelief, and still some ignored the warning about the pending invasion.

"But child, how could such a mass of Hobs gather without the Seers knowing about it?" one of the council asked.

"I am a Spear, not a Seer. To ask such a question of one with no knowledge is foolish," Bethany said.

Chail placed a restraining hand on her shoulder, but she ignored it. The insult was a good one, and she smiled inwardly at it. The council member either didn't understand it, or decided not to acknowledge it. Instead, he continued.

"Furthermore, for Hobs to have enough troops, they would have to have more than one Queen. And we know they only have one."

"And how do you know that? Is there some magic that you possess that looks into the earth, and counts all the Hobs in the Realm?" She shook her head. "We are wasting time. The Seers are needed to send the dream. To gather as many of the Spears to the town as possible so it can be protected. Is it not our duty to protect the people?"

"Young lady," the lead council member said, leaning forward in his chair. "It is not your place to question this council. We make decisions for the good of the Realm. We cannot just call all the Spears in that area to put aside all their duties and protect one town. Yes, it is important. We will send supplies and what Spears as we have available to stave off the invasion. To do more would be a waste of resources."

"And to do any less would send the wrong message to any invading force. 'Come, the Realm is open. Take what you need and leave'. It'll take three days of a forced march to make it back to the Town of Lands. In that time, four Spears may already be dead, trying to protect the very town you have deemed unworthy of our protection. Should they die in vain?"

There was a murmur in the council.

"If you fail to act, the Realm is lost. The people will know what you did here. They will revolt, and rise up against the very foundation that has built our great land."

The council stood.

"Young lady," the speaker said. "Your words will be attended to. I believe your master will have some wisdom to share with you concerning how you have dealt with us, and the words you used, however inappropriate they were. We will adjourn and discuss what you have said this day. You will now leave."

The council turned and left the small hall.

"I believe they think I will have a stern talk with you, now that they have left," Chail said, looking down at Bethany.

"I'm sorry, Master Chail. They got me so…angry." She twisted her lips and furrowed her brow. In a mocking voice Bethany said, "We'll think about saving all those lives. But we have to eat. Maybe sleep a little before deciding to talk or do anything to save the people of a small town."

Chail laughed, put his arms around her and hugged tightly. "I hear them just like that in my mind. I couldn't have said it better myself."

"Should we leave now?" Bethany asked.

"I'm a little hungry. Are you able to walk?"

"I can walk, but not very fast."

"I know of a little place…"

They sat in the kitchen of the mess hall, a boiling pot of broth on the stove.

"This is what your clutch never knew," Chail said, using a small basket to lower a thin slice of meat into the bubbling mass. "Meat in the basket, basket in the broth. You spice the broth and cook the meat. Don't leave it in too long. Pure heaven." He pulled out the basket and put it on a plate. "Try it."

Bethany took a piece and popped it into her mouth. The flavor exploded on her tongue, surprising the young Spear. "You eat like this every day?"

Chail laughed. "No, my dear. But I do enjoy food. Eat to fill yourself and wait until the next meal. Love the food and enjoy it, don't just eat to fuel your body, rejoice in it. Something Master Shail taught me when I was your age."

Bethany laughed, not prepared for this side of the man who had trained her from as far back as she could remember. Heat colored her cheeks, and the realization she was blushing made her feel even more heat rise.

"I used to have a crush on you," she said.

"I know. You and Sandra."

She had forgotten about Sandra. The girl was assigned several weeks ago, sent to Fisheries. Her mind went back to that one day they had found Michael killed by Master Dress. The day Sandra had tried out the special training with Thomasyn. Bethany remembered how the anger had boiled up in her. When Thomasyn spilled the blood of the criminal she had rejoiced inside. But the thought of how Sandra had *practiced* with Thomasyn was unsettling.

"Did you ever talk to her about the practice she had with Thomasyn?"

"That was something little ears shouldn't have heard, and little minds shouldn't have concerned themselves with. Anyway, I would rather you remember the good things that came from your training, not the bad."

Bethany smiled. "I believe Thomasyn would have called it a good thing."

Chail put another basket in the broth. "Yes, but Thomasyn was young and not really able to enjoy it, or understand the true meaning of what was being done to him." Chail straightened his vest, and grew silent.

After a short time he emptied the basket onto the plate. They ate in silence. The enjoyment of sharing each other's company was all they needed. For every day of her life, Bethany had seen her trainer, Master Chail, until she was sent away to her posting. Now, she realized just how much she had missed the man's easy smile, tender demeanour, and quick laugh.

The door to the kitchens opened, and the sound of a throat clearing announced another intruding on their time together. Chail didn't even look up.

"Yes, Con?" he said.

"The council has decided. They would like to talk to you."

"Thank you, Con. We'll be there in a minute."

"The council asked for only you to attend."

"Well, it's a good thing I don't report to the council."

"We only called for you, Master Chail."

Chail and Bethany stood in the small chamber with the seven council members sitting before them. The bare walls of the small room seemed to emphasize the scowls on the faces of each member. Each told a story, and Bethany believed it was not one she wanted to hear.

She watched them; her left hand resting on her hip. Each member seemed not to understand the disrespect they paid to the Spears, or the people of the Realm.

"She is here at my pleasure, not yours," Chail said.

"Yes. We were told of your strange ways of teaching."

"Enough. What have you decided? Will the Seers be used to call the Spears?"

The council grumbled, several of them gestured toward the two Spears in front of them. The middle council member stood and held up his arms, palms skyward. "In the name of the Five! Enough!"

With the members quieted, he sat and continued, "The council has sat and discussed the use of the Seers. Several of the members don't want to use the Seers for calling the Spears to protect the Town of Lands."

Chail started to speak, but the member held up his hand to silence him.

"The power of the Seers is limited, and if used unwisely will weaken the Seers ability to see approaching danger to the Realm. Reaching out with one's mind takes much energy, and limits a Seers's ability to function for many months. We will need to have several Seers push their thoughts. In fact, all of them will need to be engaged. Such an act will leave us blind to any threat that may desire to act while they are recovering from the exertion."

"The Seers seem to be blind to the current threat of the Hobs," Bethany said.

"Bethany! Be quiet," Chail said.

The council member nodded. "Yes, they didn't see. But as I was saying, the members of the council have voted, and we have decided to let the Seers call the Spears. The dreaming will begin within the hour, and Spears within a day's run to the Town of Lands will hear the call. They will be compelled to seek out the town, and be mindful of a possible threat. Master Chail, do you have a battle plan?"

"Yes, Counselor, we will force march in order to reach the town in as short a time as possible."

"Then commence as soon as you can, and take the little one with you. I'm sure her tongue is as good a weapon as her spear." The old man smiled, spread his arms and stood, motioning for the others to stand as well. "In the name of the Five, and by command of the king, the Spears will be called, and the Realm will defend against this oncoming threat against the people it serves."

Tess stood defiantly as she watched Bethany stuff her backpack. "You're not going."

Bethany shook her head. "Yes, I am."

"But you're still healing."

"I'll keep healing. We're not running, we're marching."

"Do you know what a forced march is?"

"Yes, I do. Do you?"

Tess took a deep breath. "It's a death march."

"If I was a prisoner. I'm a Spear. A forced march is a march over a long distance at a faster pace with little or no rest. We'll stop to eat and sleep, then pick it up again to get to the town." She stopped packing. "I'm a Spear. This is what we train for. I'm more worried for the militia men who are accompanying us. They're the ones who don't know what to expect." She resumed stuffing her pack.

"But what if something happens and your feet break open? The salve heals fast, but the skin is thin."

"Master Chail said Wooders are accompanying us on the march, to help with keeping the troop going." She finished and slung the pack over her shoulder. Bethany turned and faced Tess. "I'll be alright. Maybe, if I'm lucky, Thomasyn and Jon will have left a few Hobs for me to kill."

Tess gave a short huff of laughter, put her hand to her mouth, and then wiped away the tears. "I have missed you, Bethany." She held out her arms, and the young Spear walked into them.

"As I have missed you. I'm sure Master Chail will demand we return. Until then, remember I love you with all my heart."

"And I love you."

-3-

Chail and Bethany waited outside the quarters of the King and Queen. Three council members stood on the other side of the hall, talking quietly amongst themselves. The call to attend the King had gone out an hour ago, just prior to the dreaming to call the Spears to march.

Two hundred souls waited for them in the training grounds, ready to start the long journey to the Town of Lands.

"Why are we waiting?" whispered Bethany.

"I wish I knew, little one. I wish I knew." Chail shifted his weight from one foot to the other, nervous of what the King may ask of him. The last meeting had been months ago when he had been asked about the training, and whether it was advancing as requested.

"Maybe one of them knows," Bethany said, inclining her head towards the council members. "I bet if you ask them they'll tell you."

"Sure they will. And the Hobs invasion will wait until we get there." Chail silently hoped it was true, though. Garion and Shail along with Jon and Thomasyn could delay the Hobs with needle sharp attacks. Maybe long enough to allow the Spears time to reach them. That is all they needed, time. And it was not something they could squander at the whim of the King.

The door opened, and the High Wooder stepped into the hall. He looked at Chail and nodded, but headed towards the council members. His voice was low, but the bass sound of it cut through the silence.

"There is nothing we can do for him." The Wooder's back was turned, but they could tell it was him speaking. "His lungs have filled, and he is struggling to take in air. I doubt he will survive the night."

One of the council members murmured something that neither Bethany nor Chail could hear. The other two nodded.

"No, I don't know for sure what it is that ails him. It is like the consumption, when the body eats itself and grows dark fluid inside. But it is running quickly through him. There are nodules of flesh that have developed on his body, but they have grown in mere days, and not weeks like in others who have a similar illness."

There was more hushed talking by the three, and the Wooder shook his head.

"The King said he doesn't want to talk to the council, but he would like to talk to those two." He turned and indicated Chail and Bethany. "He said they are the only ones to enter now."

Chail, shocked at the revelation, nodded to the Wooder, and turned.

"Before you go in, Master Chail, please understand, King Savoy is very sick, and he may not last much longer. It is hard to understand him, for fluid fills his lungs and he coughs considerably. He is not contagious, so you will not get sick by being around him. His eyes are sensitive to light, so be prepared. Do not touch him, for his skin is pained at the touch, and will blister and bleed easily."

Chail nodded and turned to enter. The Wooder reached out and touched the shoulder of the Spear and whispered, "When I say he is not well, I also mean he does not look well. Don't show surprise. The Queen and oldest son are sitting with him."

Chail nodded again, and took Bethany's hand. She squeezed back, and with his other hand he opened the door to enter the King's chambers.

Bethany wrinkled her nose. The odor of the king was pungent, similar to that of dead chicken left in the sun too long. She swallowed the urge to cough and kept pace beside Chail as he walked into the anteroom.

Another Wooder waited for them, standing by the door to the bedroom.

"He is drifting in and out of consciousness, and may not recognize you immediately. Do not tire him." The Wooder reached over and opened the door, releasing more of rotting smell into the room.

Bethany still held onto Chail's hand as they entered.

She remembered how the king had looked the day before, sick but still strong. Now the skin stretched tight across his face and most of the meat had left his bones. The sharp eyes were clouded and sunken in his face, and his cheekbones jutted from the loss of flesh. The nose shone in the low light of the room, and lips pulled back from the teeth in a perpetual grin of a reaper.

The queen sat on the bed with a small, wet towel in her hand. She dabbed the king's forehead lightly. Her plump profile was a distinct contrast to the king's gaunt features.

A young man, no more than twenty, stood to the side. Dark hair ruffled and a chiselled jaw that reminded her of the king, but his eyes showed the queen's kindness. He inclined his head to Chail. His eyes flittered to Bethany, a slight smile hinted at the corner of his mouth. It was gone before it truly showed. The smile shocked her. Not knowing what to do, she looked down at her feet and shuffled her feet.

"Stop fidgeting," Chail whispered, squeezing her hand. "That's Queen Milon, and her oldest son, Prince Darious."

They waited for the queen to acknowledge them. She stared at her husband, emotionless. After a minute, Darious touched his mother's shoulder, and motioned towards Chail and Bethany. She nodded and looked toward her husband again.

"He asked for you, Master Chail. He respects you." She took a deep breath, and turned her head toward the two Spears. "He drifted off just before you came in. This is the first sleep he has had that wasn't restless. I'm worried if I wake him he'll not sleep as well again."

"I am awake, Milon." Savoy's hand reached out, shaking. He touched Milon's arm with tenderness. "Please, let him appro—" He started coughing, leaning forward.

Milon leaned over, gently pushing Savoy back into his bed. "Don't exert yourself."

His breathing was shallow, gurgling, and unsettling to Bethany. "Milon, I love you. I have not been a good husband, and for that I am truly sorry."

"You don't have to apologize, Savoy. You're my husband, and I have loved you as well."

"You lie, but thank you," he said. There was no animosity in his voice, only love. "I was not nice to you. I'm only happy we were able to have strong children, and you made sure they were honorable. I didn't deserve you."

"Enough of this talk," Milon said. "You'll get well, and we'll argue again like we have all our lives. Only this time, I'll make you come with me to the kitchens in the morning for a sweet snack before breakfast. Do you want to speak to Master Chail, now?"

"Master Chail is here?"

Chail stepped forward. "I am here, my King."

"I… I kept after you to increase the Spears, to get them ready." The king coughed again. Mucus colored the skin at the corner of his mouth, and Milon whipped it away. "Fifteen years ago the Seers came to me. Several of them had been having a recurring dream. One of the attack of the Hobs, but also an impending attack from Elves. They couldn't tell me…" He coughed again, this time it was more violent.

"They couldn't tell me when, but they knew it would be soon. I kept after you to increase the numbers of the Spears. I should have told you. I wanted to use them to attack the Elves first, but that is not to be.

"I am being punished by the Five. My desire to strike first has allowed this sickness to devour my body." Again, he coughed. Milon took away the cloth now spotted with blood. "Forgive me, Chail. I should have been more upfront with you." His head slowly turned to the side, his eyes glossing over and mouth opening. The sound of wheezing slowed, and the gargling became less pronounced until finally, after an extended exhale, King Savoy no longer breathed.

Milon wept.

Tess paced the length of Chail's office, waiting. She had heard the king was ill, but rumors were now spreading that he had died because the Five had frowned upon him. She shook her head, not knowing why someone would spread such vile rumors.

The door opened, admitting Chail and Bethany. They seemed to be bickering as they entered, but Tess didn't listen to them. She just ran to Chail and hugged him.

Chail hugged her back. "And what did I do to deserve this?"

"What's happening? Why did you get called to the King?"

Bethany spoke before Chail could. "The King died. The Five took him."

"But, just yesterday he was leaving to make sure everything went well. All he had was a cough." Tess backed away from Chail, looking him over from head to toe. "Did you touch him?"

"No. He wasn't contagious."

"That's what the Wooder said," Bethany sneered. "Can we go now? There's nothing here for us."

"Excuse me?" Chail said. "I think you speak for yourself."

"I didn't mean...You know, there's nothing stopping us now from marching on the Hobs and saving the town."

A light tapping sounded on the door. They turned, and saw Prince Darious. "Am I interrupting anything?"

"My Prince, no. Your prerogative," Chail said. "The Realm is yours now." He lowered his voice and leaned forward. "You need to be inaugurated quickly to fill the power gap. The longer we wait, the longer the council will have control."

"Is that such a bad thing?" the Prince asked. "Father always relied on their wisdom."

"Yes," said Chail. "One of the things your father was always concerned about was the council taking control. They are the ones who held up the protection of the town, and they are the ones who would block your coronation. Hold it up for as long as they can, and maybe demand that your mother remarry, thus blocking you from the throne. This would force the kingship on her new husband who may not be as kind as your father."

Darious studied Chail, one arm across his chest, hand cupping the elbow of his other arm. His free hand stroked his chin. After a minute he dropped his hands and sighed. "Yes, you are right, Master Chail," he said, standing up straight. "Before the council takes any type of control I want you to arrange the coronation. It needs to take place with haste. I don't want the council to hinder us saving the Town of Lands."

Chail looked at the man. "You seem to have a little bit of your father in you. I will have the Spears march immediately."

"Thank you, Master Chail. These orders will make it official." He handed Chail a scroll sealed with the King's seal.

Milon sat on the bed, holding Savoy's hand. Tears still ran down her cheeks, and her nose shone. Servants entered the room, cleaned and left. They didn't bother her, knowing grief needed to be played out fully before a person could heal.

The chef entered, carrying a small tray with a few lemon squares. He approached her and knelt.

"My Queen."

"Brant? You never come up here. What—"

"You came down and picked at the food I prepare. You haven't been down for a while, so I brought to you this." He held out the tray.

"Oh, Brant. They are my favorite, but right now I have no appetite." She turned back to her husband. "He never liked the weight I put on after we married. Maybe I should lose it now he is gone."

"As you wish, My Queen. I only want to serve."

"I know, Brant. But for now I want you to make light meals for me, nothing heavy. I think he'd like me to live long, and enjoy my life. He… He loved me, you know."

"How could anyone not love you, My Queen?"

"I was not kind to him."

"He never complained."

"No, he never complained."

"And why would he, my Queen? You gave him the Realm."

Milon placed Savoy's hand on the chest of his body. She then leaned forward and kissed the now cold forehead and stood. With trembling hands, the Queen straightened her dress and stepped away from the bed.

"I need to let the Wooders take the body. They'll make sure he is ready for interment." She looked over at the chef and smiled. "You have always been kind to me."

With his head downcast, he took a deep breath. "I have always loved you, my Queen."

Her gaze sought to meet his eyes, but he kept his on the cold floor. Milon wondered why he confessed what he did.

Her hand stopped trembling, and she reached up to place it on his cheek. He leaned into her touch, and then moved away quickly. She could see the heat of his discomfort rising in his face.

"I didn't mean to…"

"Brant," she said, her voice soft.

The man straightened, looking toward her but not at her. "My Queen…Please. I am a common chef, below your station. It…We are of two worlds." He held out the tray again. "One. Just one. For remembering."

Milon smiled at the man, reached out, and took one of the squares. "For remembering." She took a bite.

Prince Darious looked down on the Spear's training ground. His lips moved, he appeared to be counting, and his eyes carried a question that he could not ask.

"Master Chail," he said. "You have just over one hundred and thirty Spears. But I'm concerned; they look very young."

"The youngest is nine, oldest is thirteen." Chail turned to Darious. "Your concern is not warranted. Each one of these children has already been blooded in battle. Even the least trained has fought for their life, and killed at least one hardened criminal."

"Killed? They are so young. Must we always be so… barbaric?"

Chail looked out at the Spears, gaze landing on each one. *This is so familiar, I feel like I've done this a great number of times.* Each one of the Spears lined up below them held a special place in his heart, like the members of the Clutch he had sent off just weeks ago. Training them any other way than he had done was not a decision he would make.

"I don't know any other way to deal with a criminal than to have them help train Spears in flight." Chail sighed. "These criminals are murderers and kidnapers. The worst of the worst."

Darious glanced at the children again. He watched their feet pound against the ground; the dust swirled, not showing the blood stains absorbed by many decades of training. The targets leaned against hay stacks with spear buts protruding from them. He exhaled and shook his head. The prince took a deep breath. "We should try to reintegrate our criminals back into society. We kill, when we should understand; punish, when we should heal."

"My Prince, it is the way. They broke the rules of society. Not by stealing to feed themselves, but by murdering, killing those we wish to protect. If they don't want to be proper members of our culture, then why should they live? No, it is unfair to ask those who follow the law to support those who break it. If you asked the people to do such, you may find them rising in revolt." Chail bowed his head.

"Your father had an interesting outlook on life, and how it was to be cherished. I remember one of his edicts, so long ago. 'Let no man, woman or child take the life of an innocent. One who does forfeits their own life in exchange.' He believed the life of an innocent meant more than the life of a criminal. That still means something to the people. Yes, it is custom to place none but hardened criminals in the hands of the Spears, and he made sure they were hardened criminals. You were not there when he passed judgment on those whom he sentenced to the training grounds."

Darious remained silent.

Pushing himself away from the railing, Chail moved towards the entrance of the barracks. He stopped before entering and turned to the prince. At first he swore the young man's father was looking down at the Spears, not the boy himself. The similarities between the two stuck him, and he almost said the dead king's name when the prince turned towards him.

"What's wrong, Master Chail?"

"Nothing, Sire. It's just…Well, I see your father in you. He always looked out at the Spears with the same expression as you had just then." Chail shook his head. "But you are two different people, with different ideas."

"Yes, we are different people." Darious moved away from the railing. "Remember it, and we can move forward. I want you to keep training the Spears, and if all goes well over the next few days, return all of them to us to finish their training."

"I'll do my best."

"Yes, do your best. How many of the militia will you be taking?"

"I'd rather not take any, but the numbers say we will need to take at least two hundred."

"Why would you say that?" Darious asked.

"They're not trained." Chail rejoined the Prince at the railing. His hand gestured toward the Spears. "Each of these children is a seasoned veteran. They can run all day, and still be able to fight. The militia will be lucky to walk for half a day, and they will be tired the next day. We have to force march them for three days with little rest. March for five hours, rest for two hours, march for five hours. Some will not make it. Some will fall from exhaustion, others will just give up. What type of an impression do you think that will make on the Spears?"

"They will understand," Darious said. "You've not only trained their bodies, but expanded their minds." He put his hand on Chail's shoulder, even though he was almost half a foot shorter. "I look at Bethany, and see the training of her intellect. So will it affect them? Yes, but not the way you think. I believe they will make the militia push even harder, for the militia will see children doing what they are not able to do."

"Then we shall do it?"

"Yes," Darious said. "You will do it."

Together, they walked into the barracks.

Bethany looked at Chail. "I don't deserve to be on a horse."

Chail put his arm around her. "Then who does?"

"Any of the Masters, but not me."

"Tell me, who ran for three days to warn us?"

Bethany looked at the ground. "I did."

"And who risked her own life to get here in time to warn us?"

"I did." Her voice was barely audible.

"Bethany, you have already proven your worth to the Spears. Now, as we are about to march for several days, you should be thankful you're being allowed to come with your injuries still not healed. And if I didn't give you a horse to ride, Tess wouldn't let me hear the end of it."

"But you're the trainer of Spears, and she's your wife. Why would it make any difference?"

He squeezed her shoulder and laughed. "My sweet child, if only life were that easy. The truth is, yes, we are married. So in order to keep my life happy, I keep her happy. When you're older you'll understand. A husband will tell you, spend your time making your wife happy, and she will make sure you are happy as well."

"It's like the sacrifice of the Fifth God," Bethany said, looking up at him. "He sacrificed for us, and now we try to make him happy."

Chail chuckled. "I don't think a mere human can make a God happy."

Bethany didn't understand. She had been taught the Gods always cared about people. They relished in the building of temples, prayers offered to them, sacrifices burned for them. She didn't understand why Chail, a man she knew to be God fearing, would speak so harshly about the deities he offered up prayer to. Her head swam with the thought of Master Chail not being allowed at the feet of the Five after his life ended.

"What about the king? Do you think he's at the feet of the Five now?"

"I believe he is," Chail said, his eyes scanning the formations of troops before him. "It's unworthy of them to ignore a king."

"But they could if they wished, right?" Bethany's curiosity got the better of her. She swelled with questions concerning the Five, and even though Chail was not a priest, he was the smartest man she knew.

"I don't think the Five have any desire to ignore a soul who's made the long journey to their feet."

"Tess said her first husband died before she gave birth to her child. Don't you think he would have asked the Five to look out for her? Why did they let her first child die?" Bethany let it out before she knew what was happening. She saw the slight pain reflect in Chail's eyes, and immediately regretted asking.

After a few seconds Chail took a deep breath. "We don't know what a person's soul will ask for when it gets to the feet of the Five. First, it could be they don't speak the actual words, but are examined for the deepest desire they may have. It could be that his desire was not to be alone in the afterlife, and he wanted to have someone to love. Maybe this is why her son died of the coughing. We don't know. Maybe the Five knew if Tess lost her child she would come to the Spears, and better the lives of your entire Clutch. Have you ever thought what your life, and the lives of your Clutch mates, would have been like if she was not in it?"

"I… I couldn't think of my life without her. She's been my mother, my friend. The one who always made sure we were alright after training. She made us sit and understand what it's like to be a family." Bethany took hold of the hand on her shoulder and squeezed. "You guided us through our training, making sure we survived. I saw you cry when Elana was hurt. Remember when a splinter of wood took her eye? You held her hand and…You didn't see me. We were supposed to be practicing, but Thomasyn was concerned, and asked me to follow. I did, and you cried when you saw her."

Bethany remembered the day with clarity. The girl, six years old, had lain on the bed with a blood-spotted bandage wrapped around her head, covering one eye. And all caused by a simple training accident and a broken wooden sword.

"I remember it," he said softly.

"You and Nanny Tess are the father and mother of our Clutch."

Chail's eyes widened and he looked at Bethany. She returned his gaze. Her face reflected innocence not yet destroyed by the training, the killing, and the life of a Spear. Her purity would be enough to destroy any man's heart.

"That is the kindest thing anyone has ever said to me." He kissed the top of her head. "Now, my young Spear, it is time to get these two groups integrated. I want the old militia with the young Spears. The young ones will rally the old to move faster and keep up. The older Spears can stay with the younger men, for they will have more in common. What do you say? Want to show the militia what Spears are made of?"

Tess stood outside the gates to the Spears' training grounds. Her eyes scanned the faces of the women and children gathered there anticipating the march of the Spears and militia. Many women, holding children of all ages, had tears rolling down their cheeks in what she could only guess was a foreboding glimpse of what the future had in store for their husbands.

Like them, Tess was concerned with the possibility of losing Chail. She knew her husband's skill made him one of the best, a true fighter, a seasoned Spear with knowledge far beyond those he commanded.

When she agreed to marry him, Tess had not hesitated as she had in her first marriage. She knew this man would not be taken advantage of by muggers or brigands. No, Chail would take them and use them to train the Spears, like a true man would. She imagined him on the battle field, hundreds of Hobs bodies before him and arrows bouncing off his chest as he bellowed in victory. A smile touched the corner of her mouth. She knew Chail would return. He'd bring Bethany and the others home, and cull the Hobs so they could not attack the Realm for many more years to come.

The wailing of a woman reached her ears, the pitch high and sounding of great lamentation. She scanned faces, and finally found her. The woman wore the robes of a widow in morning. Her hair, streaked with silver, ran down her back in rivers of black. In her arms, a child, no more than a few months old, howled for attention. Tess remembered her child, the one who lasted in her arms only a few days before passing to the Five. Her heart went out to the woman.

A shriek and Tess wondered how different her life would have been if Denis had lived. Would she be the one mourning his life in the march to the Town of Lands? If she didn't know as much about the Spears as she knew now, would she still be as calm?

She wanted to reach out to the woman, to comfort and tell her all would be well, that the loved one she cried for would be taken care of. And if he survived the march, every Spear would help protect the life of each member of the militia. Tess knew that all the Spears, even with their training incomplete, would rather give their life for the lives of the ones traveling with them than return without them.

But the woman didn't know this. How could she? Even living in Capital, so close to the training grounds of the Spears, she did not know much about how they were trained. She would only know that if someone broke the law severely, they would be taken to the Spears and be used in order to teach the children how to kill. With only that knowledge, Tess understood why the woman would be wailing.

The great doors swung open before the crowd. Onlookers gasped at the display of Spears, dressed in their leather jerkins and cloaks. Even at their small size, the children moved with an air of confidence. The crowd parted out of respect for the sacrifice being made for the Realm. Mixed among the formation marched the men of the militia.

A SHARP SPEAR POINT

Five abreast, feet hitting the ground in time, the parade marched through the gates. It was the first time in many years Spears of such a young age had been called upon to protect the Realm. The first five Tess recognized from the young nine-year-old Clutch, heads held high. A sword hung on each hip. The short sword they would use when they closed ranks and were close enough to their enemy to smell their breath and feel the heat of it on their face. The small size of the sword hid the effectiveness of the weapon. It was not clumsy like a great sword or heavy like a broad sword. The children could easily deflect any blow with it, and still outswing a Hobs weapon three to one. Over their left shoulder, the throwing bone stuck out, and over the right, short spears. The bone cradled the spear in order to propel it with accuracy and force, but could also be used as a club to bludgeon an unwary adversary.

Standing out in stark contrast, the militia wore iron armor, made for them by the city smiths. Small helms covered their heads like the shells of nuts. Tines of metal stretched from the brow of the helmets to the tip of the noses. Scale mail, the armor made from small, flat pieces of metal, protected the front of each one, and ring mail covered their arms. They only protected the front, for it was well-known by all that a man in battle would protect their life by not turning an unprotected back on an attacker. The stark contrast between the shining militia and the Spears in their earth toned suits gave a stark contrast as the sun glinted off polished armor.

As the columns of the parade passed, people cheered, lamented, and offered gifts of flowers. Several women rushed into the ranks, kissing their loved ones goodbye. Tess hoped their loved ones would return.

Tess eyed Chail astride his horse, with Bethany riding beside him, and stepped out of the crowd as he approached. Chail stopped his horse beside her. Bethany, likewise, stopped beside her master and waited.

"You will come back," Tess said. Her voice was soft, but it carried the weight of a command, and she saw his eyes widen from the statement.

"I will come back to you, my love." Chail's mouth turned to a soft smile.

"You will come back to me, and you will bring the Spears home safe."

"I will bring all back with me."

Tess could barely see from the water and sun in her eyes. "You will bring Bethany back with you to heal, along with Thomasyn and Jon."

Chail shifted in his saddle. "I will bring all our children home."

She understood the meaning behind his words. He would bring them all home, dead or alive. He would not leave anyone behind. Those that fell at the side of the road during the march would be cared for, and none would be left alone. Someone would always be with them.

She stepped closer. "I love you, Chail. Come home to me when you have crushed the Hobs."

He leaned down and kissed her gently. When he straightened, his face showed the gentleness of the man she loved. He turned to look forward and shook the reins. His horse strode forward, leaving Bethany looking at Tess.

"I'll let no harm touch him. You have my promise," Bethany said, and she nudged her horse to follow Chail.

"I know you will, Bethany. I know you will." Tess watched them until all the Spears and militia had passed. She waited until the fifty Wooders assigned to them also passed. She waited until their bodies had meld into one large mass of men moving through the city. She waited until the crowd dispersed.

A SHARP SPEAR POINT

Tess left the streets as the last of the day's sun blazed in the direction of the Spears and dipped below the horizon. She waited until the gates closed. She waited until the sun threatened to close the day.

-4-

For the most part, the forced march worked. Men forced their feet forward, backs bent with strain. Every Spear in Flight, the young Spears still in training and not yet fully indoctrinated into the elite group, marched without faltering. They did not complain, they did not falter, and they did not fail. Chail understood the problems of a forced march, but no alternative was left for them if they were to save the Town of Lands. They must continue forward, marching day and night with little or no rest. The men of the militia, pushed to their breaking point, exhausted, and feeble, could only try and match the Spears. Chail mixed the militia and Spears for just such a reason, to give the soldiers something to aspire to. It would force them to keep moving, to prove their worth. A simple matter of pride would drive them forward.

Many years of conditioning had prepared them for this day. The day they would march with no end in sight. The day they marched to save the people they served.

The younger Spears had just finished a ten league run a few days prior. Each and every Spear was well trained in long distance running, knowing they could travel farther without a horse than with one. But not as fast.

In order to ensure the militia survived, Chail stopped the march every three hours to allow a one-hour rest. During the day they covered forty leagues, and after a short rest of two hours, the Spears roused and eagerly prepared for the continuation of the march under the stars.

Three of the militia could not continue, and Chail assigned a Wooder to help heal them of their exhaustion. During the night, seven Spears found them, and joined their ranks. The Spears in Flight rejoiced as seasoned Spears, lent their strength to the defense of the town.

Through the evening, five more militia fell, and Chail again allowed for a Wooder to oversee them. To bolster their numbers, twelve more Spears joined their quest. And the column of marchers swelled.

By the middle of the next day, Salman was in sight, and a contingent of forty Spears ready to reinforce the ranks joined them. All told of the same dream, a compelling need for them to meet the group on their march.

A dozen of the militia fell later that day, and again, Chail released a Wooder to care for them. Another twelve Spears joined the march.

At the end of the day they spied wisps of smoke on the horizon. Militia, downcast that they were late, grumbled about rushing to only be late while the Spears discussed rushing forward to save the Town of Lands for the Hobs now occupied it.

Thomasyn ran towards the town, his mind filled with images of protecting and saving the people living there. Beside him ran Jon, Shail and Garion. All were propelled by the same need.

For six days they harassed the Hobs. For six days they were mosquitoes to them. Never truly hurting, but always there, driving the commanders insane with the little prickling annoyance they could not get rid of. They scratched at the injury caused by the four Spears, but they never could free themselves of the aggravation.

After the seventh day of attempting to root out the cavity, the four Spears who had agitated in their ranks, they march on the Town of Lands, and overtook the buildings. They ignored the harassment of the Spears, and attacked. A small group of defenders could not stop the invaders, nor slow them down once they moved forward as one massive force.

The Spears arrived at the town ahead of the advancing foe just before the sun crested the horizon. With the town finally warned of the invaders an alarm was raised, people evacuated their homes, leaving empty buildings to stand defenseless against the horde. The people left behind anything not needed. By midday half of the town folk had evacuated. As the Hobs started their attack the remainder of the town was en route to the neighboring settlement, due south and away from the Hobs direction of attack.

Jon watched from the kalash of the temple, the highest part, as the mass of Hobs approached, and later from the pista, the porch way, as the invading force entered the town. He killed three advance scouts before meeting the others at the outskirts.

There was nothing they could do to save the buildings.

They ran from the town.

"King Savoy is dead," Chail said to Shail and Garion. He watched as the two Spears sat with their mouths hanging open.

"Dead? How? He was in perfect health last I saw him." Shail took another bite of rabbit and shook his head.

"He declined incredibly fast. It was first a cough, and then he was in bed, consumed. Not even the Master Wooders knew what happened, or how it took him so suddenly," Chail said. He turned his attention back to the fire. He watched as the remains of the rabbit spat grease onto the coals.

"Magic," Garion said as he lifted his head. "In the north eastern waste land I saw a shaman make a man devour himself from his insides before the dawn sun climbed the sky."

"It could be, but how can we be sure?" Shail said.

Garion looked down at his plate, and then lifted his finger in realization. "Who could have profited from his death?"

"The prince?" Chail asked.

"No, but it could have been someone outside the Royal Family." Shail put his plate down.

"The council delayed our departure, and three of them didn't want the dreaming sent by the Seers."

"Master Chail," Thomasyn said, as he came up on the three. "We need to talk."

"Yes, Thomasyn?"

"I would rather we talk alone." His voice was pensive.

Shail stood along with Garion. "Stay, we'll go see the Wooders. I also want to see Bethany and thank her. She did well in following the orders I gave her. She really didn't want to leave us, but I think she saw the logic even though she didn't agree with it."

They glanced at Thomasyn as they left. Chail waited, and then looked at Thomasyn. "What is it?"

"There's something wrong with Jon."

"What do you mean?" Chail asked.

Thomasyn glanced away, fingers pinching the edge of his cloak. "He's acting a little strange. Not quite like himself."

"You're going to have to be a little more forthcoming."

"I don't know how to say it."

"You just have to say it, Thomasyn." Chail stood and paced. "Look, it's only been a few weeks since you left the training center, and already you've changed a lot. Before you would hardly come forward with something like this."

"I decided something needs to be said."

"Tess told me this would happen. She said, 'Watch out for that Thomasyn. When he figures out what his voice is for he'll talk for hours.' I guess you've found your voice."

Thomasyn's cheeks turned red, and he glanced away.

"Thomasyn, the art of being a good leader is knowing when to discuss something and when to just come out and say what's on your mind."

"I think he's becoming…angry."

"What do you mean, angry?"

"I mean angry. The others have seen it as well. He seems to be taking pleasure in killing. Our first attack he was only to rile the Hobs, but instead put himself at risk in order to kill some of them."

Chail stared at Thomasyn with an intensity of a cat watching a bird. "So, have you seen something that led you to believe this is happening?"

"No. I was not present during his part. When we pulled the Hobs out of the camp he was the decoy. But I have a suspicion he did more than just kill a few of them. I think he killed a lot of them. He had scratch marks on his leggings."

"Interesting. What makes you think something is happening from this? Could he not have been surprised by a few of them?"

"It's more than a suspicion."

"You have proof?" Chail did not let the worry he felt show on his face.

"The underside of his horse was covered in Hobs blood."

"Are you sure?"

"Yes, I'm sure." And Thomasyn sat down and told Chail about all his suspicions.

The sun rose as Chail moved about the tents, knowing he would have to start waking the militia soon. The Spears had already been up for an hour, cleaning the site and preparing breakfast for everyone. He watched them move about, busy ants working through the day. Tents came down and were packed.

"Spears, assemble!" Chail's voice broke the silence as he watched all the Spears gather, some grumbling could be heard from the militia tents. "We need to set some strategy for this confrontation. Seer Nelion, is there anything from the dreaming?"

Nelion, an older woman reaching her fiftieth year, stepped forward. She leaned on her staff. The woman seemed feeble, but all knew otherwise. "There was some whispering in the dreaming last night. Something about victory, but a cost. I saw bones dance on bodies of Hobs."

The acrid smell of burning pitch hung in the air, and Pin winced.

Danton tied a cloth around his head to cover his mouth. The Hobs wandered aimlessly through the town, kicking down doors and rushing into the homes. Shouts of anger and frustration filled the air as no one was found for them to kill.

Pin stood beside Danton, face flushing a deep green. The Hobs reported to Pin one by one that there were no humans in any of the buildings.

"They knew we were coming," Danton said. "Those Spears who kept attacking us, they stalled our march enough for the town to evacuate."

"I'm hungry for the flesh of a human child," Pin said. It was not just a desire, but a need. The Hobs face was gaunt, cheeks sunken and skin stretched across his body. "I need the flesh." Power takes a toll, and Pin had realized it when he first extended Danton's life. But what else could he do? The gods demanded payment for what he did. To let the man die meant losing his position in the court of the Queen, and that was the last thing he wanted.

"We'll find something for you, Pin. We always do."

They walked down the center of town, looking for anything passed over by the others. They found nothing. The Hobs never left a stone unturned when it came to looking for human flesh. It was a delicacy to them.

"Commander!" A young Hobs ran towards them, excitement lacing his voice. "We have something."

Pin looked up. His hand reached out and curled into a fist. "Humans?"

"We think. Yes, humans." The Hobs motioned for them to follow, and they did.

The small one took them to the outskirts of town and through a field at the southern side. After walking for thirty minutes they came across a small home, the door askew.

Inside, three beds were overturned and blood splatter decorated two of the walls. A chest with its lid open had clothes strewn about. The cooking fire smoldered slightly, and the pot hanging on the hook still steamed with food.

Pin looked about. "Did they run?"

The small Hobs held up his finger to his lips. Even in a quiet whisper his voice reached Pin's ears, and the Hobs pointed towards the chest. "They are still here."

Storm clouds shaped like anvils rolled across the horizon and blotted out the sun. The temperature had dropped as well, bringing a chill that penetrated clothing. A gust of wind picked up a stray dandelion seed. Small rocks had been found in order to hold down the corners of the map from being caught up in the pending storm

Chail looked at the sky and shook his head. "This weather will either help or hinder us."

"This town is like a crucible, and pot of boiling water waiting for us to spill it." Chail stood and looked at Shail and Garion. "You've fought these Hobs. What are they like?"

"Not well organized," Shail said, rubbing the back of his neck. "They're easily distracted, quick to anger, and undisciplined. If we can provoke them into rage they will lose their minds."

Garion spoke up, "Jon made the whole army rise up and follow him, even when he was on a horse. They are berserkers."

"What can we use to fire that anger? An enemy without thought is easy to kill. If the blood lust is about them…" His voice trailed off, and he looked into the sky again, watching the shadow of the clouds falling towards them.

"We could use Jon again. He can fire their angst, tease them into a mass of murdering desire." Garion put his finger on the map, just outside the town. "Here, we can have him draw them into this valley."

Chail looked back at the map, his eyes following the line traced by Garion. The plan was good, and the Spears along with the militia would be able to lay in ambush.

"You believe we can use the valley walls? Slowly pick them off from behind?"

"Yes," Garion said. "We have enough Spears to take them down. We just have to…" His brow furrowed. "What is this formation?" His finger pointed to where the valley opened up in a circle.

Chail looked. "It seems the end of this valley is a killing hole."

Shail turned back to the map. "Should we really use Jon?"

"What do you mean?" Chail asked.

"Something is wrong with that boy," Shail said.

"You're not the first to suggest it." Chail rubbed the back of his neck.

Shail paused, his finger drawing the line across the map to the killing hole. "It's just…I think he's beginning to like killing."

Chail shook his head. "Spears kill. It's an unfortunate part of their training. They don't like or dislike it. We kill because we have to."

"No, for him there's more to it than that." Garion tapped the map again. "I read the reports, when he was taking part in the travelling. How he killed two trained soldiers without even thinking and did not care. He stuffed his face and had to be reminded about the people the brigands had taken advantage of. He seems to be taking a perverse pleasure out of killing."

"Where is he now?" Chail asked.

"With the others," Shail said.

Chail took a deep breath. "Call him in."

The three Hobs clawed at the ground outside the hut, moving dirt and wood aside as quickly as they could. After an hour they knew the only way to get into what they believed to be a chamber was through the chest. And the chest was secured to the floor. They could not move it. So they started to dig.

Claws ripped up planks of wood to find rocks. They moved aside rocks to find more wood. Dirt gave way; wood splintered under the onslaught of hands pulling at them. Rocks released their hold on the earth as fingers gripped their unyielding mass. After six feet they reached straw mixed in with the clay of the ground, and they heard the voices of humans below them.

They scrapped against the hard surface of baked clay. A muffled scream reached the ears of the diggers, echoed by more than one voice. Pin drooled. Danton knelt by the edge, watching the shoulders of the diggers work. Three feet down, they found a chamber made of hard, baked clay.

The Hobs in the pit chipped away at the surface with their knives, taking small pieces off at first, but making headway into the chamber below them. The screams increased in intensity, and Pin could tell many people hid below them.

"Ready your weapons," Pin said.

Three hands groped for their weapons and drew them.

A hole, created by the last plucking of a knife, allowed the scent of human flesh to float up to all those above. A curious hand reached into it, and felt about. His eyes grew wide, and a scream erupted from the Hobs mouth. He drew back and a stump came out of the hole, not an arm. Blood sprayed the dirt and other Hobs around him.

"Pull him out of there," Danton said.

Hands grabbed and hauled the screaming Hobs out of the hole. Three took his place, and hammered with enthusiasm against the clay. More chips fell, and after several blows the clay gave way, dropping the Hobs into the chamber below.

The screams reached a fevered pitch.

Jon stood akimbo, looking down at the map. "I can do it." The corner of his mouth curled upward.

"Do you understand what I'm asking you to do?" Chail asked.

Jon sighed, pointed to the town on the map and recited the plan. "I get the Hobs to follow me somehow, and lead them into the valley here." His finger trailed to the start of the valley. "Keeping them engaged, I get them to follow me until the end here." He tapped the killing hole. "By that time they should be fewer because you and the other Spears will be attacking the end of their formation. You'll be hiding in the woods at the side of the valley."

"Do you have a way of getting them to follow you?" Shail asked.

A SHARP SPEAR POINT

"I'll kill a couple of them," he said flatly, not looking up from the map.

"How will you do that?" Chail asked.

"Short spear or arrow. Simple enough."

"Good. Pick a horse from the ones we brought and get ready. We'll start first thing in the morning," Shail said.

Jon looked at Chail, nodded his head, and walked away.

Once Jon was out of ear shot Chail looked at the others. "He seems about the same. Like Thomasyn, he's starting to talk more, and he's coming into his own."

"But he did talk about killing without feeling a sense of loss," Shail said.

"It's what we were talking about. He needs to possibly kill some of the Hobs in order to get them to follow him. I don't think he's taking a perverse pleasure in killing."

Garion shook his head. "He's different. Different even than he was when we started traveling to the Teeth."

"He's finished his training, and now he's realizing that he's a full-fledged Spear. Of course he'll be different." Chail pinched the bridge of his nose. "Even Bethany has changed. She's not the same little girl, especially after getting to Capital and warning us. No, I don't think there's anything wrong with him."

"I hope you're right," Shail said. "We're placing a lot of trust in him for this attack."

"How many Hobs are we dealing with?" Chail asked.

"About a thousand. We did keep them in duress for the week and took down a few of them. How many Spears do we have?"

"Two hundred Spears in Flight, another one hundred and ten Spears joined us in the march. Only sixty of the militia will be able to fight." Chail did the math. This would be the only way to quell the invasion; he needed to destroy all the Hobs, and Danton as well.

"We can do it, Chail," Garion said. "One Spear can kill ten Hobs without trouble. We'll quell the invasion, and it'll take them years to recover."

It was a cave under the home. Walls, carved out of rock. Clay fired and hard. The marvel of it surprised the Hobs, for it started from the chest and worked its way down. A bar, holding the trunk in place, was easily removed once they entered the cave.

The first chamber held five children and an old woman. The Hobs took the children by forcing them into a makeshift coral. They slit the throat of the old woman, and the children screamed.

Then they moved the clothes and hanging blankets to discover more tunnels, and chambers attached to them. The Hobs cleared those as well, removing the children to the coral, and killing the adults.

"I'm taking this one," Pin said, his hand grabbing a human child from the arms of the small human female who held it. "I'll boil its bones until the meat falls off."

The human female shrieked, arms flailing out to the child. "No! Jordon!" Tears fell like diamonds from her eyes, catching the glint of torches. Her wailing became frantic as she struggled against the grip of her captor.

A clawed hand struck the side of the girls face, and her cries turned to sobs as she was dragged away.

The wailing of the child in Pin's arms continued, and he looked at the others through clouded eyes. "I need to take care of this, immediately."

"Do you need any help, Pin?" Danton asked, as he helped the Hobs out of the chamber.

"No," Pin snapped back. Before Danton could react, Pin softened his voice as he spoke through the child's crying. "I'm sorry, Danton. The pressure of making you young again weighs heavy on me. I need to regain my strength, and this pitiful creature will do that. I need time to take care of this, and the child's energy will make me whole again. The ceremony is tedious, and will need certain…special rites." He turned his back. "I will return, soon." Pin walked outside and towards the town.

Jon checked the saddle on the horse, making sure the belts were fastened properly. Once all was secure, he turned to Thomasyn who picked out his weapons.

"I only need five," Jon said.

"You should have six. I picked the best ones in the bunch. Straight, no knots in the shafts."

"And why do you want me to have so many knives?"

Thomasyn picked up one of the knives and balanced it in his hand. "Bethany wanted to make sure you had a lot of knives. She said you're such a bad thrower you'd need a lot."

Jon smirked. "Funny. I bet I could out-throw her now."

"She sharpened your sword for you. She said it felt like you were bashing it against rocks, probably the ones in your head."

"I had to kill a lot of Hobs over the last few days. I didn't have time to sharpen it." Jon took the sword from the pile and pulled it from the scabbard. He tested the edge against his thumb, nodded and put it back. "She did okay."

"Did you get enough to eat?" Thomasyn asked.

"What?"

"Did you get enough to eat? It's a simple question. I know how much you like to eat."

"Yes. Half a rabbit and some greens."

"Good. I want you to make it. I'd hate to see you stop riding because you wanted to bite into some dried meat or fruit."

"Did you put some dried meat in the bags?" Jon asked.

"Don't even laugh about that. I want you to ride hard and not take any chances."

"Well, if the Hobs stop chasing me, I'll have to turn around and entice them somehow." Jon bent over, picked up a rock, tossed it in the air a few times and put it into a saddle bag.

"Rocks? Really? Is that how your sword got so dull?" Thomasyn stood, and started handing the knives to Jon.

"A sling and a rock; don't underestimate their power to drive the Hobs insane with anger."

"Well, whatever it takes. Just make sure you come back alive."

Jon chuckled. "I will. But I would be more concerned about you and the rest. Make sure you're hidden well, so they won't know you're there. Only take out the ones in the back, will you." Jon took the knives and put them about the saddle. The spears went on his back next, and finally he strapped the sword around his waist.

Thomasyn held the reins of the horse as Jon mounted it. "You're my brother, Jon. Make sure you stay out of the Hobs' reach, and make it back safe."

Jon reined the horse and turned it. He started down the road toward the town.

"You be safe, Thomasyn. Remember, you're not the best of us."

Jon spurred the horse and galloped down the road.

-5-

Pin licked the blood off his fingers. Muscles filled out and bones strengthened. His skin no longer hung on his body and he could feel strength returning. He held out his hand, and the skin plumped up before his eyes. He no longer worried about the decrepit way he had looked. The ceremony of rejuvenation worked well, and now he could relish in the rewards. His fingers went again into the body of the human child.

The nail on the end of his index finger speared a kidney, and he lifted the organ to his mouth. The meat tasted similar to mushrooms, with a gentle texture. The kidney melted in his mouth.

"Ohhhh." Pin rolled his eyes. The sun of the morning brightened the room.

The small room was in a home near the outskirts of town, and he had secured the door with a chair pushed up against it. A little fire allowed for him to call upon his god and queen to capture the essence of the child. He had trapped the soul as it was released from the body at the moment of death. He touched the part of his stomach where his body emanated the scar of ingestion, where the child's soul now presided. It was the signature left from the reversing of aging, when he took Danton's age upon himself.

"I will save the queen after this. She will love me again once Danton is handled." He reached in the body again and speared the other kidney. It disappeared into his mouth like its twin. Pin licked his lips.

A yell penetrated the room, and he jumped to the window to find out what it was. A horse thundered through the town. Pin released the ceremony of binding, hastily moved the chair away from the door, and ran outside.

He scanned the horizon for the rider and found him moving through the streets with a spear held high. Pin recognized the Spear, the same one who drew the army away in a rampage of anger. It was a trap, he realized, but would the others realize, or would they explode with desire for vengeance?

The rider was now too far down the road for Pin to warn the Hobs not to pursue, but he still needed to do something. He watched as the horse and rider headed in the direction of the cottage. The same cottage they had found the underground caverns.

He ran into the room and yanked his dagger out of the body of his sacrifice. With sweat standing out in great beads on his forehead, Pin ran out of the home and down the street to see if he could keep the army of Hobs from running after the rider, and possibly being destroyed as a result.

Jon stood in the stirrups with a spear held aloft. An unintelligible scream escaped his lips and resounded through the streets as he charged through the town toward the Hobs army. He knew to rile the Hobs he needed to get close; once they saw him the creatures would recognize that he was the one who teased them before. They would know he was the one who had been just out the reach of their swords.

With his head turning from side to side as well as behind, Jon scanned for the main body of the invading army, but could not find it. Almost all the way through town and he had only seen three Hobs, and one of them had disappeared back into the house he had stepped out from.

Jon noticed a wisp of smoke just outside of town and turned the horse towards it. The hoofs dug into the earth as he spurred his mount.

Chail sat atop his horse. Bethany, Thomasyn, Shail, and Garion rode with him. They waited in the valley for Jon to charge in with the Hobs following. The other Spears and militia hid in the forested area lining the valley.

He knew if the Hobs were riled up enough, nothing would keep them from following. The minds of the creatures were simple and revenge something they never forgot.

Bethany broke the long silence first. "Maybe he stopped to eat?"

Thomasyn smirked, but stopped as soon as Chail glanced sideways at him. Inside the man smiled, thinking it was something Jon would do.

"Or maybe," Shail said, "he saw a fluffy bunny."

Chail barked a laugh as he envisioned Jon watching a small rabbit, brown-grey in color, hop away as he tried to string a box. Everyone in the small group laughed. Chail wondered if each one of them imagined a scene with Jon distracted from his task, stopping and cooking a meal for himself because he was hungry.

"He'd likely lose the Hobs first, then find something to eat," Thomasyn said.

They laughed again, and Chail stood in the stirrups. He scanned the mouth of the vale for any sign of the approaching Spear and his pursuers.

Jon slowed the horse to a trot once he exited the town. He frowned. A group of Hobs milled around a hut in the distance, several pots over blazing fires bubbled with a liquid that smelled foul.

"They've found someone. Damn." He pulled out a spear and felt the weight of the weapon. A twist of his wrist made rays of the sun strike the metal end and reflect into the eyes of over eight hundred Hobs.

Fingers pointed and screams sounded out.

Jon smiled. *They want blood, and I will be the one relishing in it.*

He stopped the horse, and pulled on the reins to make it rear. The move fueled the ferocity of the Hobs. His mount settled, Jon leveled the spear and let it fly at the lead Hobs. The creature took the projectile in the chest. It crumpled.

Jon let out a bellowing shout of defiance, and pulled another spear from his back. He tugged back on the reins and made the horse prance backwards. He threw the second spear.

Pin ran towards the hut, knowing that was the direction the rider went. The main force of Hobs were in the same direction, around the cave they discovered, creating food from the bodies of the humans. It was their way.

The Hobs kept moving, feeling fatigued from the spell he had woven, drained and not yet fully recovered from the magic called upon less than an hour ago.

"No! Don't follow him," he cried out. "It's a trap."

His warning was in vain. The Hobs were already chasing the rider.

The five Spears waited at the sides of the valley. They had strict orders to take the straggling ones in the back. With the mid-day sun declining in the sky, they watched.

In the distance they heard the pounding of hoof beats in the air, and then they stopped. Each Spear looked at each other, and counted. Screams echoed, and the sound of hoofs started again.

"He threw two spears," said Shail. The four agreed.

The horse sped past them, and the air echoed with the sounds of feet slapping the ground. Hobs, moving in mobs after the horse and rider, did not see them hiding in the trees. They waited until the last of them passed and, as a unit, four Spears and two of the militia stepped out from their concealment, nocked arrows, and let fly. They repeated three more times each, taking down twenty of the retreating force.

The next line of Spears stepped out, and the prior line ran forward to reinforce. Forty more fell. The next stepped in and sixty fell.

The Hobs, in their fury, did not notice their numbers dwindling.

By the time the last of the Spears and militia had joined the ambush, the Hobs army was decimated. Blood littered the ground.

Thomasyn watched as Jon approached the end of the valley. The Hobs followed close behind him, their numbers now under three hundred.

The five spurred their horses and charged, spears leveled at the approaching horde. They didn't scream nor shout. Each raced forward, aiming at the body of the pack. Not one moved faster than the other. Each wanted to hit the mass of bodies at the same time, causing the most damage.

As the five approached Jon, the young Spear turned his horse and joined the charge. He looked at Thomasyn and smiled. "I got ten with the sling!"

Thomasyn nodded and turned his attention on the approaching Hobs.

They closed the gap quickly. Chail struck one with his spear. Trampling three, Thomasyn drove his spear into another Hobs, breaking the shaft.

The Hobs split to each side, and the Spears following loosed their last arrows. The Militia drew their swords and rushed forward.

A wail erupted form the Hobs. Each pulled a sword or knife. They shouted incoherently. The mob turned and ran toward the advancing Spears. A small group resumed their chase of Jon. The riders turned. Jon held out his hand and Bethany tossed him a spear.

"Again!" Chail yelled.

They spurred their horses. Spear points came down. Sharp, deadly, accurate, the Spears erupted through the small pack of followers. A spear struck. The Hobs middle exploded. A spear butt slashed. A Hobs nose splattered. A knife tumbled through the air, burying itself in a Hobs' neck. The riders spilled out of the small force, leaving none alive in their wake.

"Dismount!" cried Chail. Thomasyn hit the ground, knowing the horses' footing would be compromised as the blood made mud out of the earth. With sword in hand, surveyed the scene as the shoulder of a Hobs was carved away by his blade. It was the last of the Hobs.

"Not much of a fight," Jon said.

"They never stood a chance." Bethany walked up between Jon and Thomasyn. Her eyes downcast. "It was too easy."

"Easy?" Jon panted as he looked at her.

"Yes, easy. And don't play coy with me." She struck Jon in the stomach with the flat of her hand. "I know that ride hardly made you sweat."

Jon stopped panting.

"She's right," said Chail. "This was too easy."

"Sir." A Spear approached, bow across his back and quiver empty. An evil gash on his arm seeped blood. "Jon appears to have made the bulk of the forces follow him. They have maybe a few hundred left in the town. What are your orders?"

"Form-up. We have a march ahead of us." Chail grabbed the reins of his horse and led it off the killing ground.

"We have time; they'll think the force is being run on a chase like the last so they will be a little skittish for the rest of the day."

Jon looked up. "Night attack?"

"Night attack," Chail said.

"How could you be so stupid, letting them run off like that?" Danton screamed at Pin.

The green tinge of Pin's face was pale. He looked at Danton and yelled accusatorily. "It was you who wanted to look at the hut. It was you who ordered them to kill the Spear. Now most of our force is somewhere we don't know where!" He pointed a finger at Danton. "You killed them. Might as well have driven a dagger into their chests." He spun and started to walk away.

"Pin!"

The Hobs stopped and spun on his heel.

Danton took a deep breath. "Hobs have no control. I couldn't have stopped them even if I tried."

"You should have tried."

"You tried, but they didn't listen. What could I have done?" Danton looked at the food pots, forgotten, contents burning. "They'll come back."

"Who'll come back?" Pin followed Danton's eyes to the horizon.

"The Spears."

Two hundred and sixty Spears and militia came out of the valley. Their focus, the remaining Hobs. The army was scattered around the hut. Bows ready and arrows nocked, they moved forward.

The Hobs, seeing the approaching horde of Spears, became frantic with fear. They scrabbled around the hut in panic. All but Pin and Danton were erratic.

The Spears let arrows fly. Hobs fell. Others scattered into the night.

"Move," Danton ordered. He was too late.

Pin cowered behind Danton. They waited for the Spears to advance. Knuckles white, Danton gripped his sword hilt.

Spears spread out and encircled the hut. Chail moved forward, his cloak billowing behind him as the sun started to set.

"Stealing lives, Danton? Or is this sniveling coward the one who steals for you?" The skies darkened. A rain storm was rolling in from the distance.

"I am here, Spear. Fight me. Give me the right to prove I am innocent of evil according to your laws. Then you must let me be free."

"You will face someone, Danton," Chail said. His hand motioned.

Thomasyn and Jon stepped forward and looked at each other.

"Two? You send two out to fight me?"

"He called me forward," Thomasyn said.

"I can fight better than you. I'll take him," Jon whispered back.

"Jon," Chail said. "Thomasyn is fighting Danton."

"I can beat him, Master Chail," Jon said.

"Yes, you probably can, but I said Thomasyn will fight him." Chail didn't take his eyes off Danton who smirked in response.

"Afraid, Master Chail? Don't want the one who tormented my army to prove his worth?" Danton took a step forward.

"You!" Chail yelled, pointing at Danton. "You stay there. Don't move."

"Master Chail, please let me fight him."

Thomasyn stepped back.

Chail's head swam, not knowing which way to turn. The two strongest fighters he had ever trained, one emotionless and the other full of want and desire. He knew the longing to achieve an end would play heavy in the outcome, but was Jon's hunger enough to fulfill the need? It was compulsory to remove Danton, or the evil in the one-time Spear would return once again with an army to fight them.

He turned, and looked at both Jon and Thomasyn. The first, red faced with fists clenched, glared at him. The latter shrugged. Both fought well, both excelled in almost every weapon, but the fire in Jon's eyes held the man for a second. Yes, he can use the anger to ensure victory.

"Jon, come here," Chail said softly.

"Yes, Master Chail." Jon stepped forward and stopped beside the Master Spear, rocking back and forth on his feet.

"Danton was one of the best. He trained over three hundred years ago, and has probably been practicing for years as well. But magic may not have made his muscles as young as he looks, and he may be over confident." Chail pulled his sword out of its scabbard, and handed it to Jon. "Use my sword. The legendary forger, Milakie, made this sword for me twenty years ago when I was assigned to the palace. It was made, and left on the summit of a mountain for the five Gods themselves to strike with lightning. Once they touched it with their souls, the smith sharpened the blade with mage fire. There is no sharper sword created by man. It's balanced well beyond what the forges make, and the edge will cut through hard wood and metal."

Jon grasped the leather bound handle. He noticed the intricate pattern of lines etched into the blade. The metal itself looked oiled, but when he touched it the surface was cool and dry. His vision could not focus on the ripples, for they appeared deep, as if they ran through the sword like undulations under the surface of water.

He balanced the blade and, without hesitation, stepped forward. Jon pointed the blade forward, grasping the handle with one hand. He motioned for Danton to advance and confront him.

Danton advanced toward Jon, drawing his sword. The straight blade glistened in what light penetrated the clouds, glowing, much like Chail's sword. "My sword was made before your master was born. By the dwarves themselves using the fire from deep in the Earth, and no sword made of man has ever been able to chip it."

They approached each other, stopping two paces apart. Blades pointed to the ground, mere inches apart. The two men circled, watching the other's eyes for any telltale of an approaching attack.

Danton stopped, reversed direction, and circled right. Jon switched hands.

With a wicked smile, Danton switched hands as well. Both combatants held their swords in their left hands. Danton taped Jon's sword lightly. The ting of the two metals touching echoed eerily in the field.

Jon tapped Danton's sword in return. The tap was a little harder, a little more forceful, and carried both just a little further from the center of the circle.

Danton stomped his foot.

Jon's sword swung up. Danton's sword responded. The two edges hit, sounding through the air. A smile lit Danton's face, and he held up a finger, waggling it. "Don't get distracted, stay focused."

With a swiftness that surprised Danton, Jon brought the sword up. It sliced the air. The surprised scream followed. Danton stumbled back, finger in his mouth. He pulled it out and blood trickled out of a small cut.

Jon smiled, nodded and backed away. "Wrap it," he said, smiling. "Remember, talking is for those not fighting."

Danton flushed. He shifted the sword under his arm and ripped part of his shirt. With care he wrapped it around his finger. "The lesson will begin."

With sword at waist level, Danton advanced. His free hand shot out sideways, away from his body. The sword whipped up. Jon countered. His sword came perpendicular. The two weapons hammered against each other.

"Good," Danton said. "Again!" His sword fell and swept up.

A sword went down horizontal. Another clash. Danton's foot struck out. Jon took the kick on his arm.

"Stay sharp," Danton said. "Attacks can come from any direction."

Jon's face reddened. He took a deep breath and let out a silent oath. "Only once," he whispered.

One foot forward, and he slashed up, twisting the blade.

Danton defended. His sword tapped the attacker's blade. Jon followed the twisting. The defensive move amplified the swing. A swish, and the sharp blade touched Danton's face. A small laceration opened under the once Spear's eye.

He screamed in anguish. He leapt forward.

Jon held his sword before him. He moved it left, right, and left again. The sword defended against the onslaught of Danton's attack. The en guard countered the attacks. He concentrated on the moves, timed them. He counted the cadence. Strike after strike blocked. Left shoulder. Lower right leg. Right shoulder. Each strike deflected. The timing changed. Jon counted again. Timed each blow. Head. Left shoulder. Lower right leg. Right shoulder. Deflect, back up, parry, breath. His sword blurred as did Danton's.

The count changed again. A split second between the end and start. He defended. The fury of the attacks continued. Jon circled right. The count once again went off. Jon circled left, the count changed. Jon stepped back, again he needed to start his count. He allowed two full cycles of attacks without fully moving. The cadence stayed the same.

Jon circled right. He counted. Danton restarted the pattern. With a quick sidestep, Jon doubled the count, stepping twice. Danton seemed to fumble, but recovered quickly. Jon took advantage and struck. The point touched Danton's sword arm. A blossom of red erupted from under Danton's surcoat.

Danton advanced, fury smoked from his eyes. Glistening beads of perspiration shown on his forehead.

He's getting tired, Jon thought, knowing the count would again change. The man was strong, and his stamina was amazing. Jon counted again. Head. Left shoulder. Lower right leg. Right shoulder. He deflected each.

Jon switched hands. The constant strikes against the sword numbed his hand. He shook it, counted the time between strikes now. The swings were not as fast. Danton was getting tired. With the attacks slowing ever so slightly, Jon revived the feeling in his right hand. He shook it, bringing back the life it had. Sweat glistened on Danton's brow.

The timing of the strikes lessened once again, and Jon took advantage of it. He switched hands. A blow toward Jon's head started, and he moved to the right fast and ducked.

Danton stumbled. His sword sliced through air. Jon tumbled and landed on his feet. He spun. The sword he carried followed a gentle arc. It cut into the fabric of Danton's shirt, nicking a chain mail link. A small piece of the mail shirt fell to the ground.

Jon smiled. His sword sang in the air. Each attack he aimed toward a different part of his opponent's body. Once he completed a pattern he changed it. Head first. Next, left leg first. Now, Right arm first. He varied the attacks, changed the timing. Slow, fast, two slow strikes with one fast. Danton defended. Block, twist, move.

Danton panted. The sweat on his brow dripped. He tried to switch hands, but Jon pressed the attack.

The swords hammered together.

Jon could hear the change in Danton's breathing. The small strike on the man's arm oozed blood. The arm of the shift Danton wore was soaked red and he backed up even more.

The blows came faster. Jon pushed. Danton retreated. The fight continued.

Slowly, as if waiting for the outcome of the fight, the sun disappeared below the horizon.

The Spears fed logs to the Hobs' fires, and shadows played across the fields. Dark shadows interplayed on the side of the hut.

Danton's sword was not as strong deflecting Jon's blows, and more blood colored his surcoat.

The sword flashed. Danton's breath heaved in his lungs.

Jon pressed harder, his swings ringing now, mechanical, rhythmic. He pushed forward.

Danton fell backward. He held his sword before him, struggling to reclaim his feet.

Jon's sword hammered downward. He struck at Danton's sword. With two hands Jon grasped the handle. Danton held his sword defensively before and it bounced from the strikes.

Jon reversed his swing.

Danton's hand twisted, the sword pushed away from protecting his body. Jon struck at the hand, removing it from the arm. Danton screamed.

The sound hung in the air. It forced its way through the bodies of everyone watching. Before anyone could do anything, Jon spun, and crouched as he drove the tip of his sword threw the underside of Danton's jaw. The force pushed the weapon through the skull. Eyes glowed red as magic erupted from Danton's body, and then went dark. The tip of the sword emerged out of the top of the dead Spear's head.

-6-

Chail walked forward. "Jon," he said.

The young man ignored him and giggled. The younger Spear's eyes did not leave the face of the dead man in front of him.

"Jon!" Chail said.

He turned and looked at Chail. "He bleeds," Jon said, a smile lighting his lips.

"Get up," hissed Chail. "Show respect. He was a Spear, for the sake of the Five. And you're a Spear. There is no pleasure in this."

Jon got his feet under him and looked down at the body. "He's nothing."

"My sword, Jon." Chail held out his hand.

Jon's eyes lingered on the hilt, the crossguard just under the chin. The blade of the weapon extended out of the top of Danton's head, separating the dead and opened eyes. He reached down. His hand wrapped around the hilt and pulled it free.

Jon's eyes roamed up and down the blade, watching the blood slowly make its way down toward the hilt. He wiped the sword against the clothes on the corpse. As he stood, he extended the handle to his Master. "I told you I could take him."

"Enough." Chail sheathed the sword, his face flushed with anger. "Join the others."

No one noticed the Hobs disappearing into the shadows as Jon walked away.

Chail sent the militia to gather firewood for the pyre. The Spears gathered the weapons of the fallen from both the victors and the defeated. The weapons of the Hobs were piled on the outskirts of the village, ready for the fire.

Chail took Danton's sword and examined it, his eyes roaming down the blade's edge. He handed the sword to Jon. "You keep it. The sword will be better in your hands then anyone who would find it. Remember it came from a Spear, and was used at one time to protect those weaker than him."

Jon thanked Chail, and returned to gathering the bodies of the Hobs for cremation.

The militia stacked great logs into a pyre and lit it. One by one the Spears took the bodies of the Hobs to the bonfire and tossed them on it. The stench of burning flesh filled the air.

Blood, deep, dark, and sticky after being on the ground for hours, caused many of the army to slip, hindering their movements. Each Spear took short steps, keeping their center of balance under them. The bodies of all the fallen slowly disappeared into the blazing inferno, sending a black cloud of greasy smoke toward the sky.

The light from the fires cast eerie shadows across the faces of the Spears, and he realized a new issue clouded his mind. He still did not know what to do with Jon.

The young man was broken, just as Thomasyn and Shail had warned him. He knew it, but when the breaking happened he did not know. The only thought he had about the issue was that it occurred during the training. Possibly with the Wooder walk. It was the only time Jon was out of the direct protection of the Clutch, and the control of the trainers. He made a mental note to discuss what happened with the Master of Wooders.

Still, they had to travel. There was a need for them to make their way to the Teeth of the World. The Spears minding the dwarves were destined to be rotated out. Maybe after several years with nothing negative to affect him, Jon could heal, and this could be a positive influence on the young Spear.

"In the morning you'll continue your journey to the Teeth," Chail said, turning to Bethany.

She nodded, and looked at the blood on her hands.

"What's wrong?" Chail asked.

"Nothing. It's just…There's a lot of Hobs blood here. The last time I had Hobs blood around me I almost died."

Chail took her hand and pulled out a water skin. He popped the cork and emptied the cold liquid on Bethany's hands. The blood sluiced off and trickled to the ground. "We'll have to get your clothes cleaned."

"I can do that on the road. The one horse died."

"I know. You'll take mine. She's from the same mare." He looked to the east, seeing the first signs of the day touching the horizon.

"Master Chail," Thomasyn said, coming up from the hut. "The townsfolk approach. A runner reports they were five leagues away when the Hobs took the town."

"Good, we can use their help." Thomasyn's brows furrowed, and Chail knew something was wrong. "Now what's on your mind?"

"Jon," Thomasyn said.

"Just keep an eye on him. Keep Shail and Garion apprised of anything that happens." Chail pinched the bridge of his nose.

"Yes, Master Chail." Thomasyn walked away.

"He's not the only one worried about Jon. All of us are. He seems to be…broken." Bethany wiped her hands on her pants. "The storm has broken up and without rain my cloak will soon look like yours, Master Chail." She let out a soft laugh.

"Tess cleans my cloak, so you better watch what you say." He smiled.

"I'll have to teach her the Spear way of cleaning things," Bethany said.

"The Spear way?" Chail asked. After years of being a Spear he didn't understand the reference.

"Yes. Give it to someone in the castle and tell them to clean it." She smiled.

Chail laughed. He could see the town's folk in the distance now, slowly moving across the field towards the fires. He wondered how they would view the massacre that took place here just last night. Would they welcome the Spears with open arms as the saviors of their town? Or will they look upon the death and destruction as too much justice? Will they understand?

He decided it was too early to figure it out. Let history decide if they were heroes or butchers. With the townsfolk approaching, he noticed how he looked. Clothes, meticulously cleaned every day, now had the scent of blood and travel on them. Dirt covered him, as well as blood and sweat. He didn't want to meet the town like this. He looked like a butcher, a killer of Hobs.

Chail, freshly clean and wearing new clothes, smiled as he drank mead from a cup.

The town had celebrated the Spears and militia even though both groups had been covered in blood. One half of the town folk took over the incineration of the Hobs corpses while the other half took the combatants to the town and set to washing. Clothes were taken and cleaned, and left out to dry in the morning sun. The townsfolk made sure every member of the group was taken into a home to rest until the afternoon.

While the Spears rested, the town gathered up their livestock and slaughtered thee hogs along with two cows. The carcasses were wrapped in flat leaves and buried with coals. The town folk left the meat to cook in the ground.

Now, with the sun setting for the day, the Spears were being celebrated for saving the town. The story of the caverns under the hut in the fields was told by a survivor, and retold again and again. Those wanting to look had done so, describing a family's multiple generational home away from the prying eyes of the town. But when a Spear or militia member came close, the topic changed slowly to how much the Spears were loved for having saved them.

Shail once again spoke of his friends at the Teeth of the World. The brothers had taught him how to drink, and tonight he was showing everyone how well he had learned.

Even the young Spears in Flight were celebrated by the town. Weak wine was served to them.

Chail stood, and moved to the boar being taken out of the ground. The members of the town waited for him to taste the meat, each hanging on his reaction.

He took a bite. The pungent aroma of spices dazzled his nose, and the taste was something he never expected. The rich flavor surprised him, and he bit into the meat a second time.

The town elders watched him and, once they saw his smile and the nod of his head, cheered. The feast started and continued through the night.

Instruments appeared in eager hands and music filled the ears of all present. The beat, light and fast, made couples come together and dance in the firelight. Chail wished Tess was with him to enjoy the celebration. He stared into the fire, his mind with his wife.

A gentle hand touched his shoulder. Chail turned to Bethany behind him, smiling.

"They say dancing frees the spirit," she said, her eyes laughing. "Come, Master Chail, dance with me."

"No, I couldn't." His heart sang with the knowledge that she loved him enough to ask for a dance.

Bethany tugged at his arm. "Come. Come, Master Chail."

She pulled at his arm and convinced him to rise. His feet followed her to the field, and he let the music take him. He watched her smile widen further as his feet moved with the beat. Bethany hopped in place and spun with joy. He laughed as she laughed. His smile pulled harder at his face and the laughter came more from his heart.

The sparkle in Bethany's eyes drew him into the music. His mind blanked and instinct took him forward to the fever of the dance. He could not tell how long they danced. Sweat stood out on his brow from the exertion, and while couples left to sit and drink, others came forward and took their place.

Chail slowed and Bethany came to his side, her eyes searching him for any problems.

"I'm good, just tired. I have to sit. Find Jon and dance with him." Chail found a man pushing a mug into his hands. He took a long swallow.

Bethany pulled at his arm again, but he resisted. "This is a time for the young," he explained. "Go, find Thomasyn or Jon and dance with them. They're your age and can keep up better than this old man."

She tugged again, but he held his ground and shook his head. Bethany hugged him, stretched up and kissed his cheek, then spun off into the field of dancers, searching for a partner.

"If only I was young again," Chail said.

"You're only as young as you feel," Shail said, coming up beside his one time student. "The exercise would have done you well, and she's a lovely young lady."

"The key word there is young, Shail. I've known her since she was a baby in my arms. Fourteen years. Some of those years changing her diapers, and other years holding her hand after she cut her finger."

"Still, she is a lovely young lady." Shail took a mug of mead from a tray, and nodded to the man who served him.

"I'm married now, and the last thing I need is to have her swooning over me. She had a crush on me when she was younger. Did you know that? Now, after she has gotten over it, you want me to try and force myself on her to couple? No, she is still a little too young."

"She's fourteen, almost fifteen. Most girls her age are already married and giving birth to their first child."

"And most of them are married to boys their own age. I'll wait till I get home to Tess, then I'll celebrate the differences between men and women."

Shail laughed.

Chail's eyes searched the dancers with their legs and arms moving to the music. Bethany was in the midst with Thomasyn beside her. They danced and weaved, moving with the music. Both smiled and laughed. Maybe they will join one day, if they knew what he knew now. He glanced at Shail to see his mentor laughing. He realized his mentor had been kidding him one last time.

"Shail, make sure you tell those two about your life," Chail said, motioning to Bethany and Thomasyn.

"My life? What do you mean?" Shail asked.

"Tell them about your life, and finding your wife. Tell them how happy it has made you. Tell them about the first time you held your child in your arms. Tell them to celebrate while they can, for times like this are very few and far between."

Shail nodded, and moved away towards a woman of middle age who beckoned him towards her.

"I will," he said. "And make sure you tell those two about love, the kind you and Tess have." He handed his mug to Chail as he moved away.

"I hope you're the right one to explain this to them," Chail said in a whisper.

The morning light crested the horizon, chasing away the darkness. The long grass was still warm from the day before, refusing to release the heat it had gathered.

Thomasyn stretched his arms above his head, touching his clothes were they had been strewn. A mass of auburn hair tumbled in waves across his chest. He didn't know when it happened, just that it did. His hand touched her hair, and Bethany tossed a little. He watched the rise and fall of her body, feeling the light tickle of her breath against his naked body.

He didn't want to disturb her, but the need to make water was overpowering him. Thomasyn twisted gently, hoping not to disturb her.

"I'm awake," Bethany said, turning her head and looking up at him.

"I have to—"

"So do I," Bethany said. She pushed up and covered her breasts with her arm.

"A little late for modesty." Thomasyn stood and moved into the tall grass. He looked over his shoulder to find Bethany had moved in the other direction and squatted looking the other way.

"Don't think this means anything," she said to him. "It was the drink."

He remembered what Master Chail had told him once, and looked down to examine himself. "Are you sure we did something?" He finished, and walked back to the spot they had slept. His eyes wandered over the ground, and finding nothing, he looked up at her smoldering eyes.

"You don't remember?"

"I drank a lot last night as well," he said. "I'm trying to find the blood."

"Blood? Thomasyn, you're not really big."

"No. Have you ever coupled with someone before?"

"No. I never—"

"Then there should be blood here." His hand motioned to the ground. He moved some of the grass around and there was no blood. "Master Chail says the first time there should be blood. Something about skin being broken."

"Well… it was my first time."

"I think we fell asleep before it happened," Thomasyn said. "We should make our way back to the town, before anyone knows we're missing."

"You say anything and I'll tell them you spilled before you touched me."

"I won't say anything."

Bethany grabbed her clothes and dressed quickly. Before Thomasyn could put on his small clothes, she was dressed and running towards the town.

Jon followed Bethany with his gaze as she ran into town. He had watched her and Thomasyn dance all night and wander off into the grass after drinking several mugs of mead.

The only thought that went through his mind was that they had coupled, and it was all he could think about the rest of the night. Bethany was supposed to be his, and Thomasyn took her. Every time he found something he was good at, Thomasyn was just a little bit better. When he wanted something, Thomasyn was given it or took it. Anger was all Thomasyn couldn't take from him.

Now, when he was ready to ask Bethany to dance, she had reached out to Thomasyn instead of him. The boy was infuriating.

The grass shifted in the field and the dark brown hair of Thomasyn moved through it. Jon could tell that loping walk from anywhere. He gauged the distance at just over twenty yards, and the boy wasn't watching the horizon like he had been trained to do.

One spear, that's all it would take.

He looked at the pack. One spear out of the three before him, the three that Thomasyn had chosen for him. Poetic justice ran through his mind as he picked one up. His finger tested the point and it drew blood. No, not today.

Shail waited for Thomasyn to join them. He and Garion had discussed the trip and knew it was best to start off as soon as possible. Their travel was already delayed, and the detachment of Spears at the Teeth of the World would be worrying about them if they don't show up near the appointed time. The young Spear was jogging into the clearing where celebrations had taken place.

The horses were tethered near a watering trough, their packs filled with supplies from the town, each saddle with spears and sword attached. Freshly washed and dried clothes awaited the Spears in the home where the horses were hitched.

"He's always late," Jon said.

"Enough, Jon," Chail said.

"Yes, Master Chail."

"Maybe he just got up?" Bethany said.

Jon scowled.

"Enough you two! Just wait."

They both went silent, waiting for Thomasyn to join them.

Running at a leisurely pace, Thomasyn arrived at the group and looked around. "We leaving?"

"Yes," Chail said. "You still need to deliver the horses."

Bethany looked at Chail. "I assumed we would be traveling back to Capital with you. Nanny Tess expects us."

Chail shook his head. "No. The horses and you five have to be at the Teeth within the next three months. It's not that hard of a journey, just a long one. The Spears at Halton Pass need to be rotated out."

"And the brothers are waiting to teach me a new drinking game," Garion said.

"We're all ready to go. The town folk have supplied us for a while," Shail said.

"Then you better resume your journey." Chail held out his hand to Shail.

The two men grasped their hands and released. Chail turned to the three young Spears. "My children. It seems we only just said goodbye yesterday. And here we are again, saying goodbye." He held his arms wide and the three hugged him. The boys released first, but Bethany still held on.

"I don't want to go. Can't I go back to Capital with you?"

"No, Bethany," Chail whispered. "No matter how much I would want you to come home with me, you have orders. There's a reason you three were picked." He kissed the top of her head. "You're the strongest, the best, and we need you there for Halton Pass."

She squeezed him, the girl he saw as his child, then backed away, wiping a tear off her cheek.

Chail's heart broke.

-7-

After two months of traveling, all Bethany could think of was getting off her horse. Her back ached. Redness colored her thighs and more than once blisters formed on her hands from the reins.

The Teeth of the World rose from the Earth like white fangs. At first the vision had been breathtaking, a marvel to behold. Now the peaks mocked her, laughed at their progress and never grew closer no matter how far they traveled. After five days Bethany swore the mountains walked away from them.

She hated the Teeth, the peaks reaching into the sky. Bethany wondered why anyone would want to travel to such an isolated place.

Shail held up his hand, and she reined in her mount. Her horse lowered its head to eat the grass.

Bethany dismounted, and when her feet hit the ground her legs buckled.

"My back aches," Shail said.

"It's a little further down on me," Garion said. The two laughed.

Her cramps were back, and she knew the bleeding would start soon. Traveling on horseback made the bleeding hard to deal with, but she knew it would have to happen. She walked away from the group.

"Where are you going?" Jon called out.

She waved him away and marched, seeking shelter from the prying eyes of the men.

The cold wind picked up again, cutting through her clothes and chilling her to the bone. She stopped and decided this was far enough. Bethany pulled down her pants, squatted, and released.

A shiver went through her. "Will the warmth return?" she asked no one in particular. All Bethany could think about was getting warm again. She hoped the men would have the fire started by the time she made it back.

She finished and dressed. The fire offered a small glow where the horses and men waited. Thunder rolled off the peaks before them and the wind brought cold, driving rain. "Even the land doesn't want us here."

"What was that?" Thomasyn asked, looking up at her.

"I said, even the land doesn't want us here." She shivered.

Jon ran up to the two of them, a smile lighting his face. "It's not rain! Look!"

He held out his hand, and on it, several small pieces of ice melted to water. "It's falling out of the sky!"

Hail moved toward the group, a few pieces at first, then more small pellets dropped from the heavens. Soon hail pelted them, and they moved quickly to set up shelters.

Shail pulled his hood tightly over his head. The wind blew his cloak behind him, and loose rocks held down his shelter. In a soft tenor he sang.

> The feet of the teeth
> Lay before me
> And time to run
> Is nigh
> For Spears are called to protect
> And send even beneath
>
> For Spears protect the lives of all
> Never forgetting who they serve
> And from shore to shore people adore them
> Knowing their life will sometimes fall
>
> The jewels of the Earth
> Are pulled from the ground
> And measured against the sea
> For a thumb is the deal
> To keep the glory
> Jewels of glitter and mirth
>
> For Spears protect the lives of all
> Never forgetting who they serve
> And from shore to shore people adore them
> Knowing their life will sometime fall
>
> Today we travel to the Pass
> And the feet of the teeth
> To spit in the eye of the dwarf's
> We take the gold

> And silver too
> All for the Realm to have
>
> For Spears protect the lives of all
> Never forgetting who they serve
> And from shore to shore people adore them
> Knowing their life will sometime fall

His voice trailed off, and Garion smiled. "I haven't heard that song for many years. What about the songs of the Dwarves? Don't they sing?"

"I can try. Their voices are gruff and unyielding to the world." Shail chuckled to himself. "Okay, I know one."

He started to hum, then broke out in a loping dance.

> Gold gold gold gold gold
> Gold gold gold gold gold
> Gold gold gold
> Gold gold gold
> Gold gold gold gold gold

They all laughed as the weather drove the hail against their bodies with more ferocity. Doubled over, the five travelers finished erecting their tents and let the horses graze on the ground's bounty.

Once they had the tents up, Thomasyn and Jon scavenged for more firewood. Bethany stayed behind with Garion and Shail, pulling rocks to form a makeshift firebreak for cooking. She removed cured meat and dried fruit from a pack.

"We still need water," Shail said, looking at Bethany.

She turned her face to the sky. "Easily done." She stood up and moved toward her tent. Soon she came out and placed a cloth on the ground, putting rocks on the corners. She waited.

Bethany collected the falling hail, putting it in a water skin until all were full. She placed them inside the firebreak. Shail nodded.

Jon and Thomasyn brought armfuls of wood. The two dropped their bundles and fed the fire. Once sufficiently hot, the cured meat was placed on rocks along the edge of the fire. Their dinner cooked as they passed dry fruit between them.

They moved in silence, having nothing new to talk about. But the hail added to their day and it was the topic of discussion between all of them.

With the flat land stretching for leagues, the three young Spears used the hail to quench their thirst and asked questions of the two older ones.

Bethany was first to ask a question. "What makes hail?"

Garion shook his head. "Well, it is said the hail is really rain that started too close to the mountains. The cold air caused it to freeze and fall to the ground. Others say it is the tears of the Fifth God, dropping to the Earth and freezing as it comes closer to his cheek."

"But the Fifth God became one with the earth, spreading himself to us as souls," Jon said.

"There are as many thoughts on this as there are people," Shail said. "It is best to just let your thoughts think what they may, for any can be right." He threw more wood on the fire and reached for some of the cured meat.

"Master Chail never told us about hail," Thomasyn said.

"There are many things that Master Chail never told you," Garion said. "Why the fish swim in the water, or how birds fly in the sky. How about what the clouds are made of, did he tell you that?"

"No," Bethany said. "He told us how the skin keeps the blood in the body, and the way to cut a muscle so it doesn't work without killing a person."

"We are all taught that by our Masters, and if we are good we don't have to use it." Shail chewed the meat and smiled at her.

"Don't have to use them?" Jon asked. "I don't understand why we would need to learn something and not use it."

"Because it is better to find the right way out of a situation rather than kill to resolve it," Shail said. "As Spears, we are to use our minds to deal justice, not our ability to kill."

Garion joined in, "If you come across two children fighting on the street, one obviously winning but not relenting in his attack, what would you do?"

"Talk to the winner and tell him to stop, for he has won," Jon said.

"And if the loser tells you the winner had stolen coins from them? Who is right?" Garion asked.

"He's the victim, and the one that needs protection," Jon said.

"But why do you think that is?" Garion asked.

"Because why would someone lie about being robbed?" Jon asked.

"Why indeed. One could say the boy beating the other was trying to settle a bet that he could win. The other child was fighting to gain money as well, but had nothing. So who is right? We don't know, so why interfere at all?" Garion smiled.

The puzzlement on Jon's face amused Bethany; she looked at Garion and said, "Take both aside and question them separately. Compare what each is telling you and see who actually has money on them and who does not. The loser, if he has money, is sent away and the winner, if he has no money, should he be given the talk about not fighting."

Garion nodded.

They ate in silence for a while, chewing the cured meat and drinking the water with different herbs in it. The meat, sweetened by the curing, and the freshness of the water contrasted well. When one felt the coldness of the day chill their bones the heat of the water warmed them up.

As the last of the light gave out, the five Spears retired to their tents and bundled up against the cold.

The howling of the wind continued through the week, slowing their progress. The horses suffered the most, for once warmed from the walk they shivered at night as their bodies cooled.

At the end of the twelfth week, the travelers could see their destination. It took another two days to finally make it to the mountain path that led to Halton Pass. The well-worn road twisted and turned until it came to a plateau. The face of the mountainside at the plateau revealed a large cavern worked into the stone itself, and the town of Halton Pass lay in the mouth of the cavern.

The group of Spears assigned there and several dwarves came forward. The thick beards of the dwarvs were combed down the front of their chest and tucked into their belts. Heavy helms sat on their heads, with great tufts of hair escaping the sides. They stood just over four feet and seemed almost as wide.

Each wore leather vests and pants stained with dust from the stone they had been excavating.

The three young Spears gawked at the dwarves until Shail cleared his throat. They looked away, their cheeks coloring.

"Master Shail. It has been a long time." The tallest of the Spears stepped forward, extending his hand to Shail.

"Willum, it has been many years since you were sent here. Good to see you again." Shail gripped the hand, smiling.

A dwarf stepped forward towards Garion, his arms outstretched. A voice erupted from his throat as if it had traveled through gravel before coming from his mouth. "You remember your oath?"

Garion fell to a knee and embraced the small man. "The blood holds us together, and blood will never betray our friendship. Gran, it is good to see you my friend. How many years has it been?"

"Too many," Gran said. He released Garion and stepped back, looking him over. "Life seems to have treated you right."

"As you, my friend. Shail, this is Gran, one of the brothers I told you about."

Gran bowed. "I hope you didn't tell him too much about me. I like to keep myself mysterious to strangers. But if he's a Spear brother of yours, he's a brother to me as well."

Gran held out his hand, and Shail shook it.

"Friendship is always a pleasure to have, but a brother is a joy," Shail said.

Willum gestured to the other Spears. "Master Shail, Garion, I would like to introduce you to Matthew, Rachel, Jason, and Parsons. Our hosts, Hull, Pon, Gron, and of course you know Gran."

A SHARP SPEAR POINT

Each of the party bowed slightly, never taking their eyes off the five Spears. Hull came forward, shadowed by Pon.

Like the other dwarves, Hull's voice grated from across rocks when he talked. His words slurred and sounded like they were mashed together before pushed from his mouth.

"We have rooms for you inside. While you're here I want you to have the best of living spaces. You will need for nothing," Hull said, and Pon looked down at the ground. "The weather will turn soon. Come."

The dwarves motioned the group toward the mountain face, and into an opening. The Spears followed in a line and after fifty paces the corridor opened into a grand space with arching columns. Each of the columns decorated with intricate scroll work, a wide base, and intricate carvings.

The vaulted ceiling stretched 300 feet above them. The whole chamber felt warm, so they dropped their heavy cloaks.

Many dwarves gathered to follow the newcomers, and Hull talked about the work the dwarves had done to create the great hall they walked through. Further on the ceiling approached them from above. As it closed in on them, the hall became a corridor again.

"We have many metal workers through this area. Blacksmiths and artists. Each one training to be a master of their trade. Tomorrow I'll show you our forges. For now, I'll show you your beds."

He directed them through corridors and small halls with workers until he came to a large barracks. Sections were closed off and Hull motioned to them. "These rooms are for you."

"I thought we would be in the barracks outside the caverns," Jon said.

Hull shook his head. "Those are for outsiders. Garion is family, and those who travel with him will be treated as family also." He moved to one door and motioned to Bethany. "This is yours."

She opened the door and started to cry.

Bethany turned Thomasyn, squeezed his hand and ran forward to the enormous steaming bath. Heat emanated from the coals under the tub, and she turned to see a bed laid out for her taking up most of the other end of the room.

The water was scalding hot, but she lowered herself into it nonetheless. She untied her hair from its braid next, and scrubbed it with the soap she had found. It felt good to have the grime removed.

Bethany sang.

It was not a song with words, just a melody of enjoyment. It was the first time in months she felt good. It was the first time in months she felt clean. She scrubbed at her skin to remove dirt that was no longer there.

She inspected her wrinkled fingers. "No, not yet." She giggled and resumed singing.

Just over an hour prior, dwarf women had taken her cloths away to be cleaned. They had promised to return them in two hours, saying the heat of the Earth's blood would dry them quickly.

The water was still just short of bubbling. She leaned back and slept.

Thomasyn submerged himself in the water one more time. He remembered years ago when Jacob had danced in a tub at the training grounds, showing off his spear. His mind thought of that day. It was the day Master Chail had married Nanny Tess.

He stood and dried himself with a rough towel. An image of Bethany came to his mind just the way she was when they had awoke that day in the Land of Towns. He smiled. She was a beautiful woman. If only…No, they were Spears, and in the same Clutch. He would not allow anything to happen between them. But if something could happen between them…It was all he could think about now.

Thomasyn threw the towel aside. There were clothes on the bed. Thick and scratchy robes. A quick shrug and the largest one slipped over his head. The shoulders were too large, and it ended at his knees. He laughed. All they had done, and the one thing they couldn't have figured out was the height difference between a dwarf and a man.

One hand pushed the top of the bed. It was soft and yielded to his weight. He climbed onto it and fell asleep.

Jon searched his room. He did not find anything to eat. It was infuriating they would leave him here without something. He searched again.

The bath sat in the room with steam rising off its surface. He ignored it. His stomach grumbled. The pack. Food was still there. Not much, but something. He dumped the contents on the bed and searched through them. Some dried meat fell out of the pack. He ate it.

There was not much, just enough. His stomach no longer grumbled.

He removed his clothes and jumped into the tub. His hands scrubbed the last of the dirt from his skin which had not seen soap in many months. Bathing was not a pleasurable experience. Something in his mind rejected the need to be clean, and he didn't know why.

The door to the room opened, and a Dwarven woman scooped up his clothes.

"They'll be cleaned and returned in two hours," she said, and closed the door as she left.

Jon stood just as the door closed. On the bed sat a robe. It looked inviting, but the fabric also looked as rough as the towels. He was not yet clean, but the desire to submerge himself was not there. It would have to be done, so in the tub he went again.

Thomasyn sat on the floor with his eyes closed, absorbed in the silence. A heavy knock on the door interrupted the peace; he stood, walked over to the door, and opened it. A serving woman stood waiting, a plate of food in her hands. It was not much, just bread, cabbage, and carrots with fish. He did not enjoy the fish.

He had been in the room for five days now, and he wanted to get out. But the door was fastened from outside and nothing he could do would force it open. After the second day he stopped trying.

Each day he had tried to talk with the serving girl who dropped the food off. Each day she said nothing until, at the end of the third day, she opened her mouth and shown him an empty space with no tongue. He stopped trying after that. The frustration of not knowing why he was locked up threatened to overtake him until he started to meditate.

He took the food twice a day and ate it sparingly. Every morning he woke up to the knocking, ate, and shadow sparred for an hour. He would then practice with his sword.

The serving girl showed him how to refill the bath. A spigot at the bottom allowed the water to drain through a grate. Another spigot concealed in the wall allowed for cold water to fill the tub. It only took twenty minutes for the fire to heat the water, another ten for it to be near scalding. It was a good system.

Thomasyn relieved himself in the hole beside the grate and ran more water. He wondered how Bethany was doing, and how Jon was putting up with such meager rations. His main concern was with Jon. His friend always seemed to need food. More than anyone else he knew. But he was not the only one. Others had the same problem, a need to eat all the time.

Jon had told him if he did not eat he would get headaches. Sometimes light ones, but most of the time very trying ones that split his head in half. He said one day it made him so sick he promised to never go hungry again. The need to constantly eat drove him to be better hunter. Thomasyn knew Jon was a better hunter, but did not know if it made him a better fighter.

He drew his sword and practiced.

"There's not enough food here," Jon exclaimed. The small Dwarven woman just looked at him, her large eyes glossy with tears ready to pour forth as she backed away from the angry Spear.

He was not angry at the woman, he was angry at the dwarves for keeping him in the room. For five days they had kept him locked in the room with little or no food. His stomach grumbled, and he took the plate from the woman.

"Tell them I need more than this."

Her mouth opened to speak, but he closed the door on her.

He scowled and picked up the fish. It was salty and dry.

"They'll starve me to death."

It had been five years since he was this hungry. And in that day he had killed two large men to save a young girl. He remembered the day clearly, for after helping save the girl he was able to eat. Even then, the Wooder, Juliette, only let him eat for a short period of time, and then she had called the villagers in to feast. His headache had been monstrous before eating, but the food had helped.

Now, with only two small meals a day, and most of it vegetables, the beating of a stick had been hitting his skull for the last three days. Sleep had not come to him the previous night. Instead, the pain made him stay awake with his palms pushing against his temples. He wondered if submerging himself in the hot water would help. At least it would not hurt.

Jon walked over to the tub and looked at the coals under it. They glowed softly, with very little heat. He grabbed his sword and poked at them. They flickered and pushed upward ever so slightly, touching the bottom of the tub, crunching the ash away and throbbing with heat. He was fascinated.

The glow of the coals increased and small puffs of heated air pushed forth. It was a wonder. How the coals grew baffled him.

He stood and opened the spigot.

The Dwarven woman smiled.

"Oh, come in." Bethany moved aside, and this time the woman entered. "Thank you for the food. Just sit on the bed, and we'll see what we can do."

She closed the door. The woman already sat sitting on the bed. A smile lit her face.

"I'll start, and when I'm finished you can do me, agreed?"

The woman nodded and turned her back on Bethany when the Spear sat on the bed. A brush from the side table quickly appeared in her hands and the woven hair of the Dwarven woman became untied from its leather binding. The brush made its way through the tangles, pulling the small knots loose.

"I'm sorry," Bethany said. "I'll try not to tug too hard."

The woman made a noise, but without a tongue it was unintelligible. But Bethany understood what was being said. She heard the same noise every time the woman tried to say thank you.

"I'm curious on how long the king will keep us here. I doubt you heard anything yet." She softly tugged out another knot. "But I'm sure it will happen." She popped a carrot into her mouth. "Do you know how long we'll be kept in like this?"

The sound was air breaking silence.

"Well, I'm sure there's a reason for it. It's just… I really miss Jon and Thomasyn. Are they okay?"

The dwarf's head turned sideways, and she stuck her chin out. A "Hum" sound came from deep in her throat.

"I bet Jon complains about the food."

The woman giggled.

"Is Thomasyn okay?" Bethany's hands worked deftly to tie the hair into a braid. She weaved five braids at first, and then braided the five together. The look was elegant, and when the woman saw it in the mirror she clapped her hands.

"Okay, me next." Bethany sat on the bed with the brush held out. The woman frowned, sadness mirrored in her eyes. "Don't worry. I just want my hair brushed out and tied to the right. It's easy." The dwarf spread her hands. "I'll show you. Come." She tapped the bed. "We can talk."

The woman came over and untied Bethany's braid. She ran the brush through the hair.

"I don't think Thomasyn is suffering any. He's probably practicing or something. Jon's probably sulking. I bet he's only bathed once." The dwarf giggled again. "Yeah, I thought so. Just a couple of strokes more and I'll show you how to do the braid."

After the braiding was done the woman turned to Bethany and smiled. She took the Spear's hands and squeezed. The woman then leaned forward and kissed her on the cheek, stood, and walked toward the door.

"You're leaving already?"

The woman smiled and nodded, but there was no pleasure in her expression.

"Will you be back later today?"

She shook her head.

"Then who will bring food?"

The woman smiled and made a walking sign with her hands, then an eating sign.

"We're going to be released?"

Again, she made a sign Bethany knew as "I don't know."

"Well, whatever happens, thank you for being kind."

The woman rushed toward Bethany and hugged her.

Hull cleared his throat, but Thomasyn ignored the dwarf and continued the patterns he worked on. The sword whistled through the air. In mid-swing he switched hands. The strike changed to a low sweep. His momentum carried him to his toes and around. The sword came down. The cut ended just before the floor.

"I would not want to face you, young Spear."

Thomasyn stood and sheathed the sword. "You have left me in this room for five days. I hope there is a good reason for it."

Hull took a deep breath. "The decision was not mine. Our king wanted to make sure a feast was prepared for you and yours, and the tunnels made safe for your inspection."

The Spear turned and walked to the bath. He opened the spigot and watched the water fill the tub. "And when am I supposed to come to this feast?"

"Just over an hour. I'm just letting the others—"

"And you are telling me just now? Have you told Bethany yet?"

"As I was saying, I'm just letting the others know about the feast. I have told Bethany, but you are being told before the arrogant one."

Thomasyn nodded. "Get me last. I want to bathe before eating."

"There'll not be time," Hull said.

"I don't care. My workout today was three hours, and I want to be comfortable when the king meets me." Thomasyn tossed his sword onto the bed. "Your people have not been very gracious to us. So don't expect us to be gracious to you. I will be ready when I'm ready. Please go, and I'll let you know when I'm ready."

Jon heard the door open. Feet moved about the room, as if the owner was looking for something lost. They shuffled to the tub, stopped, then one of the feet tapped against the floor. The feet moved toward the bed.

He stayed under the bed, looking at the feet like a cat watching a mouse. His head pounded with pain, and the bath had not helped him at all. The thought of stabbing out at the stubby appendages crossed his mind, but he could hardly move from lack of food.

"Hello?" The voice of the dwarf sounded in the stillness of the air. Jon smiled. He started to form a plan.

The feet moved to the side of the room and the cabinet door opened. There was a huffing of breath. The doors closed.

"Where could he be?" mumbled the dwarf.

The feet came back to the bed, turned and the mattress bent under the weight of a body sitting on it. The bed creaked. The slabs of wood holding the mattress up bowed and pressed against Jon's back. He could not move.

An upside down head appeared to look under the bed. "Oh, there you are. There is a feast in an hour."

The word feast echoed through Jon's empty stomach. He wiggled out from under the bed and rolled to his feet.

"I'm ready now," he said.

Hull laughed. "You're barely dressed!"

Jon looked down at his small clothes. "I'm ready."

"You'll not see the king looking that way."

"But I'm hungry!" Jon sat on the ground. His mind whirled, trying to make sense of what he saw and heard. "You've fed me hardly anything and my head hurts."

"Get dressed, and we'll feed you."

Jon's nod was almost audible.

Thomasyn watched as Garion talked to Hull in hushed tones.

Bethany's hair was washed and combed to perfection, while Jon looked ragged, and had lost weight over the last few days. He wondered if the restricted diet had caused his friend any difficulties.

Garion turned and approached them. "There is a feast, but pay attention to the customs of the people here. They are different from what you are used to."

They all nodded.

Hull led them through the corridors and into the Great Hall. The room had been transformed into a feasting area. One hundred tables formed two rows with chairs about them.

Three round tables on either side of the rows stood empty. Several dwarves entered the hall carrying trays of food. Two pairs of dwarves with a roasted pig between each came into the room and placed them on the tables. The pigs had apples stuck in their mouths, and the skin was all but burnt and blistered. Great splits in the skin showed wonderful white flesh underneath.

Next the roasted lambs, covered in herbs, were deposited next to the pigs. The legs stuck straight into the air with their cavities filled with corn.

Next dishes of steaming vegetables from squashes to potatoes, all cooked and spiced with brown herbs were placed on the tables. Breads followed, light and dark with grains on top. Designs had been cut into the tops of the breads.

Pies were brought in. Some had feathers stuck into the top while others had hooves carved into the crust. Several of the pies had fins sticking out of the upper crust, designating that they were fish pies, and next to them were lamprey pies, steaming with flavor.

Thomasyn realized how long it had been since his stomach had been full and could only imagine what Jon was going through. He looked at Garion, who pointed at the potatoes and carrots.

"Spiced with the blood of the earth," Garion said. "And you'll not believe the flavors of the food they have here. Those other pies, well they are fish and lamprey. Baked in ovens hotter than those in Capital. Your time in seclusion will teach you about how important family is, and the restricted diet to savor the food you receive. I'm sorry that I did not warn you, but it would be a violation of the customs."

Jon moved first and headed directly to the table containing the lamb roast. With a plate in hand, the young Spear used a knife to skewer slabs of meat and deposited them on his plate.

Hull stared, his mouth agape.

"Jon!" Bethany hissed.

He stopped and looked over at her, his eyes wide and brows furrowed. His mouth formed the word "What."

Thomasyn pointed towards Hull. Jon shrugged.

"The meal needs to feed all," Hull said. "We are not a rich people. It took several days to collect this feast, and it must feed a thousand mouths. Children are the first to eat. In our culture, the adults sacrifice for the clan's children. We usually go hungry so our children can flourish."

Bethany turned to Hull. "But you mine all the riches of the mountains. How could you be poor?"

Garion cleared his throat.

"It's the contract," Hull said. "But it's not my place to say. The king will want to talk to you."

Children, small and quick, moved about the hall and swarmed the tables. The food started to disappear as the children fed.

Thomasyn could hear Jon's stomach growl, and a child snatched the plate from his hands. Soon the children left, and the tables looked ravished.

"Come, the children have finished," Hull said, motioning them toward the tables.

As they approached, Bethany picked up three plates and handed one to Jon and one to Thomasyn.

"You eating flies?" Bethany said.

"What?" Jon asked.

"If you stand there long enough I'm sure, even in this cold, a fly will find your mouth and land in it. If you chew fast enough, maybe you'll catch one or two."

Jon closed his mouth, and Thomasyn laughed.

"I'm hungry," Jon said.

"Hush, child," Shail said. "You'll wait your turn like everyone else."

And wait they did. After ten minutes they finally made it to the tables, and very little was left. Jon mumbled to himself while he placed more vegetables than meat on his plate, and shuffled his feet in response. Both Bethany and Thomsyn took sparse portions, and waited until most had taken their need before picking at the remains.

Thomasyn made his way to the front most tables and stood behind a chair, just like the dwarves did. He watched as confusion raced across Jon's face.

Jon stood staring at the remains on the table. His mind raced across the problem of food. A spike was driving its way through the back of his skull. All it would take was a plate full of food to quell the pain in his stomach, and chase away the pounding inside his head. Meat would be best, but very little of it was laid out before him. With a shaking hand he took as large a piece of pork as he could find, and scraped cuttings of the lamb onto his plate.

A sliver of fish pie was next, along with potatoes and carrots. The food was just half a plate more than the rations they gave him through the last few days, but it would do. It had to do.

He joined the others and stood behind the seat opposite Hull. The dwarf looked at Jon's plate and scowled. The plate was laden with twice as all the others. Jon's hand went to the plate and took a little piece of lamb. Bethany slapped his hand.

There was a murmur from the assembly as a dwarf, wearing a suit of leather bearing the colors of all the gems in the world walked forward. His high helm with four point antlers sported ribbons and bells. He stopped, and struck the butt of his staff against the ground three times.

"All present be advised, the King of the Dwarves, the King of us all, the King under the mountain is about to present himself for the feast of the Spears."

His staff struck the ground three more times and he stepped back.

All eyes turned to a dwarf walking slowly toward the table. His small frame, stooped from the weight of the mountains, shuffled forward. The beard on his face was long and streaked with gray the same as the sparse hair on his head. The small circlet on his head was two bands of metal, one gold and one silver. They twisted around each other like a rope and the ends were joined without seams.

The King took very little and joined the main table. He placed his plate down and raised his hands above his head. When he spoke, his voice boomed like a bass drum.

"My brothers, let us pray," he said, bringing his hands together above his head and lowering them in front of him.

"The Five Brothers, gods of our world, we beseech you for your favor. We are not worthy, but the people suffer. Our need is mighty and gratitude unending. We pray to you, the one who lit the sky, the maker of the stars. We implore you, the one who created the sun and makes it rise every day. We beseech you, the one who gave us the earth from his body. We plead to you, the one who gave us the tress and birds and beasts. We petition you, the one who gave us life. Our people need you, and we will always praise your honor."

The dwarves stomped their feet in time and slapped their hands together as one, four times.

The king sat and motioned the others to do so.

Jon settled and picked up his fork. Hull stared at him. Bethany elbowed him. Once again the bellowing voice of the king sounded.

"As tradition tells us, the dwarves of old fought between themselves. Brother fought brother, cousin fought cousin. Blood spilled blood. Now, we are older and wiser. We share our lives and loves. To continue our sharing, we share our food. Now is the time of sharing."

Jon watched as each dwarf exchanged their plate with the person opposite them. Hull held out his plate to Jon, and waited.

"I don't want to change my plate," Jon said.

Bethany exchanged her plate with the dwarf opposite her. "You do it now, and smile," she hissed to Jon.

He looked at the plate held out by Hull. It contained carrots and potatoes, with a little gristle of meat. The plate was opposite from what he had.

"Do it now," Bethany said.

Grudgingly, Jon picked up his plate and handed it to Hull, taking the plate offered to him. He smiled.

"Now," the King bellowed. "Now we return that which is given as we respect the sacrifice the other has suffered."

Jon held out the plate, and Hull smiled, handing back the one he was given.

"See," Bethany said. "You got your meat back. Be happy, and stop your whining."

"Eat!" called out the King.

Jon bent his food toward his plate as did others. Food disappeared. Jon devoured his plate, worried the king would call for another exchange.

The herald came and spoke to Garion. "The king would like to meet with the new Spears after they have toured the mountain."

"I'm sure we all can—" Garion started, but the herald cut him off with an upraised hand, palm facing the older Spears.

"The king would like to meet with the new Spears, not the old. I'm sure you'll understand."

Garion glared at the dwarf. "I understand what you're saying. Maybe you don't understand what I'm saying. We'll all be able to set time aside for the king after dinner."

The herald nodded; the bells on his antlers rung out with high pitched and clear sounds. "Enjoy your meal, but understand the king only wants to talk to the new Spears."

Garion shook his head and dismissed the herald with a wave of his hand. He stabbed a spiced potato with his fork and put it in his mouth. A smile crossed his lips.

Jon bit into the potatoes and the flavors of cinnamon and cloves exploded in his mouth.

Bethany looked toward Hull and nibbled at the food on her plate. "Master Hull?"

"It's Chancellor, really. But just call me Hull, Miss Bethany. I don't stand much on traditions or titles."

"Okay, Hull. Please, just Bethany. I wanted to know more about the legend of the dwarves. How did everything come to be?"

Hull popped a piece of carrot into his mouth and stared into the distance. Jon grew quiet and leaned closer to hear. Hull looked back at Bethany and raised a finger.

The dwarf took a deep breath. "I guess you've been told about the 'Human' story of why we are here?"

"Yes, we were told your king tried to fool our king, and the dwarves were tricked into returning to mine for the Realm." Bethany gazed at Hull.

"Yes, what most are told. If I were to explain it is not the full truth, what would you think?"

Finally Bethany said, "I would say it wouldn't surprise me."

The dwarf smiled and nodded. "I was hoping you were intelligent, but wise did not enter my mind."

Her cheeks blazed red, and she looked down. "You honor me, Hull."

"No, you honor me with your curiosity. It is refreshing, for the humans we trade with are close-minded. But still, I don't think—"

"Tell her," Garion said, as he speared another potato. "I think it will do her good to understand how things have been decided for your people."

Hull looked at Garion, then back at Bethany. "It may change your outlook on the Realm, finding out more than you intended."

"I'm sure I can decide if it makes a difference or not," Bethany said. "Besides, if I don't like what I hear I can always just disregard it."

"You will probably do that when you hear this, but regardless of your thoughts I will tell you." Hull bit into the squash. He chewed and swallowed, took his cup of mead and drank. "You've been told a long time ago the king of the Realm wanted the riches of the land for his own. That is true, but it is not told to you that the Realm did not include the Teeth of the World. We, the dwarves, live in the Teeth. They are our home. We have lived here for centuries, and will always live here. Look at this hall, this Great Hall. Do you think it was created in a few decades? No, it was not. Those pillars there are Corinthian. They started as Doric, and over the years we adorned them.

"No, you don't have to say anything," he said, holding up his hand. Jon looked and saw Bethany bite back her words. "I know you want to say something, but let me explain. Yes, we have lived here in the mountains many generations, and for all those years we toiled to create this Great Hall.

"With our meeting hall created, we then tunneled into the heart of the mountains, finding small veins of ore at first but staying with the earth, for we knew the riches were here. And at one point we found the blood of the earth, the heat that runs through the earth from the blood of the Third God. We tapped it, learned how to harness its ability to blend metal that is light and strong."

Hull took another drink, and then looked into the cup with wide eyes. Bethany watched him, and he smiled, turning the cup upside down.

"I need more mead to finish this story. Sit, I'll return in a minute."

Bethany took a breath and nodded at the dwarf. He stood and walked away.

"He's pulling at your leg, you know," Jon said. "Everyone knows their king was taken because he tried to take the Realm."

"Hush, Jon. I don't know why, but I think he's telling us what he believes is the truth."

"Maybe he is trying to build sympathy for the dwarves. I still think they deserve what they have," Jon said.

"Enough!" Garion slapped the table. "You don't know these people like I do. Dwarves are honorable. They work hard and give much to the Realm. I suggest you listen to their story and make a decision based on that."

They stopped talking and let the words sink in. Jon realized what Garion had told them—that he was a brother to several of the dwarves. He waited for Hull to return and finish his story.

The dwarf came back to the table with two mugs of mead. He covered his mouth and let out an echoing belch.

"Sorry, the mead builds up gases in the belly. They must be released lest one explodes." He laughed and took the last of the squash from his plate and ate it. "Our king was shrewd, but not as shrewd as our current king. Back then the Realm was just expanding and taking all of our great land. The Elves were pushed out and others, like the Hobs, went underground.

"The king of the Realm saw value in the dwarves, and he took the daughters of our king, holding them ransom. The king agreed to pay it once his children were released, but the king of the Realm decided he wanted the ransom first. Our king kept sending gold and gems, but was told there was not enough.

"The dwarves took this as a great insult and refused to send any more, demanding first proof the children were still alive. But instead of proof of life, the heads of the children were sent, with a curse to echo through millenniums. Our people are cursed to always find the treasures of the earth but not to keep them. Our lives are extended, and we live for many a years past what we once did, but we are destined to poverty unless the ruling king of the Realm releases us from the curse."

"So, you send the gold and jewels to the king of the Realm so you can live longer and in poverty?" Bethany asked.

"Yes, we have been sending all the gold and jewelry to the Realm." He drank down one of the mugs of mead. "If we were released..."

Jon nodded. The dwarf lifted the other mug and drank. On the third gulp mead started to spill, and his laugh bubbled through. His mug hit the table, and Garion laughed as well. Jon watched them, confused.

"I actually think she believed me!" Hull said, and slammed the table with his hand.

Garion sat with one hand over his mouth. Small puffs of laughter escaped through his fingers. "Yes, you fooled her."

Jon watched Bethany's anger climb. Not because she was angry with Hull. No, he knew her better. She was angry with herself. She had allowed the dwarf to take advantage of her, and spin her around his finger in a tale she should have seen through.

Jon placed his hand on her arm and smiled in pleasure, for the pounding in his head had subsided. "Remember what Master Chail said? I think this could be one of those moments."

-8-

The heat was stifling, and sweat trickled down Jon's back. An unrecognizable acrid stench was in the air and he wrinkled his nose.

Hull led them through a downward slopping tunnel. The dwarf's short legs moved in short, fast strides. The three Spears almost needed to run in order to keep up.

"We are entering the apprentice area," Hull said. "I want you to see how they form the metal."

Jon wiped his brow. "How much further?"

They had been walking for almost an hour, and he could feel his stomach growling. A voice spoke to him.

You need more food.

Jon stopped, shocked at hearing a voice from inside him. He looked around, and saw no one besides Bethany, Thomasyn and Hull. He ignored the voice.

"Not too much longer," Hull said.

When do we eat again?

"When do eat again?" Jon asked.

"Eat? You just ate!" Hull said.

You didn't get very much to eat, and you hunger.

"But I didn't eat much—"

"Jon!" Bethany said.

"What?"

"Be respectful," she said. "We ate more than most of them did."

"It was a nice feast," Hull said. "The king made sure we had more than usual. It was good you came."

They passed another hanging lantern. Shadows cast their dancing darkness against the wall.

"It was good food," Thomasyn said.

"Yes, good food," Bethany agreed.

"Just not much food," Jon said.

"Stop it!" Bethany said.

"Well, it wasn't," Jon grumbled under his breath.

"We've arrived." Hull stopped in front of an opening in the tunnel. "Spears, I would like to introduce you to Grang, a newly promoted apprentice."

The opening led into a small cavern. The dwarf, Grang, was naked to the waist. His arms bulged with corded muscles, thick and strong. In his left hand he held a glowing rod of metal and in his right a large hammer. Grang moved to the back of the cavern and dipped the metal into the stream of molten rock.

Hull led them into the room. "He will work on several pieces for days, molding the metal into a sword. See how he uses the blood of the Earth to heat it hotter than any forge of the Realm could?"

Grang pulled out the metal and shook off the molten rock. He went to the anvil and pounded the piece. Sparks showered down to the ground. The odd glint struck the chest of the dwarf, but he did not flinch at the heat.

"Here." Hull motioned toward a stack of swords against the side of the cavern. "Some of the work he has already completed."

The Spears glanced at the stack of weapons. "Looks like a small armory," Jon said.

"It is good work," Hull said. "When he has completed at least three masterpieces this pile will be melted down for the next smith, and Grang will apprentice with another master."

Jon walked over to the weapons and picked one up. The weight surprised him, for the sword was larger than his, but weighted much less. "These are very light."

"And sharp. Here, let me show you." Hull took the sword and approached the anvil. Grang backed up. Hull drew the edge against the side of the anvil. A sliver of metal came away. "As I said, sharp."

"A very good blade," Thomasyn said.

"Worthy of a Spear." Bethany nodded.

"No, not good enough," Hull said. He tossed the blade into the molten lava. It glowed crimson, and then melted into liquid metal. "It is close to the third level of apprenticeship, but it can be better."

They watched as Grang bowed his head. "Yes, unworthy." The Spears looked at the smith.

Hull walked forward and placed his hand on the other dwarf's shoulder. "But much better. Your work improves each day. Soon you will be in the depths with the hottest of Earth to temper your blades."

Grang's face brightened like a full moon rising over a dark lake. He bowed.

Jon turned back to the pile of weapons.

Pick one up.

His hand reached out to touch a blade but hesitated.

Go on, do it.

"Those are poor blades," Hull said from behind Jon. The Spear turned. Hull was at his side, looking at the blades with his head bowed, eyes downcast. "Grang is a good smith, but not at the quality of our masters near the heart of the mountain. Do you want to see really good blades?"

One single thought went through his mind. "I would rather see some food."

Bethany smirked.

"But we have eaten alre—"

"Excuse, my eminence," a dwarf said rushing into the room.

Hull looked at the intruder. "What is it?"

"The king would like to see the Spears now."

The headdress of the herald sat propped against a stack of paper. His bald head gleamed in the torchlight, and he mumbled to himself as the pen danced across a page, leaving runes in its wake.

Behind him and to the left, double iron doors barred an egress. A breeze blew through the room, fed by a shaft to the outside. In the middle of the room, a fire pit blazed and cast warmth throughout. Eerie shadows performed a macabre dance against the walls.

The candle on the herald's desk flickered as it pulled the last wax to fuel the flame.

Bethany, Thomasyn and Jon waited for the dwarf to recognize their presence. Jon shifted from foot to foot, his head darted back and forth. Thomasyn cleared his throat.

The herald put his quill down, and rubbed the top of his head. "You are waiting to see the king?"

"Yes." Thomasyn stepped forward.

"He's not here."

Jon sighed. "This is a waste of time."

"Jon," Bethany hissed.

"No, not this time. Everyone wants me to be quiet, listen to what's being said. 'Be respectful, Jon. Don't upset anyone, Jon.' Well, how about they do the same thing for us? Herald, be respectful to us. Recognize Spears are here to see the king who asked for us. You are showing disrespect and upsetting us by making us wait."

The herald rubbed his chin. "And what do you expect me to do about it, Spear?"

"Tell the king we are here and let us enter," Jon said.

"I can't."

"And why not?"

"He's not in his chambers." The herald leaned back in his chair.

"Then why are we here?" Jon said, raising his hands in the air.

"Because he asked you to be here."

"But he's not here!" Jon spat.

The herald leaned forward. "Exactly."

Thomasyn shook his head. "I don't understand."

With a deep breath, the herald put both hands on his desk and pushed away. He stood and walked around to face the Spears directly. "Some things are done for a specific reason. It's not to make you angry, or to show disrespect. There is more happening here than you could imagine."

"Then tell us," Bethany said.

The herald's hand reached out, fingers splayed, then he brought it back to stroke his chin. "I am not a fan of this new king of yours. He is quick to anger and seems to have an agenda that he does not share with others. My concern is for the people he is sworn to serve."

Jon started to say something but Bethany nudged him.

The herald continued. "There is general unrest in our population. And many of us grow angry that the Realm has much more than they need, while we have little to show for our efforts."

"Do the dwarves want a war?" Jon sneered.

The herald shifted his gaze toward Jon, and a small smile crept across his mouth. "Does the Realm?"

"Our temple of the Five Gods," the herald said as he spread his arms wide.

Bethany and the others followed the dwarf through the main chamber and into the living areas of the tunnels. Children ran through the corridor. Smoke drifted in the air, making its way to the shafts in order to escape to the outside world.

They marveled at the smooth walls, the craftsmanship of the floors, and how all the dwarves shared what they had with each other, not demanding more than they needed to survive.

The entrance to the temple contained double doors with metal work inlaid. Small handholds decorated the stone portal.

The herald pushed open the doors, exposing the interior to the Spears.

Candles lit the large chamber. They hung suspended from the ceiling on chandeliers and on shelves of rock carved out of the walls. Polished rock reflected the light and bounced it through the empty space.

Several dwarves worked at removing spent candles from a chandelier as it rested on the floor. They pulled the nubs and placed them into a bag, sticking new candles on the spikes. The workers looked up as the Spears entered. They gathered up their belongings. In silence they lit the candles, hoisted the chandelier to the ceiling, and left.

The floor sloped, allowing for the benches on either side to see the raised dais in the middle. The whole chamber resembled an amphitheater, but cut out of the rock. The dais itself was ornamentally carved rock with a pulpit in the center.

Five banners hung from the ceiling and draped behind the dais, each depicting the sacrifices of the Five Gods. The color blazed in the candlelight, showing the artistic abilities of the dwarves who created them. Under each banner, an alter lay with flower petals strewn about them.

"This is amazing," Bethany said.

The herald looked about him. "This is nothing. You should see some of the smithies. They are the power of the dwarves."

A few dwarves came in and sat on benches.

"But this chamber, it's one of the most impressive I've seen," Bethany said.

"Yes, very impressive," Thomasyn said.

"This is truly nothing." The herald walked past them, followed by more dwarves. "Our love for the gods is great, but we love each other more."

Dwarves filed past them and filled the chamber, until all the seats were occupied. Bethany, Thomasyn and Jon looked behind them at a sea of dwarves. They were pushed forward toward the dais. At first they struggled against the motion of the crowd, but soon realized it was futile and allowed themselves to be herded forward.

Soon they were at the foot of the dais with dwarves seated behind them. The herald climbed onto the stage. He raised his hands and spoke.

"All present be advised the King of the Dwarves, the King of us all, the King under the mountain is about to preside over you and the Spears of the Realm."

The faces of all the dwarves turned to the back of the room. The king, moving with his back bent and shoulders hunched, walked slowly toward the dais. He leaned heavily on his wooden staff and limped. Plated mail covered his body, and a sword on his belt reflected the candlelight. His crown glinted, and his beard hung only an inch off the ground. Each dwarf stood and bowed to the king as he made his way to the dais and climbed the stairs. Bethany swore he had aged many years since dinner.

Ten dwarves entered after him, each pair carrying a cloth-draped litter. Bethany could see the outline of bodies under the cloth. The pall barriers followed the king to the podium and placed each litter on an altar, then joined the masses.

The voice of the king boomed through the air.

"Let us pray." He bowed his head. "To the Five, we beseech you to look upon this conclave and see your five fallen creations. They toiled all their lives and never complained about their station. With hands bare, they dug through the earth in search for what you left, and now, after a collapse of the caverns far below, they lost the spark given to them at birth. Our flesh has fallen and bones broken, but we will remember them. They will forever be with us in our hearts. We, all of us present, wives, sons, daughters, fathers, and mothers, ask you to take them into your arms and show them the love they deserve. In the name of the Five."

A great chorus of voices echoed out. "In the name of the Five."

Two dwarves came forward.

"Pon was my brother. For years we dug together, unlike others. We were like one, digging and searching. There was not much we wanted in life. Full bellies and the love of a wife. Pon found Brera, made her his wife, and she is now heavy with child. Now Brera must work, for it is our way."

The dwarf beside the speaker turned, and her round belly was obvious to all who saw her. Tears swelled in her eyes. "Pon was a good husband. He worked hard and always brought home much for us." Her voice cracked.

One by one a dwarf stood and talked about a fallen brother. One by one a wife stood and displayed a swollen belly or crying children. Bethany's heart felt heavy from the words.

The king raised his head, and Bethany noticed a tear in the corner of his eye. "The ceremony of rebirth will begin."

Five hooded dwarves came forward. Each approached an altar and raised their arms palms facing the ceiling. Together they spoke.

"Every dwarf is given a piece of the Five, a spark of life for them to protect. They are to cherish and grow it. And they will be taken to the seat of the Five."

The king spoke, "We will repeat the edict of life."

All the dwarves stood. Each of the hooded figures pulled the covers off the bodies on the dais. Each face of the dead was scraped and bruised, showing signs of the trauma they went through. The hooded dwarves spoke and the congregation repeated all they heard:

> We are but a shell
> A container for the Five

Once again the congregation repeated. The dwarves on the dais crossed their arms.

> Our lives are but a spark of the Five
> Cherished as a gift from those above
> And as we walk through the world
> We must always remember to feed the spark
> For it is unknown when it will return

The five dwarves removed the clothes from the bodies. Dust billowed in the air and settled quickly. Each came forward and formed a line in front of the dais. They each took turns speaking:

> Why art thou cast down, O my soul?
> And why art thou disquieted in me?
> Hope thou in the Five; for I shall yet praise Them
> Who is the health of my countenance and my Gods
> I will lift up mine eyes unto the hills
> Which made heaven and earth
> They will not suffer thy foot to be moved
> They that keepeth thee will not slumber

One of the five stepped forward. "My fellows, the roll of the digger has been called, and five dwarves have not answered to their names. They have laid down their picks and shovels, and with them they have left the mortal part for which they no longer have use. Their labors here below have taught them to divest their hearts and conscience of the vices and superfluities of life, thereby fitting their minds as a living stone for that spiritual dig–that tunnel not made with hands, eternal in the heavens. Strengthened in their labors here by faith in the Five, and confident of expectation of rebirth, they have sought admission to the seat of the Five above."

Another of the five stepped forward. "Let our hearts be lifted up by the words of those whom from ancient times have trusted in the love and power of the Five." He raised his hands to the heavens. "The Five are my guilds; I shall not want. They make me to lie down in rich rocks and soil; they lead me to still waters. They restore our souls; they lead us in the paths of righteousness in their names." He dropped his arms and stepped back. The third one stepped forward.

"My fellows, the thoughts of this hour are, and should be, solemn thoughts. But they should not be heavy with a weight of woe nor clouded with the darkness of hopeless grief. They should rather be solemn with the moving of the great ideas and deep emotions which stir to life in the hours when we are brought face to face with the great realities which underlie our existence. Companionships are temporary in this world of change. It is not possible that the associations of a lifetime should be broken without a pang of pain and a wrench of parting which seem to rend our very souls. Finding one day that one we have loved is no longer with us, we are as these under a new earth–all things are changed."

Bethany could not believe the spirituality of the dwarven people. She had not seen anything like this in Capital, not for any of the funerals she had attended. As the third dwarf stepped forward to speak the assembly aped the movements of the speaker's hands.

"At such a time the teachings of the Five come back to us with renewed force. The Five, Immortality, Friendship–these are what we strive for to keep before the eyes and in the members of our congregation. These are the thoughts that have power to comfort and uplift us now.

"In the Five we live and move and have our being. In the Five we learn to rejoice in our lives. In the Five we learn to release the pain of parting. In the Five we are reborn." From under his robe he produced a clay bowl. "When the bowl is broken," he said, smashing the bowl on the floor, "we move on in life." He produced a small jug. "And when the fountain is broken at the cistern, the body fails." He broke the jug on the ground, and pulled out a silver cord and unwound it. "And when the silver cord is loosened, and the pickaxe is a burden, and the spark of life returns to the Five who gave it. We remember there is no death, for life is transient. All that is beautiful and good and true in dwarven life is no more affected by the shadow of death than by the darkness that divides today from tomorrow."

The fourth dwarf came forward, and he held up his hands, palms to the heavens. "O Gods, our Fathers, grant that we sorrow not for those who know not the promises contained in the Holy Books; but may we look forward to the great gathering of thy grace that we may live as the heirs of this blessed and glorious hope which thou hast so graciously set before us."

He lowered his hands and bowed his head. "May the blessing of the Five go with you all."

The congregation spoke together. "And also with you."

With a step back the dwarf returned to the alter of the body he stood next to. The fifth dwarf spoke, but didn't move. "We give to those passing what was needed in life. A pick axe, to help them through the rock to the seat of the Five." He took out a small hand pickaxe and placed it on the body. The other four aped the symbolic gesture as well. "A comb to brush out the rocks from the beard and be respectable to the wife on returning from the dig." He took a small comb of bone from his cloak and placed it on the body. The others continued to mimic his movements. "A smock of white made from the wool of a newborn lamb, to protect their clothes from spots and stains." A smock, rolled and tied, was placed on the bodies. "And a grain of gold, to pay their way from heaven to the earth to be reborn." He dropped a grain of gold on the body, placed both his hands in his sleeves and stepped back.

Five more hooded figures stepped on the dais and pulled the sheets over the bodies. They nodded to the king and stepped back to stand beside the other five. The king came back to the dais and took a deep breath.

"My friends, my loyal friends. It is with great sorrow I tell you five of our brothers have lost their lives. Gran, Hull, Pon, Gron, and Dans were excavating in the lower chamber of North East when a pocket of gas was found. They tried to plug up the break but in doing so succumbed to the poison. Their bodies failed, and the gas touched a torch. The result caused the gas to ignite and the ceiling collapsed on our brothers.

"We have lost many from the digging of the mountains and received very little in return." The king lowered his head. "We have lost too much.

"Many years ago, before we were born, a king, not unlike myself, stood in the small chamber that became our great hall and made a mistake. He tried to take advantage of a new alliance of towns who called themselves the Realm. The king then used poorly constructed language in an attempt to trick the new alliance, and take advantage of one he plied with mead.

"Now, generations past, we find ourselves still locked in this contract. We toil for emptiness, and live in squander. Our children fed, we find nothing left for ourselves and most of us starve." The king reached under his breast plate and pulled out a scroll. "This is the original contract between the King of the Dwarves and the King of the Realm signed so many years ago. It is old, it is fragile, and it no longer should be valid. Contracts that hold our race to draconian terms without end are invalid in our eyes. We are dwarves! We dig the Earth! We shall be free!"

The king unraveled the scroll, took the top of it and ripped the yellowed paper down the center. The contract came apart in a jagged line. Bethany watched with her mouth open.

"We reject this contract. We, the dwarves, will dig no more ore, pry no more gems, or transport jewels to the Realm until they decide to treat us fairly and justly."

The king looked at the three Spears. "This is the ruling of the King of the Dwarves."

The crowd of dwarves cheered.

The temple emptied, save for the three Spears and five guards at the door. The king told them to wait as he followed his people out of the temple, his back bent.

Jon stomped back to his companions "This is wrong. They have no right to refuse to work. They have a contract with the Realm." Jon punctuated each sentence with a slight pause.

"Jon," Bethany said. "You need to sit and calm down."

"No. I didn't do anything wrong. Why should I be locked away in their temple as they decide what to do with us? If anything their king should be charged and thrown in jail."

Bethany shook her head. She walked over to the seats and looked at the roughness of the rock. A small section of the stones were worn smooth from the hundreds of bottoms that had sat there. She climbed half way up and sat in one of the seats.

From the vantage point she could see the whole dais, and the banners stopped just short of blocking the view. The smallest noise made by Jon and Thomasyn echoed up to her ears. Even the lowest of Jon's mutters could be heard, and she could actually understand what he mumbled if she concentrated on his voice. Something about a mouse with no legs.

Bethany shook her head and stood. She looked over at the guards and wondered how long it would take her to overpower them. Five dwarves. It would take too long, more time than she could afford, for one or two of them could get word out that trouble had arisen. Too much time and reinforcements would be there to subdue all three of them. If all of them attacked at once...

To test her idea, Bethany went to the end of the row of seats and turned toward the guards. After three steps the guards lowered their pikes in a defensive posture. She stopped and studied them. Each held their pike as if born with it in their hands, not a tremble, nor reluctance in action. They were trained well.

"What are you doing?" It was Thomasyn's voice. He was still at the bottom of the chamber.

Bethany returned to the dais, but stopped five rows up. She whispered, "Jon, can you hear me?" She listened, and not hearing a response, motioned Thomasyn to come up the stairs. When he joined her, Bethany spoke in a hushed tone, "I figured if Jon couldn't hear me from here, our voices wouldn't make it to the guards."

"Why are you whispering?"

"To keep the guards from hearing. I think Jon is right about this. The king has shown treason here, and we need to warn our king. We need to get out of here. A rush on the guards, taking them by surprise, could gain us our release. But we would have to act fast. Did you keep any weapons?"

He stared at her.

"You did. A knife?"

"What do you have in mind?"

Bethany glanced at the guards. "One knife can take one, two knives … Knowing Jon, he has at least one knife hidden as well. It'll leave us with even odds. We can take the weapons off the dwarves and escape."

"Didn't you keep a knife back as well?" Thomasyn asked.

A smile lit the corner of her mouth. "Three throwing knives. I could have kept more, but the guard outside the herald's room saw a few of them when I took off my sword."

He nodded slightly.

"What are you talking about?" Jon asked. He had snuck up behind Thomasyn.

"We're thinking of taking the guards," Bethany said.

"Ha!" Jon said.

"You have a better idea?" Thomasyn asked.

"Yes, we wait."

Bethany shook her head. "I don't understand you. First you want us to attack or rebel and now you want us to just sit still and wait? Why?"

"Okay, say we overthrow the five guards; then what?"

"We go through the doors and make our way out to the surface," Bethany said.

"How many guards are outside the doors?" Jon asked Thomasyn.

"I don't know, three or four."

"And what if there's ten?"

"We'll figure it out when we come to that," Bethany said.

"It's not worth it." Shail's voice boomed in the empty air. All three turned to the dais, and Bethany couldn't believe he stood there, watching them. The Spear held out his hand and jumped off the stage, making his way over to the three. She saw a flickering candle and noticed a seam in the wall, a hidden door. "I know what you're thinking, but there are twenty on the other side. Each part of the king's guard. Each trained in the use of pikes and swords. If you make it out to them you'll get killed by the outside guards."

"So we just sit here?" Bethany asked.

Jon turned away from the group.

"We need to do something other than wait," Thomasyn said.

"There's nothing we can do. King Gimladovan is adamant about no longer digging the riches for the Realm. He wants a share that is fair, not draconian," Shail said.

"But that was the contract they tried to impose on us? It's just we turned it on them," Jon said.

"Jon's right. They wrote the contract and tried to take advantage of us but it was turned to take advantage of them, how can they complain?" Bethany said.

"Because it's been over two thousand years." Shail rubbed the back of his neck. "It's not a legal issue, it's a moral one. At what point do you stop punishing a people because of what their ancestors did? Bethany, if I discover you have a child and then you steal money, say thirty gold points, and die before paying it back, should your child then be responsible to pay it back?"

"No, but that's—"

149

"Exactly what is happening here. You know the law limiting length of contracts, right?"

Thomasyn looked up. "Yes, five years. One cannot enter into a contract with a limitation exceeding five years. All contracts over five years immediately expire at the end of the first five years, and must be renegotiated."

"Exactly," Shail said. "And that was put in place by the last King of the Realm. It was put in place to protect those who were being taken advantage of."

Jon turned. "It's not protecting those who signed contacts before then."

"Right," Shail said. "Any contract prior to that date is still enforceable, still valid."

"So the dwarves are looking at changing the contract?" Bethany asked.

"That is something the king wants to talk to you three about."

Thomasyn waited for the others to say something, but they just stared at Shail. The man waited. It seemed like an eternity but the silence only lasted a few minutes.

"So what do we need to do?" Bethany asked.

"Go to him," Shail said. "I'll take you there, but you'll have to talk to the king and find out what he really wants. What kind of concessions are on his mind, and then it has to go to the Realm. Understand that they won't mine any more until their needs are met."

"So, we need to take care of this?" Thomasyn asked.

"Yes, you need to take care of this," Shail said.

"Why us?" Jon asked.

"Because you are the young Spears. You're the ones who can understand what they are going through. Garion and I are just part of the old Spears who have enforced the contract for years. And even with the friendships we have here, we are still the bullies, the bad humans who make them live up to what the contact says, regardless of how we treat them or feel." Shail rubbed the back of his neck, his voice softer. "We tried to take the issue to the king years ago, but the council refused to have it heard. In many ways, the old king listened to them. Now, our new king may have the ability to change, especially when ones near his age report what we have been saying for years."

Thomasyn touched Shail's arm. "You believe in this, don't you?"

Shail looked into Thomasyn's eyes. "Yes, I do."

"Then you better take us to the king."

Shail smiled.

Shail opened the door to the herald's office, and escorted the three young Spears in. The herald sat behind his desk, transposing notes to a new contract. He held up his hand to hold back the Spear from talking until he finished the part he worked on.

"We've been here before. This… herald does nothing to help out but make snide remarks," Jon said.

"I made snide remarks, young Spear, in order to show you there was more to what you see." The herald pushed away from his desk and grunted as he stood. "There are always things more important than the desire you think is important."

Thomasyn noticed a resemblance to one of the five dwarves who had been killed in the accident, and the large bags under his eyes told a story of loss. The herald limped, and when he reached for the door behind his desk the dwarf all but stumbled.

Moving swiftly, Thomasyn came up beside the old dwarf and helped open the door. The herald looked up and smiled, giving a node of appreciation. They both swung the doors open.

A long hall, thirty yards deep and five yards wide, vast ceilings and great arching columns stretched before them. Thomasyn felt small in comparison, and hesitated taking the first step forward.

-9-

The heat was stifling, and sweat trickled down Jon's back. An unrecognizable acrid stench was in the air and he wrinkled his nose.

Hull led them through a downward slopping tunnel. The dwarf's short legs moved in short, fast strides. The three Spears almost needed to run in order to keep up.

"We are entering the apprentice area," Hull said. "I want you to see how they form the metal."

Jon wiped his brow. "How much further?"

They had been walking for almost an hour, and he could feel his stomach growling. A voice spoke to him.

You need more food.

Jon stopped, shocked at hearing a voice from inside him. He looked around, and saw no one besides Bethany, Thomasyn and Hull. He ignored the voice.

"Not too much longer," Hull said.

When do we eat again?

"When do eat again?" Jon asked.

"Eat? You just ate!" Hull said.

You didn't get very much to eat, and you hunger.

"But I didn't eat much—"

"Jon!" Bethany said.

"What?"

"Be respectful," she said. "We ate more than most of them did."

"It was a nice feast," Hull said. "The king made sure we had more than usual. It was good you came."

They passed another hanging lantern. Shadows cast their dancing darkness against the wall.

"It was good food," Thomasyn said.

"Yes, good food," Bethany agreed.

"Just not much food," Jon said.

"Stop it!" Bethany said.

"Well, it wasn't," Jon grumbled under his breath.

"We've arrived." Hull stopped in front of an opening in the tunnel. "Spears, I would like to introduce you to Grang, a newly promoted apprentice."

The opening led into a small cavern. The dwarf, Grang, was naked to the waist. His arms bulged with corded muscles, thick and strong. In his left hand he held a glowing rod of metal and in his right a large hammer. Grang moved to the back of the cavern and dipped the metal into the stream of molten rock.

Hull led them into the room. "He will work on several pieces for days, molding the metal into a sword. See how he uses the blood of the Earth to heat it hotter than any forge of the Realm could?"

Grang pulled out the metal and shook off the molten rock. He went to the anvil and pounded the piece. Sparks showered down to the ground. The odd glint struck the chest of the dwarf, but he did not flinch at the heat.

"Here." Hull motioned toward a stack of swords against the side of the cavern. "Some of the work he has already completed."

The Spears glanced at the stack of weapons. "Looks like a small armory," Jon said.

"It is good work," Hull said. "When he has completed at least three masterpieces this pile will be melted down for the next smith, and Grang will apprentice with another master."

Jon walked over to the weapons and picked one up. The weight surprised him, for the sword was larger than his, but weighted much less. "These are very light."

"And sharp. Here, let me show you." Hull took the sword and approached the anvil. Grang backed up. Hull drew the edge against the side of the anvil. A sliver of metal came away. "As I said, sharp."

"A very good blade," Thomasyn said.

"Worthy of a Spear." Bethany nodded.

"No, not good enough," Hull said. He tossed the blade into the molten lava. It glowed crimson, and then melted into liquid metal. "It is close to the third level of apprenticeship, but it can be better."

They watched as Grang bowed his head. "Yes, unworthy." The Spears looked at the smith.

Hull walked forward and placed his hand on the other dwarf's shoulder. "But much better. Your work improves each day. Soon you will be in the depths with the hottest of Earth to temper your blades."

Grang's face brightened like a full moon rising over a dark lake. He bowed.

Jon turned back to the pile of weapons.

Pick one up.

His hand reached out to touch a blade but hesitated.

Go on, do it.

"Those are poor blades," Hull said from behind Jon. The Spear turned. Hull was at his side, looking at the blades with his head bowed, eyes downcast. "Grang is a good smith, but not at the quality of our masters near the heart of the mountain. Do you want to see really good blades?"

One single thought went through his mind. "I would rather see some food."

Bethany smirked.

"But we have eaten alre—"

"Excuse, my eminence," a dwarf said rushing into the room.

Hull looked at the intruder. "What is it?"

"The king would like to see the Spears now."

The headdress of the herald sat propped against a stack of paper. His bald head gleamed in the torchlight, and he mumbled to himself as the pen danced across a page, leaving runes in its wake.

Behind him and to the left, double iron doors barred an egress. A breeze blew through the room, fed by a shaft to the outside. In the middle of the room, a fire pit blazed and cast warmth throughout. Eerie shadows performed a macabre dance against the walls.

The candle on the herald's desk flickered as it pulled the last wax to fuel the flame.

Bethany, Thomasyn and Jon waited for the dwarf to recognize their presence. Jon shifted from foot to foot, his head darted back and forth. Thomasyn cleared his throat.

The herald put his quill down, and rubbed the top of his head. "You are waiting to see the king?"

"Yes." Thomasyn stepped forward.

"He's not here."

Jon sighed. "This is a waste of time."

"Jon," Bethany hissed.

"No, not this time. Everyone wants me to be quiet, listen to what's being said. 'Be respectful, Jon. Don't upset anyone, Jon.' Well, how about they do the same thing for us? Herald, be respectful to us. Recognize Spears are here to see the king who asked for us. You are showing disrespect and upsetting us by making us wait."

The herald rubbed his chin. "And what do you expect me to do about it, Spear?"

"Tell the king we are here and let us enter," Jon said.

"I can't."

"And why not?"

"He's not in his chambers." The herald leaned back in his chair.

"Then why are we here?" Jon said, raising his hands in the air.

"Because he asked you to be here."

"But he's not here!" Jon spat.

The herald leaned forward. "Exactly."

Thomasyn shook his head. "I don't understand."

With a deep breath, the herald put both hands on his desk and pushed away. He stood and walked around to face the Spears directly. "Some things are done for a specific reason. It's not to make you angry, or to show disrespect. There is more happening here than you could imagine."

"Then tell us," Bethany said.

The herald's hand reached out, fingers splayed, then he brought it back to stroke his chin. "I am not a fan of this new king of yours. He is quick to anger and seems to have an agenda that he does not share with others. My concern is for the people he is sworn to serve."

Jon started to say something but Bethany nudged him.

The herald continued. "There is general unrest in our population. And many of us grow angry that the Realm has much more than they need, while we have little to show for our efforts."

"Do the dwarves want a war?" Jon sneered.

The herald shifted his gaze toward Jon, and a small smile crept across his mouth. "Does the Realm?"

"Our temple of the Five Gods," the herald said as he spread his arms wide.

Bethany and the others followed the dwarf through the main chamber and into the living areas of the tunnels. Children ran through the corridor. Smoke drifted in the air, making its way to the shafts in order to escape to the outside world.

They marveled at the smooth walls, the craftsmanship of the floors, and how all the dwarves shared what they had with each other, not demanding more than they needed to survive.

The entrance to the temple contained double doors with metal work inlaid. Small handholds decorated the stone portal.

The herald pushed open the doors, exposing the interior to the Spears.

Candles lit the large chamber. They hung suspended from the ceiling on chandeliers and on shelves of rock carved out of the walls. Polished rock reflected the light and bounced it through the empty space.

Several dwarves worked at removing spent candles from a chandelier as it rested on the floor. They pulled the nubs and placed them into a bag, sticking new candles on the spikes. The workers looked up as the Spears entered. They gathered up their belongings. In silence they lit the candles, hoisted the chandelier to the ceiling, and left.

The floor sloped, allowing for the benches on either side to see the raised dais in the middle. The whole chamber resembled an amphitheater, but cut out of the rock. The dais itself was ornamentally carved rock with a pulpit in the center.

Five banners hung from the ceiling and draped behind the dais, each depicting the sacrifices of the Five Gods. The color blazed in the candlelight, showing the artistic abilities of the dwarves who created them. Under each banner, an alter lay with flower petals strewn about them.

"This is amazing," Bethany said.

The herald looked about him. "This is nothing. You should see some of the smithies. They are the power of the dwarves."

A few dwarves came in and sat on benches.

"But this chamber, it's one of the most impressive I've seen," Bethany said.

"Yes, very impressive," Thomasyn said.

"This is truly nothing." The herald walked past them, followed by more dwarves. "Our love for the gods is great, but we love each other more."

Dwarves filed past them and filled the chamber, until all the seats were occupied. Bethany, Thomasyn and Jon looked behind them at a sea of dwarves. They were pushed forward toward the dais. At first they struggled against the motion of the crowd, but soon realized it was futile and allowed themselves to be herded forward.

Soon they were at the foot of the dais with dwarves seated behind them. The herald climbed onto the stage. He raised his hands and spoke.

"All present be advised the King of the Dwarves, the King of us all, the King under the mountain is about to preside over you and the Spears of the Realm."

The faces of all the dwarves turned to the back of the room. The king, moving with his back bent and shoulders hunched, walked slowly toward the dais. He leaned heavily on his wooden staff and limped. Plated mail covered his body, and a sword on his belt reflected the candlelight. His crown glinted, and his beard hung only an inch off the ground. Each dwarf stood and bowed to the king as he made his way to the dais and climbed the stairs. Bethany swore he had aged many years since dinner.

Ten dwarves entered after him, each pair carrying a cloth-draped litter. Bethany could see the outline of bodies under the cloth. The pall barriers followed the king to the podium and placed each litter on an altar, then joined the masses.

The voice of the king boomed through the air.

"Let us pray." He bowed his head. "To the Five, we beseech you to look upon this conclave and see your five fallen creations. They toiled all their lives and never complained about their station. With hands bare, they dug through the earth in search for what you left, and now, after a collapse of the caverns far below, they lost the spark given to them at birth. Our flesh has fallen and bones broken, but we will remember them. They will forever be with us in our hearts. We, all of us present, wives, sons, daughters, fathers, and mothers, ask you to take them into your arms and show them the love they deserve. In the name of the Five."

A great chorus of voices echoed out. "In the name of the Five."

Two dwarves came forward.

"Pon was my brother. For years we dug together, unlike others. We were like one, digging and searching. There was not much we wanted in life. Full bellies and the love of a wife. Pon found Brera, made her his wife, and she is now heavy with child. Now Brera must work, for it is our way."

The dwarf beside the speaker turned, and her round belly was obvious to all who saw her. Tears swelled in her eyes. "Pon was a good husband. He worked hard and always brought home much for us." Her voice cracked.

One by one a dwarf stood and talked about a fallen brother. One by one a wife stood and displayed a swollen belly or crying children. Bethany's heart felt heavy from the words.

The king raised his head, and Bethany noticed a tear in the corner of his eye. "The ceremony of rebirth will begin."

Five hooded dwarves came forward. Each approached an altar and raised their arms palms facing the ceiling. Together they spoke.

"Every dwarf is given a piece of the Five, a spark of life for them to protect. They are to cherish and grow it. And they will be taken to the seat of the Five."

The king spoke, "We will repeat the edict of life."

All the dwarves stood. Each of the hooded figures pulled the covers off the bodies on the dais. Each face of the dead was scraped and bruised, showing signs of the trauma they went through. The hooded dwarves spoke and the congregation repeated all they heard:

> We are but a shell
> A container for the Five

Once again the congregation repeated. The dwarves on the dais crossed their arms.

> Our lives are but a spark of the Five
> Cherished as a gift from those above
> And as we walk through the world
> We must always remember to feed the spark
> For it is unknown when it will return

The five dwarves removed the clothes from the bodies. Dust billowed in the air and settled quickly. Each came forward and formed a line in front of the dais. They each took turns speaking:

> Why art thou cast down, O my soul?
> And why art thou disquieted in me?
> Hope thou in the Five; for I shall yet praise Them
> Who is the health of my countenance and my Gods
> I will lift up mine eyes unto the hills
> Which made heaven and earth
> They will not suffer thy foot to be moved
> They that keepeth thee will not slumber

One of the five stepped forward. "My fellows, the roll of the digger has been called, and five dwarves have not answered to their names. They have laid down their picks and shovels, and with them they have left the mortal part for which they no longer have use. Their labors here below have taught them to divest their hearts and conscience of the vices and superfluities of life, thereby fitting their minds as a living stone for that spiritual dig–that tunnel not made with hands, eternal in the heavens. Strengthened in their labors here by faith in the Five, and confident of expectation of rebirth, they have sought admission to the seat of the Five above."

Another of the five stepped forward. "Let our hearts be lifted up by the words of those whom from ancient times have trusted in the love and power of the Five." He raised his hands to the heavens. "The Five are my guilds; I shall not want. They make me to lie down in rich rocks and soil; they lead me to still waters. They restore our souls; they lead us in the paths of righteousness in their names." He dropped his arms and stepped back. The third one stepped forward.

"My fellows, the thoughts of this hour are, and should be, solemn thoughts. But they should not be heavy with a weight of woe nor clouded with the darkness of hopeless grief. They should rather be solemn with the moving of the great ideas and deep emotions which stir to life in the hours when we are brought face to face with the great realities which underlie our existence. Companionships are temporary in this world of change. It is not possible that the associations of a lifetime should be broken without a pang of pain and a wrench of parting which seem to rend our very souls. Finding one day that one we have loved is no longer with us, we are as these under a new earth–all things are changed."

Bethany could not believe the spirituality of the dwarven people. She had not seen anything like this in Capital, not for any of the funerals she had attended. As the third dwarf stepped forward to speak the assembly aped the movements of the speaker's hands.

"At such a time the teachings of the Five come back to us with renewed force. The Five, Immortality, Friendship–these are what we strive for to keep before the eyes and in the members of our congregation. These are the thoughts that have power to comfort and uplift us now.

"In the Five we live and move and have our being. In the Five we learn to rejoice in our lives. In the Five we learn to release the pain of parting. In the Five we are reborn." From under his robe he produced a clay bowl. "When the bowl is broken," he said, smashing the bowl on the floor, "we move on in life." He produced a small jug. "And when the fountain is broken at the cistern, the body fails." He broke the jug on the ground, and pulled out a silver cord and unwound it. "And when the silver cord is loosened, and the pickaxe is a burden, and the spark of life returns to the Five who gave it. We remember there is no death, for life is transient. All that is beautiful and good and true in dwarven life is no more affected by the shadow of death than by the darkness that divides today from tomorrow."

The fourth dwarf came forward, and he held up his hands, palms to the heavens. "O Gods, our Fathers, grant that we sorrow not for those who know not the promises contained in the Holy Books; but may we look forward to the great gathering of thy grace that we may live as the heirs of this blessed and glorious hope which thou hast so graciously set before us."

He lowered his hands and bowed his head. "May the blessing of the Five go with you all."

The congregation spoke together. "And also with you."

With a step back the dwarf returned to the alter of the body he stood next to. The fifth dwarf spoke, but didn't move. "We give to those passing what was needed in life. A pick axe, to help them through the rock to the seat of the Five." He took out a small hand pickaxe and placed it on the body. The other four aped the symbolic gesture as well. "A comb to brush out the rocks from the beard and be respectable to the wife on returning from the dig." He took a small comb of bone from his cloak and placed it on the body. The others continued to mimic his movements. "A smock of white made from the wool of a newborn lamb, to protect their clothes from spots and stains." A smock, rolled and tied, was placed on the bodies. "And a grain of gold, to pay their way from heaven to the earth to be reborn." He dropped a grain of gold on the body, placed both his hands in his sleeves and stepped back.

Five more hooded figures stepped on the dais and pulled the sheets over the bodies. They nodded to the king and stepped back to stand beside the other five. The king came back to the dais and took a deep breath.

"My friends, my loyal friends. It is with great sorrow I tell you five of our brothers have lost their lives. Gran, Hull, Pon, Gron, and Dans were excavating in the lower chamber of North East when a pocket of gas was found. They tried to plug up the break but in doing so succumbed to the poison. Their bodies failed, and the gas touched a torch. The result caused the gas to ignite and the ceiling collapsed on our brothers.

"We have lost many from the digging of the mountains and received very little in return." The king lowered his head. "We have lost too much.

"Many years ago, before we were born, a king, not unlike myself, stood in the small chamber that became our great hall and made a mistake. He tried to take advantage of a new alliance of towns who called themselves the Realm. The king then used poorly constructed language in an attempt to trick the new alliance, and take advantage of one he plied with mead.

"Now, generations past, we find ourselves still locked in this contract. We toil for emptiness, and live in squander. Our children fed, we find nothing left for ourselves and most of us starve." The king reached under his breast plate and pulled out a scroll. "This is the original contract between the King of the Dwarves and the King of the Realm signed so many years ago. It is old, it is fragile, and it no longer should be valid. Contracts that hold our race to draconian terms without end are invalid in our eyes. We are dwarves! We dig the Earth! We shall be free!"

The king unraveled the scroll, took the top of it and ripped the yellowed paper down the center. The contract came apart in a jagged line. Bethany watched with her mouth open.

"We reject this contract. We, the dwarves, will dig no more ore, pry no more gems, or transport jewels to the Realm until they decide to treat us fairly and justly."

The king looked at the three Spears. "This is the ruling of the King of the Dwarves."

The crowd of dwarves cheered.

The temple emptied, save for the three Spears and five guards at the door. The king told them to wait as he followed his people out of the temple, his back bent.

Jon stomped back to his companions "This is wrong. They have no right to refuse to work. They have a contract with the Realm." Jon punctuated each sentence with a slight pause.

"Jon," Bethany said. "You need to sit and calm down."

"No. I didn't do anything wrong. Why should I be locked away in their temple as they decide what to do with us? If anything their king should be charged and thrown in jail."

Bethany shook her head. She walked over to the seats and looked at the roughness of the rock. A small section of the stones were worn smooth from the hundreds of bottoms that had sat there. She climbed half way up and sat in one of the seats.

From the vantage point she could see the whole dais, and the banners stopped just short of blocking the view. The smallest noise made by Jon and Thomasyn echoed up to her ears. Even the lowest of Jon's mutters could be heard, and she could actually understand what he mumbled if she concentrated on his voice. Something about a mouse with no legs.

Bethany shook her head and stood. She looked over at the guards and wondered how long it would take her to overpower them. Five dwarves. It would take too long, more time than she could afford, for one or two of them could get word out that trouble had arisen. Too much time and reinforcements would be there to subdue all three of them. If all of them attacked at once…

To test her idea, Bethany went to the end of the row of seats and turned toward the guards. After three steps the guards lowered their pikes in a defensive posture. She stopped and studied them. Each held their pike as if born with it in their hands, not a tremble, nor reluctance in action. They were trained well.

"What are you doing?" It was Thomasyn's voice. He was still at the bottom of the chamber.

Bethany returned to the dais, but stopped five rows up. She whispered, "Jon, can you hear me?" She listened, and not hearing a response, motioned Thomasyn to come up the stairs. When he joined her, Bethany spoke in a hushed tone, "I figured if Jon couldn't hear me from here, our voices wouldn't make it to the guards."

"Why are you whispering?"

"To keep the guards from hearing. I think Jon is right about this. The king has shown treason here, and we need to warn our king. We need to get out of here. A rush on the guards, taking them by surprise, could gain us our release. But we would have to act fast. Did you keep any weapons?"

He stared at her.

"You did. A knife?"

"What do you have in mind?"

Bethany glanced at the guards. "One knife can take one, two knives … Knowing Jon, he has at least one knife hidden as well. It'll leave us with even odds. We can take the weapons off the dwarves and escape."

"Didn't you keep a knife back as well?" Thomasyn asked.

A smile lit the corner of her mouth. "Three throwing knives. I could have kept more, but the guard outside the herald's room saw a few of them when I took off my sword."

He nodded slightly.

"What are you talking about?" Jon asked. He had snuck up behind Thomasyn.

"We're thinking of taking the guards," Bethany said.

"Ha!" Jon said.

"You have a better idea?" Thomasyn asked.

"Yes, we wait."

Bethany shook her head. "I don't understand you. First you want us to attack or rebel and now you want us to just sit still and wait? Why?"

"Okay, say we overthrow the five guards; then what?"

"We go through the doors and make our way out to the surface," Bethany said.

"How many guards are outside the doors?" Jon asked Thomasyn.

"I don't know, three or four."

"And what if there's ten?"

"We'll figure it out when we come to that," Bethany said.

"It's not worth it." Shail's voice boomed in the empty air. All three turned to the dais, and Bethany couldn't believe he stood there, watching them. The Spear held out his hand and jumped off the stage, making his way over to the three. She saw a flickering candle and noticed a seam in the wall, a hidden door. "I know what you're thinking, but there are twenty on the other side. Each part of the king's guard. Each trained in the use of pikes and swords. If you make it out to them you'll get killed by the outside guards."

"So we just sit here?" Bethany asked.

Jon turned away from the group.

"We need to do something other than wait," Thomasyn said.

"There's nothing we can do. King Gimladovan is adamant about no longer digging the riches for the Realm. He wants a share that is fair, not draconian," Shail said.

"But that was the contract they tried to impose on us? It's just we turned it on them," Jon said.

"Jon's right. They wrote the contract and tried to take advantage of us but it was turned to take advantage of them, how can they complain?" Bethany said.

"Because it's been over two thousand years." Shail rubbed the back of his neck. "It's not a legal issue, it's a moral one. At what point do you stop punishing a people because of what their ancestors did? Bethany, if I discover you have a child and then you steal money, say thirty gold points, and die before paying it back, should your child then be responsible to pay it back?"

"No, but that's—"

"Exactly what is happening here. You know the law limiting length of contracts, right?"

Thomasyn looked up. "Yes, five years. One cannot enter into a contract with a limitation exceeding five years. All contracts over five years immediately expire at the end of the first five years, and must be renegotiated."

"Exactly," Shail said. "And that was put in place by the last King of the Realm. It was put in place to protect those who were being taken advantage of."

Jon turned. "It's not protecting those who signed contacts before then."

"Right," Shail said. "Any contract prior to that date is still enforceable, still valid."

"So the dwarves are looking at changing the contract?" Bethany asked.

"That is something the king wants to talk to you three about."

Thomasyn waited for the others to say something, but they just stared at Shail. The man waited. It seemed like an eternity but the silence only lasted a few minutes.

"So what do we need to do?" Bethany asked.

"Go to him," Shail said. "I'll take you there, but you'll have to talk to the king and find out what he really wants. What kind of concessions are on his mind, and then it has to go to the Realm. Understand that they won't mine any more until their needs are met."

"So, we need to take care of this?" Thomasyn asked.

"Yes, you need to take care of this," Shail said.

"Why us?" Jon asked.

A SHARP SPEAR POINT

"Because you are the young Spears. You're the ones who can understand what they are going through. Garion and I are just part of the old Spears who have enforced the contract for years. And even with the friendships we have here, we are still the bullies, the bad humans who make them live up to what the contact says, regardless of how we treat them or feel." Shail rubbed the back of his neck, his voice softer. "We tried to take the issue to the king years ago, but the council refused to have it heard. In many ways, the old king listened to them. Now, our new king may have the ability to change, especially when ones near his age report what we have been saying for years."

Thomasyn touched Shail's arm. "You believe in this, don't you?"

Shail looked into Thomasyn's eyes. "Yes, I do."

"Then you better take us to the king."

Shail smiled.

Shail opened the door to the herald's office, and escorted the three young Spears in. The herald sat behind his desk, transposing notes to a new contract. He held up his hand to hold back the Spear from talking until he finished the part he worked on.

"We've been here before. This... herald does nothing to help out but make snide remarks," Jon said.

"I made snide remarks, young Spear, in order to show you there was more to what you see." The herald pushed away from his desk and grunted as he stood. "There are always things more important than the desire you think is important."

Thomasyn noticed a resemblance to one of the five dwarves who had been killed in the accident, and the large bags

171

under his eyes told a story of loss. The herald limped, and when he reached for the door behind his desk the dwarf all but stumbled.

Moving swiftly, Thomasyn came up beside the old dwarf and helped open the door. The herald looked up and smiled, giving a node of appreciation. They both swung the doors open.

A long hall, thirty yards deep and five yards wide, vast ceilings and great arching columns stretched before them. Thomasyn felt small in comparison, and hesitated taking the first step forward.

-10-

Jon fastened the flaps of his tent and lay in his blankets. He was cold. A thought went through his mind. *Bethany may have seen my last kill.* He didn't care. Too much time had passed between taking a life, and his desire had reached a breaking point. It was only a rat, anyway. *Soon I will find a way to examine the inside of something bigger.*

But she could have seen.

"She may have seen, but would she understand?" Jon said.

She will find out.

"She may have suspicions."

He took out one of the packages of meat out of his pack and placed the pack on the ground. One hand propped up his head, and he unwrapped the cloth and took a piece of meat out. Once in his mouth the spices used in the drying spread over his tongue. Jon could feel the meat plump with his saliva, and he sucked to draw out all the flavors.

Each package was marked with a different color of cloth, not much of a difference unless you knew what to look for. And Jon knew what to look for. The slight brown coloring on the end of the twine or a soft discoloration on the edge of the burlap told him it was a package he wanted. Yes, he had all the specially flavored meat.

Don't let them know you have them.

"They saw me pack and wouldn't take my food."

They would if they were hungry.

"I wouldn't let them."

There are two of them. You are only one.

"Then I will hunt and gather so they don't need mine."

After finishing his food Jon decided to listen. He heard Bethany agreed to share Thomasyn's tent, and now they talked. Jon made the sounds of sleeping as he listened.

They spoke, and he could barely hear them. Something was said about him, and a loss, but he couldn't discern anything else over the howl of the wind.

He kept up the sleeping sounds, and pulled the blankets around him. The dwarves knew how to make weapons, but the ones who made their blankets needed a lesson in softness. The things itched at his skin, and he just wanted to crawl out and burn them. Slowly his mind found peace in sleep, and the voice faded into the background.

Jon didn't know when the wind stopped. One side of his tent was dark, buried in snow. His stomach grumbled.

You need to eat.

"I realize that."

The small package still held a few pieces of meat, and he ate them quickly to still the pangs that would come.

He had to get up, so he threw off the blankets and allowed the cold to attack his body. After a few seconds he wrapped himself in the cloak and packed up the blankets. His frosted before him in the air.

Jon's fingers fumbled on the knotted leather straps, and once they were undone he rolled the flaps back. The sticks holding up the tent came down next. Fighting against the wind, he rolled up the tent and the blankets went inside his pack. He was ready, but both Bethany and Thomasyn still slept.

"Lazy," he said, looking at the first rays of the sun cresting the horizon.

Let them sleep.

The wind still whipped across the tundra, but no snow fell. Swirls of white curled across the plains. Jon breathed on his hands and shoved them in his cloak. "Do I have to wait for you two?"

A snort erupted in the silence, and a deep yawn rumbled.

"Thomasyn, will you get up. I'm starting off now, heading south. When you two are ready, just follow me."

"You're up? Bethany is still sleeping, but I'll wake her. Just wait."

After a short pause Bethany's voice came through the tent's walls. "I'm getting up. Look away, now!"

Jon shook his head. "Catch up when you have a chance." He turned and started to walk south.

Good. Leave them. Make it home before them.

"Jon! Just wait. We'll be out in a little bit," Thomasyn called out.

He kept walking. He just wanted to get to a warm place. His hands hurt from the bitterness of the weather, and if he kept a good pace it would only take two weeks to get to the southern area of the Realm.

Why did he want to leave them behind? It wasn't long ago that he wanted to always be around his friends. The two would support him, but for some reason the constant praise of his abilities had started to wear on him. Did they think he didn't know what was going on? They wanted to build him up, to make him think they were his friends, only to stab him in the back.

They don't deserve your friendship, the voice said.

"No, they don't."

So you should make it back before them. Tell the king about the new contract. Be the hero.

"I will."

Yes, you will.

It felt right. His so-called friends, the two he left behind, should have been ready. Master Chail would have had them up early. That is why he always woke up when he did. He should have waited, should have helped them take down their tent and pack everything up. They did stay up later than he did, so he could have helped.

No, you did the right thing.

"I should have waited."

Would they have waited for you? Or would they have waited until you left?

"They would have waited."

You don't know that for sure.

"Yes, I know that for sure."

Then you could have been the sweet one, and cleaned up after them.

No, it was their responsibility to clean up after themselves. He took care of himself and didn't need someone to follow him around. But they did care for him. It was obvious that they liked being around him or was it just the orders that were given. Did Master Chail tell them to stay close to him? Yes, he must have. Now they were traveling back to Capital, back to the heart of the Kingdom. He didn't want to go back there. Not after all those years of training, of what they had made him do.

We could make our way south, then east away from the others.

"But I have to report back—"

To the people who don't love you?

But Master Chail loved them all. Nanny Tess also loved him. She always showed him kindness, didn't she? But every time he saw her, Bethany and Thomasyn both were there. How could he be sure she was not being kind to them, and he was only there as an afterthought. Why would she do such a thing?

See? They don't love you. All you are is a dog begging for table scraps.

No, it is not true. Jon knew he was loved; he had been told that many times, and it was something he could believe. Every time he was injured during training they took care of the injuries.

Like they did with all the others who were injured.

"Everyone gets injured."

Not everyone. Two were never injured during the training.

Didn't they cause the injuries, all of them? Each time he was pushed harder to be stronger and faster than the opponents they provided. Each of the trainers making him fight faster, move between the spinning blades. And when he was facing them with swords, they would cut his arms to show how they could penetrate his defenses. No, now they can't get past his defenses. They trained him too well. He was the Master and they were the students. His mastery of the sword, the spear, and the bow could not be bested.

You are the master. It is you they should be getting to train the new Spears.

They even taught him how to disappear using the magic of the cloak, and he was the best at that as well. He blended faster than Thomasyn, he threw a spear better than Bethany. So why did he feel like he needed to measure up to them?

You don't need to measure up to them. They need to measure up to you.

Jon shook his head, clearing the fog from his mind. Why am I thinking like this? Something has happened to me.

"Jon, you all right?"

Thomasyn's hand touched his shoulder, and Jon shuddered. He turned to look at Thomasyn. Concern clouded his friend's face. "I'm all right." He shrugged away so the hand no longer touched him.

"You were just standing there," Bethany said. She was a pace behind Thomasyn, and her gaze penetrated him.

Jon took two steps back. His hand reached to his forehead and he rubbed it. He looked down to the ground. "I…I don't know…We need to get back to Capital. The king of the dwarves is counting on us."

He watched as the two gazed at him. He turned. "We need to travel. Run to keep us warm?"

"No, we walk," said Thomasyn.

Jon could hear the sound of the voice inside him. "I want to get home."

Bethany followed the two, measuring her footsteps, so she neither gained nor fell behind. Two to three weeks walking would get them to the Teeth's edge, a plateau leading to the warmer region of the Realm.

"Tell us, Bethany. Tell us about the naming of the Realm," Thomasyn said as they walked. "It'll pass the time."

She remembered the talks of the Speaker of the Spear, and the meaning behind the simple name. The Realm. Each region argued, each region demanded, each region threatened, but in the end…

"The Speaker told it better," she said. "Anyway, it's cold and I'm hungry."

"So you don't want to speak?" Jon said. "That's different."

"Shut up, Jon." Bethany took a deep breath. "So you want to hear the story of the naming of the Realm? Okay, I'll do it."

The two slowed. Bethany caught up and walked between them. Her mind searched for the story. She focused her mind and recited the story as it had been told to her.

"Many centuries ago the Realm didn't exist. The land was in turmoil and many fought against their brothers. The towns claimed dominion on the people within their reign. The people suffered.

"One man, a land owner of the peninsula at the southern area of the land lay claim to the continent, promising to bring all together. He called all together and held a great feast, disclosing his plans to those who came. Each agreed the land needed a ruler and each wanted to be that ruler.

"The one man, recorded by the scrolls as a king by his own proclamation, held a contest to show he was the one who should be the King of the Realm. To prove his worth that man had his name struck from all records. He was erased from history to be unknown by all.

"All the others proclaimed the man was not worthy for he was no longer known, and therefore had no claim to the throne. Others laughed at him saying he threw away his life and had nothing to show for it. All said he was no longer one who would be accepted as king."

Bethany pulled out her skin and took a sip. The mixed water and cream slid down her throat. She put the skin back on her pack.

"The man, now with no name, proclaimed he would never again have a name. He would always be a king of the people, for they had names and he no longer did. The kingdom would be his name and he would protect them. The others, he proclaimed, were self-righteous and self-serving. They needed to have humility and look to serve others. They didn't listen.

"Each took turns insulting the man. They called him by his name. He only looked at them and said he had no name, so their insults meant nothing. The man with no name tried to talk to them about the needs of the world, but they found it more enjoyable to insult and complain. Finally, after all had grown tired of insulting the man, they no longer had the energy to fight among themselves to decide who would be best to have the of the new king.

"The man with no name called for a vote among the people, and his was the only hand raised as one willing to be a king with no name. The others just watched and could not understand what happened. He explained they didn't want to be the king, for the king gives up his name in order to serve the people. And when the others demanded to know the name of the new kingdom the new king said they should all decide.

"But each wanted to call it after the name of their town, claiming it was the best name one could use. None could agree so they argued for days, then weeks, then months.

"Once the arguing had finished, the new king turned to them all and proclaimed them to be a council, but only to suggest and recommend. So the King said the land was finally a realm and those within were the subjects. And keeping with him not having a name, the realm would be named after him and have no name at all. Hence the name of the realm is the Realm."

The two were silent as she recounted the teachings of the Speaker of the Spears. He was the old man who was always kind to them. He was the one in her thoughts. She could still see him clearly, wispy hair and sparse beard. Cloak gray as an overcast sky.

Bethany allowed the silence to grow between them. She wanted to bridge the gap between the two and bring their family together.

The silence between them lasted for hours, and as the sun started to dip in the horizon they called a halt to their march.

They pulled off their packs and pitched tents. The hard day's march showed on them, and the cold bit through Bethany. Bethany nodded to Thomasyn and Jon, entered her tent and ate some of her food supplies before wrapping blankets around herself to sleep.

Seventeen days. They repeated the cycle of walking, talking, and stopping to sleep for seventeen days. The mundane task of traveling the leagues to Capital took their toll, and each reacted differently. Bethany snapped at the boys, Thomasyn grew more silent and Jon seemed distant.

When the snow no longer littered the ground, and trees reached toward the sky, the three knew towns would start to appear. With towns would come people, and people would welcome them with warm meals. Bethany looked forward to the possibility of a warm bath, and to washing properly for the first time in weeks.

The eighteenth day they came across a forest thick with trees. A path led through the trunks and they followed it. From mid-morning to late afternoon they walked through the trees. Signs of game showed, and Jon's head darted back and forth.

"I'm hunting," he said, taking a spear off his back.

"Jon, I think one of us should go with you," Thomasyn said.

"Why? So you can scare away the food? No. I'll catch something and meet you further down the path." He moved into the woods, leaving Thomasyn and Bethany behind.

"I'm worried about him and don't know what to do," Thomasyn said.

"I'm worried about those we left behind. Jon will survive his little hunt, and we'll make it back to Capital, but what will happen after that?"

Thomasyn shook his head and walked down the path.

After an hour, the forest thinned to a cultivated field that stretched out before them. Bethany smiled and ran forward to the top of the hill. As she crested the small hill, she spied the straw-thatched roofs of huts. In the center of the makeshift town several people pulled water from a dug well.

"Thomasyn, come!" she called over her shoulder. She ran down toward the settlement, and several of the people looked up. Two pointed at her, and the others ran towards their respective huts.

Bethany slowed as the two stood pointing at her. She tracked one of the runners as he disappeared into a hut. She knew the well held water, and they had gathered very little since they left the Snow Belt. The possibility of a warm meal also entered her mind; she was tired of the dried meat and hard, stale bread.

When she was within hailing distance, Bethany slowed to a walk. The pointers lowered their arms but kept an eye on her. *I must be a sight.*

"My name is Bethany, and I'm a Spear. My companions and I are traveling back to Capital and are in need of shelter for the night."

"No further," said the tallest of the men.

"I'm a Spear. There is no reason to be afraid of me." She took a few more steps closer to the group with her hands raised shoulder high, palms out and open.

The tall one drew a knife, and the other copied him. "I don't want to hurt you, or your companion there." He hesitated, biting his lower lip. "Put your weapons down."

"Sure, but I'm not going to hurt you." Bethany reached up, took the four short throwing spears from her back and placed them on the ground in front of her. She opened her cloak, and unbuckled the sword at her side. Then she emptied the small pockets inside her cloak of the throwing knives she carried.

His eyes grew wide. The man's reaction didn't surprise her. Once all her weapons were placed in front of her, Bethany held out her hands palm up to show she was unarmed.

"Tell the other one to come here and do the same." The man pointed towards Thomasyn.

Bethany turned and signaled Thomasyn to join her. When he was within hearing, she told him what to do. His brows furrowed as his head tilted to one side. He didn't understand why, but without hesitation he followed her instructions.

The pile of weapons in front of him matched what Bethany had. Hesitantly the tall man came forward and examined the weapons, toeing the spears to make sure they were the only ones there.

"Satisfied?" Bethany asked. "We just came across your village and would like to wash and fill our water skins."

The man just looked at her.

"Can we fill our water skins?" Bethany asked again.

The other man came up to the tall one and whispered in his ear. The tall one nodded.

"Josh here will fill your water skins," he said, nodding toward the other man.

Bethany unslung her two skins and handed them over. Thomasyn did likewise. The two watched the man take them to the well and fill them. Once finished, the skins were handed back without ceremony.

"Can we share a meal?" Bethany asked.

"No," the tall man said.

"But we're Spears. The people of the Realm always open their homes to help the Spears when they are in need."

"No. You have water, now go."

Bethany reached for her weapons. "Stop! You go now. These you will leave." The man waved toward the weapons.

"We need those weapons," Thomasyn said.

"You came here; you're taking our water. This is the payment."

Bethany signaled Thomasyn with her hand, and sidled two paces to the left. "But we only had a small amount of water. Certainly not worth all these weapons."

"We set the price. It's our water."

"But if you wanted to charge us for the water wouldn't it be proper to tell us that in the first place?" She took another three steps, hoping that Thomasyn would now be out of the man's line of sight.

"You came to us."

"The law says if you mean to sell, you must first tell," Bethany said. She knew there was no such law, but maybe the man didn't. She hoped to resolve this without any violence, just like Master Chail would do. And they needed those weapons to survive.

Why did they want our weapons?

"Stop moving," the tall man said. Bethany had moved him just enough to take Thomasyn out of line of sight. It was enough.

Bethany clenched her fist twice very quickly, signaling Thomasyn.

He rolled forward, taking his sword with one hand and a knife with the other. With a swift move, he jerked the sword out of the sheath. He rolled forward to Josh's feet. Thomasyn stood. The knife lay against the man's neck. He was behind the villager, sword pointing toward the tall man.

"No," the tall man screamed, as he turned and stepped toward Thomasyn.

Bethany dived to the weapon pile. One hand grabbed her sword hilt. The other grabbed the scabbard and pulled it away from the blade.

The tall man stood there, mouth agape. Bethany landed just in front of his feet and she squatted there. The tall man, with the point of Bethany's sword under his chin, lifted his arms and dropped his knife.

"Now, we have your attention," Thomasyn said. "You can tell us why Spears of the Realm are being treated like common beggars and turned away with nothing, not even what they came with."

"Tell them, Daylin," Josh said.

"No! We were warned," Daylin said, a bead of sweat forming on his brow.

Bethany saw how nervous the man was. The small trickle threatened to fall down the side of his nose.

"Tell us, Daylin. What has made you act improperly?" Bethany asked.

Daylin pointed to the tip of the sword, and Bethany lowered it slightly. He nodded toward Josh. "The boy there was in the woods a week ago when he found a small cache of gold."

"It was just lying there," Josh said.

"He didn't know better. All he did was take a bit of it to help the village. How could he have known?"

"Known about what?" Thomasyn asked.

"Trolls," Daylin said.

The rabbit tracks led Jon deeper into the forest, but he didn't care. He wanted to eat. Moving swiftly, he followed the small animal's trail. The disturbed ground led haphazardly through the forest.

A small bent twig indicated he was moving in the right direction. The way the leaves were disturbed, brushed aside with some strewn about told him the animal had passed in a hurry. Mud showed actual paw prints, and he knew it was a fair size for a rabbit. In five minutes he had found his prey sitting and nibbling on the leaves of a small shrub.

His right hand reached behind him and pulled a spear from the holder built into the side of his pack. He spun around and hefted the weapon. The butt of the spear pointed toward his prey. He threw the spear.

Standing up, he walked toward the body of the small creature. The spear had struck a glancing blow on the head just like he wanted it to. The body still moved, breath still shuttering in and out. Jon smiled as he picked up the spear and placed it back in the holder. Anticipation seized him.

Oh, look what you have here.

"I have dinner for the three of us."

You have something to examine. Slice off the skin and see what's inside.

Grabbing the ears, Jon lifted the creature and moved a few paces to a small riverbed. He picked up a good-sized rock.

A small leather strapping twisted in his fingers, retrieved from a hidden pocket of his cloak. Delicately, he laid his trophy on its back and tied the limbs open. Jon smiled.

Yes, this will do nicely.

"Quiet! Let me do this now, before it dies."

He took out a knife and stone and ran the edge along the scratchy surface to hone the blade. Periodically, he tested the blade to see how sharp it was. Satisfied on the edge, Jon moved back to the rock to see the rabbit grunting against the bindings.

Don't let it get away.

"It won't be able to break the bindings."

It can bite through them.

"It can't get them near its mouth."

As long as it doesn't get away...

Jon noticed the eyes of the animal, so wide the whites showed. It tried desperately to reach the straps holding it down but to no avail; its captor had done this before. The animal would not escape.

The tip of the knife touched the skin of the rabbit just below the rib cage and it squealed, sounding like a small child. As it tried to get away, Jon seized its body to hold it still.

A little pressure and the tip of the blade penetrated the skin, and he pulled upward. Again the animal cried. He grasped the skin, slit the body downward, and separated it with his fingers. Blood spilled out. His fingers explored the animal's insides and the creature let out one last, desperate shriek before its lifeblood spilled. Jon kept exploring.

Name the parts.

"Lungs, heart, stomach, intestines."

With the rabbit no longer moving he was able to use both hands. He opened the body cavity and took out the entrails. Heart, lungs, liver, stomach, kidneys, intestines, all came out slowly as he felt the consistency of each item. He was done. The skin separated with a good pull. Dinner, for him at least, was ready for a fire.

He pulled out a small game bag from his pack and placed the body inside. One more; that was all he needed. One more.

After ten minutes searching he came across another set of tracks. He followed them through the bush and found another rabbit. Trapping it was easy, and Jon named all the parts inside as the creature's heart beat its last.

Satisfied, Jon started to make his way back toward the road when he noticed the small pile of gold. It was there, sitting out in the open. No one around. No one watching. He didn't have a need for it. The Realm supplied him with everything he needed. But gold. The small glinting pebbles enticed his eyes. An itching of his palms made him rub his hands together.

Take one. Take two. Take three.

"I don't need them."

But if you have them maybe you can show her. Show Bethany. You could have her. Take her away from him. Show you are better.

Nervously, Jon's eyes darted back and forth looking for anything. No sign of anyone around him. No sign of animals present. He walked toward the gold. A shaky hand reached out and touched a small piece. He took it. Looked at it. Smelled it. The weight of it was surprising to him. He put it into a pocket in his cloak.

Jon stood. He started to turn but the glint of another piece of gold caught his eye. He reached out for it and put the small treasure into the same pocket. Another went in after it. And then another. Twelve pieces of gold now weighed down his cloak, but he didn't mind. The heavy treasure represented a lifetime of riches.

He stood again and turned toward the road. A heavy hand clasped his shoulder.

"Trolls?" Thomasyn asked.

"Yes, trolls," Dayton said. The man shook. "Josh took their gold, but instead of killing him they offered him life if he showed them the village."

"So he brought them into town?" Bethany asked.

"Yes," Josh said. "I had to. They said if they found the town without me they'd kill everyone in it."

Thomasyn remembered some of the stories he had heard about trolls. The large creatures collected whatever shone in the moonlight. They treasured gold the most. If it gleamed they wanted it.

"How many?" Bethany asked.

"What?" Dayton said.

"How many trolls?"

"At least twelve," Josh said.

"You saw them?" Thomasyn asked.

"No, only the two who caught me. The rest were back at their cave," Josh said. He shifted from foot to foot, not meeting their eyes.

"They said twelve, but you only saw two." Bethany looked over at Thomasyn and smiled. He returned the gaze, knowing full well that even a small force of villagers could defend against two trolls.

Thomasyn took a deep breath. "You have been lied to. There were only two. When four trolls gather they fight amongst themselves. The Speaker of the Spears told us such years ago."

He remembered the speech as if it was yesterday. The old man had them all enthralled as he spoke. When he showed a painting of a troll they all gaped. The creature was depicted as over six feet tall, with bristly hair covering most of their bodies, and arms that reached to their knees. He said they had a grip like the mountain and were single-minded. The skull surprised them, for it was twice the size of a man's.

The truth of the statement sank into the two men, and they stared in disbelief at the two Spears. "No more than four?" Dayton stood with his mouth open.

"No more than four," Bethany said.

"We didn't know," Josh lamented.

"Unless you knew about trolls, you couldn't have," Thomasyn said.

"How...how do..." Dayton stumbled with his voice soft, as if he was trying to come to terms with their folly.

"You don't, we do. We are Spears. It is our duty to protect your town." Thomasyn lowered his blade and walked to his weapons. He picked up his belongings. "It would have been better to have told us about the trolls to begin with.'

"They said to tell no one. Just collect what they had and send them down the road as if it was the way out," Dayton said.

Thomasyn straightened as Bethany gathered her weapons. "They have a taste for fighting, but more importantly, they love to kill. Did they come and collect the belongings after the travelers had passed?"

"Yes," Dayton said. "They collected everything, but usually the next day."

"There are three of us traveling to Capital. Once our companion joins us we can take care of your problem," Bethany said.

Thomasyn noticed a few of the villagers had emerged from their huts. They stood talking amongst themselves while pointing toward the four of them.

"How many of you are in the village?" Bethany asked.

"Seven families," Dayton said.

"Who is the leader?" Bethany asked.

"I am," Dayton said. "Logan was, but the trolls pulled his arms off, and he died soon after."

"How long have they been holding your town?" Bethany asked.

"Long. For seven years." Dayton fell to his knees. "They have made us sacrifice to them."

Thomasyn came to the man, and knelt in front of him. "Yes, but no longer."

Tears welled in Dayton's wide eyes. "By the Five." The skin on his face was drawn taught with anguish. "How can I face my children?"

"It is not you who needs to answer for this, it is the trolls. We'll find the trolls and bring them to justice."

Jon spun on his heal, right hand clasping the hilt of his sword. He pulled it free. The blade sliced through the air and looped around, stopping just before cutting into the flesh of the troll's neck. He looked into the eyes of the creature and only saw sadness. The creature had lifted its head, exposing a long neck ready to accept a death stroke. The pitiful look of the eyes with drooping lids spoke to Jon's soul.

It wants you to kill it!

Slowly, the troll's hand came up and lightly grasped the blade, moving it toward her neck. She nodded at Jon and lifted her chin.

"No," Jon said.

But it wants you to!

A whimper started in the deep recesses of the troll's body and became a grumble. Jon looked the troll over. She seemed gaunt, skin falling from bones with no substance. The grey matted fur of her body was sparse. He guessed she was old and in pain. Her eyes were cloudy as well.

With a thump she dropped to the ground in a sitting position. Air rattled into her lungs.

Jon sheathed his sword, eyes searching for other trolls but found none. Moving slowly, he picked up some fallen branches and built a fire. One green branch was broken from a tree and served as a spit for the rabbits.

The troll sniffed the air and edged closer to the fire. She sniffed again, and drool traced a line from her mouth through the dirt on her face.

You should open it up.

"Who are you?" Jon asked.

As if in response, the troll tilted her head and turned to him. Her eyes searched until one part, not as cloudy as the rest, pointed at him. She reached out one gnarled hand, palm up with fingers curled slightly. A rumbling noise escaped her mouth as she tried to speak.

Jon took a knife and sliced off a leg of one of the rabbits. He handed it to the troll. She took it in her hand after two attempts to grasp it. Small pieces of meat came off the bone as she pulled at the flesh. The troll ate slowly, even trying to bite into the bone itself.

He fed her more.

Why are you feeding her? You could be exploring. Seeing what's inside of her.

Soon the two rabbits were done. Jon finished cutting them up and fed the troll a fair share. He ate half a rabbit and snuffed the fire out. The troll made motions with her mouth and seemed to want to communicate but was not able to form words. The troll had very few teeth and a tongue smaller than he would have thought. It led him to believe the creature's tongue had been removed.

He watched as the troll's head bobbed a little, and its eyes grew heavy. Once it was asleep Jon stood, walked behind it, and drew his sword. His blade sliced through the creature's neck.

He wiped the blade against the body of the troll and sheathed it.

"I kill when I want to," he said. "No one tells me when to strike."

He threw dirt on the fire and smothered it.

"You said the trolls told you to send travelers down this trail?" Thomasyn asked.

"Yes," Dayton said. The man looked nervous, and Bethany watched him with unblinking eyes.

"How many have been sent down here?" Thomasyn asked.

"Just over two dozen men," Dayton said. "Not all at once, mind you. Sometimes a small group of two or three, but mostly one or two."

They walked down the path, following the padded dirt as it twisted through the trees. Enough light streamed through the canopy so she could see everything, but the patches of light helped obscure the shadows. Bethany tilted her head, and realized the forest had fallen silent.

"Here's something," Thomasyn pointed to the ground a few paces into the forest. "I think I've found one of the travelers."

Bethany looked into the forest and spotted something white. They walked toward it and after ten paces they came across the remains of a man. Thomasyn uncovered the bones, and Bethany picked up a femur. She noticed signs of gnawing, and held it out to Thomasyn.

"Looks like they ate the travelers," Thomasyn said.

"Something did," Bethany said.

"There are more bodies scattered about. From what I can tell, about two dozen. Seems our trolls didn't want anyone to escape and tell the rest of the Realm." Thomasyn sighed and stood up.

"If they let anyone through, the Spears would have been sent to investigate," Bethany said. "It would have ruined their little plan."

"I don't understand something," Thomasyn said. "Where are the trolls now?"

Bethany stood and looked around, hunting the shadows and trying to see if anything moved. Nothing did.

"We should return to the village," Dayton said.

"Don't worry," Bethany said. "If the two trolls attack, Thomasyn and I can defeat them."

"What if there are more than just the two you think there are? What if they have a dozen?" Dayton asked.

"We'll take care of it," Thomasyn said. He motioned toward the bones in front of Bethany.

Not knowing what he meant, Bethany first glared at him and shrugged. He raised his eyebrows slightly and gazed toward the torso of the skeleton. She followed his eyes and stared at the rib cage. Her eyes did not find anything at first, but then she saw it. Notch marks between two of the ribs. Perfect alignment. She reached out her hand and ran her finger over it.

Bethany bent closer. Examining the skeleton, a number of problems revealed themselves. The skull was cracked in two places. The neck bones were stretched and separated unnaturally. More of the notch marks showed on the back of the ribs, as if the body had been stabbed multiple times.

She stood and wiped her hands on the inside of her cloak. This was not an attack of a troll; they didn't use weapons. What she saw were the remains of a man struck down by a knife attack, stripped, and left for the forest to devour.

A realization struck her, and she looked up at Thomasyn who nodded inconceivably.

"We should get back to the village and see if Jon shows up." With that, Thomasyn turned and walked back to the path.

Bethany waited for Dayton to move. She didn't want him following her. Keeping him between the two of them was the best idea. The man smiled nervously at her and held out his hand inviting her to go before him.

"I'm the Spear, remember? You first."

The man hesitated, then bowed to her and started toward the path.

She watched him move for the first time. He didn't seem to be worried or concerned. His stride was sure and unhurried. He moved between the trees easily and once he was on the path, he didn't look around to see if he was alone. The man just headed toward the village.

Thomasyn, was just in front of them. He stopped and waited for the two to catch up. He nodded to Dayton as he passed and started walking when Bethany reached him.

"You saw," he said, keeping his voice low.

"Yes. What does it mean?"

"There are no trolls."

"Why would a village use such a ploy?" Bethany asked. Why would a person lie to a Spear? They helped people and ensured justice was served. In all her years of training nothing had prepared her for people misleading her.

"I'm not sure. Maybe to collect all the wanderers had. Maybe they did it to stay away from the rest of the Realm. Either way, they have been in a conspiracy. The whole town is probably involved."

They grew quiet. Feet shuffled along the path, trampling on packed dirt. As the village grew nearer they both placed a hand on their sword hilts. Bethany glanced at Thomasyn.

"Are we expecting trouble?" Bethany asked.

Thomasyn raised his head and Bethany followed his gaze to see the 20 villagers around the well. "Maybe," he said. "Look at them. They're armed now."

Bethany realized a few had swords, and all had daggers. They wore a scattering of strange arms, from small short swords with straight edges to one large two-handed sword on the back of a monster of a man. "That one could be trouble," she said.

-11-

Having never seen a troll up close before, Jon examined the body. Short, gray tufts of fur covered it. The arms were mostly sinew with little muscle left. The fur on the legs was thick and long, and when he checked the left leg he felt stickiness on the flesh.

Moving the hair away, he examined the leg. The fur had been worn away around the leg. The skin was red from being irritated and abrasions marked the ankle. Jon wondered if they were rope burns.

"Someone was not very kind to you."

And you were?

Jon slowly cut through the skin with his knife and examined the muscles. He cut away the muscles and looked at how the bones joined together.

You should name the bones.

"I already know what they are, why would I name them?"

Practice.

He had never been left alone long enough to truly examine such a large creature. Even when he found the small rodents others had been around him to make sure he didn't do anything. During the journey to the Teeth he had no time to examine any of the small animals he had found.

A howl cut through the air.

Jon looked up and tried to locate the noise. It sounded similar to the sound this troll had made when he had stumbled upon her, a short guttural sound. He stood and found the direction. Deeper into the forest, that was where he needed to go.

Taking great care to clean his knife, Jon removed all traces of blood from his person. He rubbed dirt on his hands first and then wiped them on the fur of the troll. The howl penetrated the air once again.

His interest was piqued. Something else was around for him to examine. Maybe, just maybe, this one would be in better health, and he could take its life properly.

Elation flared. It would be young and strong. The troll could put up a good fight, and Jon really wanted a good fight.

One foot in front of the other. All he had to do is keep up the pace.

Don't get too excited.

But he did. His exhilaration rose and made the hairs on the back of his neck prickle. The distance moved quickly, and soon he could hear the howling clearly.

He slowed. The distance was no longer great, and if he just charged in, there could be an issue. If more than just one… He stopped just shy of a clearing. One tree stood directly in the line of sight between him and the prey. Jon pressed his back against it and waited for the next howl.

A few seconds later it punctured the forest's stillness. Jon looked around the trunk of the tree and saw the troll. It stood over six feet tall and the fur was as gray as the older one's. A rope was tied around its leg and secured to a rock. Just out of reach of the troll's large hand stood a man with a stick. The point thrust out and struck the troll in the stomach. The troll howled.

With a lunge, the troll grabbed at the stick, but the man pulled it back. Jon could hear the man speaking.

"Where is your friend?" he said. "Where did she go?"

"Whry whon't whrow," the troll said.

"Oh, I bet you know." The stick jabbed out again.

Jon stepped from behind the tree. "Enough!" he said.

The man froze, his eyes grew large, and he dropped the stick.

Jon grinned as he approached the man. The troll looked towards the Spear and back at the man. Its leg jerked the rope. It waited.

The man stumbled back a pace, then another.

Before Jon reached him, the troll grabbed the man. One hand wrapped around his head and the other grabbed the lower jaw, fingers gripping with the strength of an enraged animal. With a jerk, the troll pulled.

"No!" Jon yelled.

At first, the man's eyes widened in terror. Skin ripped at the corners of his mouth. A popping sound broke over the gurgle as man's lower jaw came away from his head. The body spasmed for a brief second.

"No!" The troll threw the limp body aside.

Jon pulled his sword and approached the troll. To his surprise the creature didn't cower or defend. It stood there, waiting for the inevitable.

The sound of a man calling out to a companion reached Jon's ears as he raised the sword to deliver a killing blow.

"Forlorn. Forlorn! Where are you?" The voice carried across the floor of the forest.

"Was that Forlorn?" Jon said, looking at the troll. The creature grumbled and lowered its head.

"You won't tell him I'm here." Jon pulled the hood of the cloak over his head and backed up to the closest tree. He concentrated to invoke the power of the cloak. To the visible eye the form of the Spear molded into the tree and took on the color and texture of the bark.

A figure crested the ridge and walked down toward the captive troll. The man was within thirty yards when gaze locked on the body sprawled on the bloodstained ground. He stopped.

"Forlorn," he said, mournfully. The man bent his head and walked toward the corpse. "I told you we needed to end this. Oh, Forlorn. Why did you get so close to it without me here?"

The man knelt beside the body. With a sigh he stood up and unfastened a long pole from his back. Holding the implement in one hand he stood, and moved towards the troll.

"Now we do what I suggested." He struck the troll's chest with the pole. It backed up. The man repeated the thrust, pushing the creature back to the rocks.

The troll slapped at the pole, trying to get past it, but the man kept moving it. He untied the knot, and put distance between himself and the troll. The man heaved the end of the rope over a branch seven feet over his head. Grabbing the rope, the man took the end around a tree and pulled.

A thump sounded as the troll landed on its back, and the rope pulled the tied leg into the air. The troll howled. It swatted at the rope, but lacked the ability to reach and untie its leg.

Jon decided to act. He moved away from the tree, the cloak taking on its true form once again. He drew his sword. With a swift movement he sliced effortlessly through the rope holding the troll. The man fell backwards. Jon rushed forward. The man scrambled to his feet.

In one heartbeat, the tip of Jon's sword was at his throat.

"You're a Spear!" the man said in a gasp. "Protect me against the beast."

"From what I can tell it is the beast who needs protecting." Jon touched the tip of his sword against the man's chin, and used it to bring the man to his feet. "Why are you torturing this creature?"

"Torture? Look what he did to Forlorn. I…I'm just serving justice."

"Justice is for the Spears to serve. What's your name?"

The man gulped. "Keller."

"What were you going to do to him?"

"I…I was going to kill it." Keller grew bold at the statement.

"What gives you the right?"

Keller stumbled, losing confidence. He looked about him and felt his body with fumbling hands. "They said we needed to get rid of it. No more taking…" He stopped. With wide eyes wide and trembling jaw, and looked at Jon.

"No more taking what?" Jon said.

Keller's eyes took in the sword as Jon used the point to guide the man to where the troll had been tied.

Sneering, Jon motioned for Keller to sit. He wanted to show this cowardly person just how unimportant he was. "Finish what you were saying."

"No! We all promised."

"Promised what?"

"Promised never to tell."

"Tell what?"

Keller's mouth turned down and opened. His eyebrows squeezed together, and he squinted. The man's face was that of one desperate to find a way out of his situation.

"Are…are you going to kill me?"

"Not me." Jon stepped aside. Warm breath finally stopped hitting the back of his neck.

The troll moved forward.

"No! I'll tell you. It was all Dayton's idea. He said we could use the trolls to take from travelers. Have them drop all their belongings and kill them once they had left town. He said it would be easy, and no one would be the wiser." Keller blinked as sweat stung his eyes. "Call it off!" he screamed.

Jon reached out and touched the shoulder of the troll. At first it didn't budge, just stood there and breathed on the man as drool fell from its mouth. Jon tightened his grip.

The troll snapped its head toward Jon and snarled. Spittle flew from its mouth, and Jon could smell the foulness of its breath.

"No," Jon said softly.

Lowering its growl to a whimper the troll backed off.

Smart! Intelligent! Another one to examine.

Jon ignored the voice.

Keller relaxed.

Jon turned to him and his sword tip touched under Keller's chin again. "So how many did you kill?"

"I…none. Dayton killed them." Keller spat the name out like a curse. "He always tries to come up with ways to make money."

"Why not trade for money, or whatever your town needs?" Jon said.

"Because Dayton thinks it's below us. Too much work and we'll get conned out of what we have and get nothing in return." Keller stood taller, not hunching over anymore.

With a sigh, Jon turned and stared at the troll. Drool fell from its mouth and the breath carried the odor of a swamp.

"Why keep the trolls?"

"Dayton would have us release them for people to see. He wanted to show them to the two Spears…" Keller cut himself off.

Jon brought the tip of the sword back to the man's neck. "The two Spears?"

Keller's Adam's apple bobbed, almost hitting the sword point. "T-t-two Spears came into town today. Dayton told me to get a troll and bring it to the pass. I think he wanted to let it loose. Maybe to take out the Spears, or have them take it out."

Two Spears? Did the man mean Thomasyn and Bethany? Did they make it to the man's town? He shook his head when the troll growled. Pain exploded at the back of his head and his eyes closed.

"He's hiding something," Thomasyn whispered. "Watch the left."

Bethany's scanned the forest. Thomasyn eyed the right, glancing to Dayton every few seconds. The man walked with an easy gate, humming.

The hairs on the back of Thomasyn's neck stood, and he didn't like the feeling. For a man who claimed trolls roamed the forest Dayton didn't seem too concerned with getting to the security of the village. The woods started to give way as they approached the huts. Dayton's head turned from side to side as if he searched for something.

"Is anything wrong?" Bethany asked.

The man's gaze moved quickly about the small village and finally back at the two Spears. "No, just wondering…"

"Wondering what?" Thomasyn asked.

Dayton's head spun around. "I thought I heard…"

Thomasyn stopped next to Dayton and saw the man's eyes scanning the forest. He was looking. "I don't think there's anything out there to see."

A howl erupted from the forest behind them.

"I-i-it's the trolls," Dayton said.

The howling grew closer. Bethany came up beside Thomasyn. There was still no sign of any creature, just the sound.

Dayton stood behind them. "You will protect our village? You're Spears. You protect the people."

"Yes, we protect the people," Thomasyn said.

They waited.

The branches shook. A white blur crossed an open space, and he started to doubt his assumption that the town was involved in a cover up. Another howl penetrated the air. Thomasyn pulled his sword from its scabbard. The sun glinted on the metal as he drew his sword.

He lifted the weapon and held it just in front of his face. With a twist, the sword became a mirror for him to see behind him. Thomasyn glanced over at Bethany and she was doing the same. Their eyes met and their thoughts were in sync, years of training allowed them to communicate without words.

Thomasyn's eyes darted back to the sword. Dayton was no longer where he had been. He moved the blade away from him to see a different angle. The cudgel flashed by the sword. All went black.

Jon swore a dwarf used a hammer on the inside of his head. The lancing pain short through him as he raised his head. He pushed himself to ignore the throbbing and open his eyes.

He listened, heard nothing and opened his eyes. The stones that had held the troll blocked his vision. He turned his head. Nothing but trees.

"Why am I still alive?" he asked. His mind swam. The man had made a mistake by leaving him alive. Jon wouldn't have done it. The first thing he would have done was cut his throat. Take out the possibility of being followed.

Jon sat up. The sun hung high in the sky; mid-day. He had been unconscious for over an hour. The pain concerned him. He touched behind his right ear and the sting intensified. Wetness spread on his fingers, and when he pulled back his hand it was red with blood.

With a groan he heaved himself to his feet. He wobbled, caught himself on the rock, and got his feet under him. With a deep breath he leaned against a tree for a moment, his eyes searching. Two sets of prints, disturbed leaves, and broken twigs, signs of a disturbance. The prints headed southeasterly.

"Is that the way to the village?" Jon asked.

Of course it is. Where else would it lead?

He followed the trail moving from a slow walk to a run. The pain in his head throbbed with every jarring footfall.

Ten minutes. That was all it took before the howl reached his ears. There was something wrong. It was not the same noise the female troll made; it was something else. It spurred his thoughts and made him reach back into his memory. It was the noise made by the troll who had been tied up, when the first man had poked it with the stick.

Jon followed the howl, his feet striking the ground rhythmically as he made his way through the forest. Blood trickled down the back of his neck.

"What could they want with a troll?"

I told you to kill it.

"Why did they have them tied up?"

To use them, like you should have.

"Both were old. They must have cared for them but to what end?"

The same reason you could have, to learn.

"Trolls eat meat, and they eat a lot of it. So how did they keep them full?"

Like you would. They would hunt.

The questions, along with the voice's responses, rumbled through his mind as he ran. Another howl. Their position had changed. He followed the new path, working through the branches and leaves. At one point the trees thinned, but then they thickened once again. He caught a glimpse of Keller in front of him, walking with his pole and a rope in his other hand, the troll in front of him. Every few seconds the pole shot out, and the troll yelped.

A shock of white against the forest floor made Jon glance down. Bones of a man lay strewn on the floor of the forest. Jon stayed behind Keller, watching, waiting.

He didn't have to follow long. Keller pulled sharply on the rope to stop the creature. Another howl escaped the beast. Jon moved behind a tree and wrapped his cloak and hood around him. He blended into the forest. His breathing slowed.

Keller tied the rope to the trunk of a tree and backed away, watching the troll.

"I'll release you when they're close. You take out the young ones." The troll growled and reached out to Keller. Two inches separated them. Keller smiled and snickered. "I'm not as stupid as Forlorn. You'll not get me that easily." His hand shot out and he slapped the top of the troll's hand. "You can stay away from me, you smelly bundle of hair."

The troll gnashed its teeth at Keller.

A rustling sounded in the distance, and Jon slowly shifted his attention to it. A group of people was making its way toward them. One really tall man followed by a group of men and women walked with purposeful steps, carrying two litters with bodies on them. He counted. Eight men, five women, no children.

"Dayton," Keller said. "What took you so long?"

"We had trouble. Two Spears," Dayton said, motioning to the litters.

Keller moved forward and looked down. "She's pretty."

"She's a Spear. Dangerous. You can't just take her into your bed and be done with it." Dayton walked toward the troll.

"I wouldn't if I were you. It tore apart Forlorn before I got to it. Another Spear was there and had it set free. I took care of him," Keller boasted, thrusting his chest out.

"Bring the litters," Dayton said.

The two litters were laid just out of the reach of the troll.

"You're going to rip these two apart," Dayton said to the troll. "Rend them limb from limb. And once you're finished you'll bite them and chew the meat off their bones."

The troll sniffed at the bodies, grumbling a little as it did. Its hand reached out, but fell short. A whimper escaped the creature.

Keller stepped forward and smacked it across the face with his stick. It howled. The people stepped back except for Dayton and Keller. They laughed.

Jon reached to his side, slowly pulled out a large dirk, and placed his right hand on the hilt of his sword. He waited.

"Okay, we have to get rid of these two. Doric, run back to the holding area and make sure that the Spear's body is brought back here. Take Reegas with you."

Two men bowed and ran off in the direction Jon had come from.

"Five years ago I came to this village, hoping to help you with your problems. Not enough people and neighbors who hated you. They wouldn't trade and thought you were below them. So now, with the increased riches we have from the travelers and the threat of the troll, we can trade once more. They look at us and wonder. None know how we gain our riches. Not a one would guess how we have weapons. Arsent there is now engaged to one of the prettiest girls in the region! His dowry paid from our riches."

Dayton smiled at the people, his face beamed with pride. "Soon we will send out an invitation to the town Wellslin, asking for a bride for Reginald. His dowry paid the same way. The town will not refuse our request."

The villagers nodded and mumbled among themselves.

Dayton turned to Keller. "Get the troll riled up." He walked away.

Keller smiled and turned to the troll. He used the stick and poked at it. The creature backed up, swatting at the weapon, but Keller circled around and made it back up to the edge of its leash. He poked and whacked at the beast. The troll kept hitting at the stick, howling with anger and frustration. Keller knew what to do, and when the troll reached out again at the stick he whipped it around and struck the hand hard. Soon blood started to show and the troll's teeth gleamed as drool frothed around its mouth.

The man edged the beast away from the litters. Once they were away from them, the villagers moved the litters within reach of the beast's leash.

Jon knew he needed to act now. He stood, dissolving the magic of the cloak and revealing himself.

"Stop!" Jon said.

The villagers stood agape. Jon drew his sword, and with his dirk in hand, he approached the litters. Keller lifted a short sword and rushed toward him. With a grunt he swung at Jon. The Spear rolled to the side. He swept his leg out, tripping the attacker. Keller sprawled. He started to get up. Jon stepped on Keller's wrist and kicked away the sword. The hilt of his weapon came down on Keller's chin.

Keller's eyes glazed over. The troll grabbed Keller. Fingers found flesh. Nails dug into eyes. Keller screamed.

"No!" Jon said. He rushed forward. A desire to change what would happen fueled his thoughts, even though he knew what was needed; Keller needed to die. The troll dropped Keller and watched the Spear. Jon ducked under one of the arms. His sword lashed out. The metal came away bloodied. The troll fell forward, its stomach laid open.

Jon, having stopped in a kneeling position, stood. He walked toward the troll and knelt by it. The grass by the creature's mouth stirred from its breath. The gentle hand of the Spear reached out and stroked the hair away from the eyes. "I didn't want to. Why did you have to kill another?"

The troll's hand came up slowly, and then fell to the ground; the once-powerful beast's body shuddered and grew still.

Bowing his head, Jon gave a silent prayer to the Five and closed the eyes of the troll. He stood and turned to the villagers.

"Who is responsible for this?" He indicated the litters. There was no response. "Was it Dayton?"

Several of the people looked back and forth at each other. One stepped forward. "Yes. He said we could become an important village in the area if we did this."

"Why would you follow him?" Jon asked.

A woman came forward and took the man's hand. "He come in and helped dig the well. It was Dayton's idea to place it in the middle of the village, and move the priv to the outskirts of the cleared area."

"We not get sick anymore," another man said.

A second woman came forward. "He knows hunting, and gaming. We eat good."

Bethany stirred. Jon went to her side. "Are you okay?" He put his hand on her forehead.

"I-where am I?" Bethany asked.

"Near the town. Don't move." Jon pushed lightly against her shoulder to keep her from sitting up. "I was afraid you were both killed until Dayton ordered the troll kill you."

"Troll? But the villagers have been killing travelers who've gone through." Bethany moved his hand out of the way and sat up. She wavered, and Jon steadied her.

"You need to stop. Let your head catch up to your thoughts," Jon said as he tried to keep her down.

"Jon! Look out!" It was Thomasyn's voice.

He spun around. Jon's hand went to his sword. Several villagers rushed toward him, brandishing weapons, the lead man extended a push blade.

Jon faced them with his sword drawn. "Get back," he said. The mob stopped.

"They're ruining everything!" Dayton said from the back of the crowd. "They'll take everything away from us!"

It was going to be a fight. These twelve people were about to die, and a small smile crossed his lips.

"Now!" Dayton said. The villagers charged.

The lead man lunged. Jon ducked and side stepped. His sword flashed upward in an arc. The man screamed, clutching at the bloody stump of his arm.

Jon spun and blocked the clumsy swing of a man with a large broad sword, sending the weapon into the face of the woman to the man's right. The woman collapsed.

Moving quickly, Jon shot out his left leg, caught the sword wielder in the stomach, and knocked him to the ground.

Jon tucked and rolled. He came up and struck the shin of a man with his sword pommel. One sidestep and he eyed Dayton. He wanted to drive his sword through the man's belly. It was unspeakable what was done to his friends, to two of the Spears, to his clutch mates.

Dayton was only two more villagers from him.

Jon was on his feet once again, facing a large man who towered above him. The villager wielded a sword almost as long as he was tall. The man's arms bulged. His greasy hair hung across his face, and an evil grin mocked the Spear.

The villagers backed away and gathered their wounded, leaving only the large man in front of him. Thomasyn and Bethany struggled to get off the litters.

"He's not to get past you," Dayton ordered.

With a grunt the man stepped toward Jon. The sword didn't sway in his hands.

This man has training.

"I know," Jon whispered

Unlike most large men, this one walked cat-like, not lumbering, but on the balls of his feet. Their eyes never left each other. The man wore boiled leather, with scale mail stitched on it. Chain mail covered the joints of the man's armor, and a gorget protected his neck.

The man stood five feet away from Jon and leveled his weapon. Jon lifted his sword and stood there. He waited.

"Kill him," Dayton hissed.

Jon stepped to the left, and the man followed. Jon stepped to the right. The man aped him. The man inched forward. Instead of retreating, Jon came forward and smacked the other's sword to deflect it. The man, surprised by the quick stunt, jumped back quickly.

A nod and a smile from Jon made the man grumble in his throat. He came forward again, and thrust to hit the Spear.

Jon parried, drawing the man's sword downward. Jon's guard caught the blade, and he turned his sword sharply. It snagged the other sword. Jon torqued his sword. If the man hadn't had a steel grip on his sword, he would have lost it. Instead he grunted and almost twisted Jon's sword out of his hand.

Jon disengaged and stepped away. The man repositioned his hands on his sword. As he did so, Jon leapt. Striking with his sword, making the man parry, Jon kept up the blows. Low strike, step forward. High strike, step left. Thrust, step right. Jon kept making the man defend with his sword in an unending assault. Rivulets of perspiration formed on the man's brow. Less than a minute into the fight the man showed signs of slowing.

Jon swung at the man's right knee. When it was parried, instead of swinging high or mid, Jon spun and placed his sword against the inside of the man's leg. He pulled the sword back.

With eyes wide the man stumbled backward. He looked at the sword in his hands, and then at the sword in Jon's. Blood colored the edge.

Jon stepped forward. He knew the man could not last much longer. His sword weighed too much for constant attack. The realization colored the man's eyes, and the folly of using such a large weapon was going to be his downfall.

Jon started the attack again. The man retreated, a trail of blood colored his footfalls. Slash, thrust, slash, slash. The blade wove an intricate pattern of movement back and forth, pushing the man and making his arms tire.

The man went to a knee. His breath heaved. Jon kicked the sword from his opponent's hands. He strode toward Dayton.

Hands thrust out, Dayton dropped to his knees. "No! I beg you. Spare me."

"Jon!" Bethany said. She stumbled forward.

"Let me live!" Dayton said.

"No, Jon!" Thomasyn said. "He must be judged!"

Jon swung his sword, taking Dayton's head.

-12-

Jon wiped his blade on Dayton's remains. The man's head rested two feet from the body. Thomasyn stood wondering if his friend was all right.

The man Jon had bested, who wielded the two handed sword, sat on his haunches crying.

"Thomasyn," Bethany said. "We need to tell Master Chail about him killing without judging."

With a nod, Thomasyn turned to Bethany and held out his hand. She took it and stood. "Yes, but how will he take it?"

He turned back to look at his friend. Jon smiled. The sun sank behind the treetops. Thoughts of how they all worked together in childhood lanced through his mind. All the training, all they had achieved seemed lost. Now, his friend moved from emotion to emotion, broken instead of hardened, and he knew of no way to fix him.

Bethany's hand touched his, and squeezed. He let her go. It was going to be a long walk back to Capital. Thomasyn felt honor bound to carry the news to the king in order to help the dwarves. They were members of The Realm, and thus deserved protection.

He needed to get Jon to Capital, and Master Chail. Maybe their teacher would be able to find some way of curing the wild mood swings Jon suffered from.

Jon stopped in front of him. "We need to serve justice to the rest of the village."

"No," Bethany said. "How do you know they weren't coerced into this?"

"Yes, but they have free will and could have stopped it." Jon clasped his fist in front of him. "Justice must be served."

"Justice? Or vengeance?" Bethany asked.

"Justice," Jon said. "The law says all must pay for their part in any crime. They've killed a lot of people. How many remains have you counted?"

"It doesn't matter. I'm talking about the spirit of the law, not the letter." Bethany took a deep breath. "Remember the Speaker of the Spears? He tried to tell us about serving the people, keeping the peace, and ensuring the law didn't see tall or short people."

"It only saw people," Thomasyn said. "Remember what he taught us, to see the basic truth it supplied? He wanted us to serve." Thomasyn turned from them and took three paces towards the village. "These people are simple, and Dayton may have manipulated them. Remember the Speaker's words? Protect those who cannot protect themselves. Maybe the villagers couldn't protect themselves from him, and the murder of many travelers was the result."

"They need to pay for their crimes!" Jon said.

"And do you know who killed whom?" Bethany asked.

"No, but that doesn't make a difference. They were all involved in the conspiracy. The deaths are on all of their shoulders." Jon turned to Bethany. "They all are guilty."

"And the children? Are they guilty? Should we kill them as well?" Thomasyn asked.

"No," Jon said. Hesitation showing in his voice. "They're just…children."

"And what about the sick? Should we kill them also?" Thomasyn asked.

Jon hesitated again, looked toward Bethany. His eyebrows knitted together high on his forehead and eyes wide. "They couldn't have taken part in it. They wouldn't have had the strength."

"So, the law needs to be interpreted, not the letter, but the spirit," Bethany said, reaching out her hand and took Jon's. She pulled him into her arms and hugged him.

"I…Bethany, I want to go home." Jon wept.

Thomasyn watched as she held their friend. Her eyes sought his and pleaded with him. The message was simple, let's go home. He nodded. The city, Capital, was their true home, the only home they knew. It was a months' travel, and hardships still lay ahead of them. The world was not as the Speaker of the Spears made it out to be.

"We need to get our belongings. I'll head back to the village and secure them. Also, I will talk to the people there about what is going to be done. They will need to select a leader who will ensure this doesn't happen again." He motioned to the ground in front of them. The bodies, the wasted human life. Even the troll could have survived for years and lived a full life. The way it had turned out sickened him.

He turned toward the village. It didn't take long, only a few minutes to reach the path and move along it until the clearing was in plain sight. To his surprise, the villagers were there, waiting for him.

As he neared, one of the villagers broke away from the rest. He was of average height, just a little taller than Thomasyn. His body was lean and muscular, but also robbed of the great mass the sword fighter's body had. His clothes hung on him like rags, and a scruffy beard erupted from this face in defiance of his angular jaw. Blue eyes looked at Thomasyn, and then at the ground to his side. Piled there were Bethany's and his belongings, including their cloaks.

"We gathered them…for you, Spear. Dayton had them packed away…in his hut," the man stammered.

Thomasyn buckled on his sword, and donned his cloak. The man shifted from foot to foot, waiting.

"What is your name?" Thomasyn asked.

"Fletch, sir."

"I want you to take the spoils out of Dayton's hut. Share them evenly with the other members of your village. Once that is done, tear down the hut and burn it with the remains of the men. Let it be a lesson to all of you, never to attempt anything like this again. And if someone comes to you with such a plan, show them the remains of the hut, and the bones. Let them know the Spears are aware of what happened here, and tell them of this day." Thomasyn shrugged on his pack.

"Yes, Spear…sir. We'll make sure of it."

"The other Spear, he wanted to serve justice to all of you for your part in what happened here. Do you know what that means?" Thomasyn looked at the faces of the people. He saw some swallow and others look at the ground.

"I do, sir." Fletch didn't flinch. "If it's the desire of the Spears, it should be done."

"Not today," Thomasyn said. He turned to go but hesitated. "If a traveler comes by seeking assistance, you are to treat them well. Do not turn them aside or cheat them. Indeed, you should be thankful for their company and offer them what you can without putting yourselves in need. Share what you can, warn them of any perils that could be encountered on their travels and ensure they are told the Spears look out for them."

Fletch brightened. Obvious relief spread through the crowd. It was the right effect.

"My friends and I are in need," he said, turning back to Fletch. "There is a long journey ahead of us, and our food supplies are low."

Fletch smiled. "I know what your need is. Please, stay here for a moment." He rushed away to the group and talked in hushed tones to them. Each dispersed and headed towards their huts. Thomasyn waited.

Soon, people emerged from their homes. Two carried large sacks, others food and skins. They placed supplies in the bags and gave it to Fletch.

"We have supplies for the Spears," Fletch said. He came forward but didn't hand over the sack. "I will accompany you to Capital."

Thomasyn looked at him. "It's a long road. Why do you want to go to Capital with us?"

"To learn," he said. "Someone needs to lead our people, and they all want me to be the one."

The corners of Thomasyn's mouth moved slightly upward. "The road is long. It will take a month to get to Capital."

"Less, if we run part of the way," Fletch said, thrusting out his chest. "I am ready to travel with you."

"I can't promise it will be easy. We could face problems on the road." Thomasyn waited for the man's eyes to falter and look away. He didn't know what it was about Fletch, but something did not seem right.

"I can run fast and far. I've made the trip to the next town several times, and always faster each time I do it."

"We'll need to hunt for food at times, and go hungry when there is nothing to find."

Fletch didn't waver. "I'm a good hunter. I know what we can eat. Berries are just now coming out. Soon fruit will be on the trees."

Thomasyn's smile grew.

"I can carry a lot. There's no need for me to have weapons or armor. I have a pack…" and with that said, Fletch turned and ran towards his hut. In half a minute he was out with a leather pack in his hands. "I can carry the food." He started putting the food in his pack.

"Fletch, you can stop now," Thomasyn said, reaching out a hand to touch the man's shoulder.

His eyes fell and great sadness washed over his face.

"You don't want me to come. You're worried I'll be like Dayton and take advantage of someone. I…I understand."

Thomasyn sighed. "It's not that." He reached out and lifted the man to his feet, taking the sack from his hands. "No one is a slave to the Spears; we share our own weight among each other. All I would ask of you is to carry Bethany's belongings back to her, and once that is done we will divide up the food evenly with each other. You do not have to serve the Spears the way you think, just be there with us to share the journey."

Relief flooded Fletch's face. He nodded, gathered Bethany's belongings, and placed them in her cloak. He bundled everything up and cradled it in his arms like a newborn babe.

Thomasyn started down the path. "Come, travel with us as an equal," he called back to Fletch.

Bethany held Jon in her arms as he sobbed. Her hand stroked his blonde hair to comfort him. Slowly his sobs turned to sniffling.

"It's okay, Jon. I'm here." She rocked back and forth a little.

Jon wiped his nose. He let his hands drop, and Bethany allowed him to pull away. She kept her hands on his shoulders, and studied his face. Two steel-blue, blood shot eyes stared back at her.

"We're going home soon. We'll see Chail and Tess and eat lemon squares and boiled beef. And maybe get Con to smile," Bethany said.

Jon started to smile, and wiped his face with the inside of his cloak. "I need to collect my pack." He shrugged off her hands and went to where he had dropped his pack, near the tree he had hidden next to.

Bethany watched him. She took a deep breath and let her shoulders slump. Jon returned and sat on his haunches. His hand reached into the pack and pulled the last package of dried beef out. He opened it and held the small bundle up to Bethany. "It's the spicy one."

She smiled, reached out, and took the smallest piece. Jon took the largest piece and put it in his mouth. Bethany sniffed hers and then followed his example.

"Two pieces left," Jon said.

"Save one for Thomasyn," Bethany said.

He folded the package and put it in a pocket of his cloak. She turned at the sound of rustling leaves.

Thomasyn was approaching them with a man walking beside him. Five other villagers followed them at a respectful distance.

"This is Fletch; he'll be traveling with us to Capital." Thomasyn went to Jon and squatted in front of him. "We good?"

Jon reached into his cloak and produced the small package. "Last of the dwarven meat. I've been saving it. Two pieces."

"Can I share with Fletch?" Thomasyn asked.

"Sure. He's joining us, so why not?" Jon held out the package, and Thomasyn accepted it.

Thomasyn took the smallest, and then offered the package to Fletch. The man stared at it, then picked up the last portion of meat, and chewed.

"The villagers are going to bury the dead and burn Dayton's body. I want to get a lot of distance between us and here." Bethany was by their side now, concern showing on her face. She brushed the hair aside on the back of Jon's head. "We'll have to do something about that, but not here. These woods are wrong. They feel full of death. It's not sitting right with me."

The two Spears stood. Jon motioned towards the path. "We can get moving any time you want."

Bethany looked at Fletch. "How far is it until we're out of the forest?"

"Not far," Fletch said. "Maybe another seven miles."

"A quick run," Jon said.

"Or an easy walk," Bethany said, massaging her neck. The pounding of a hammer echoed inside her skull. A run would only aggravate the injuries they suffered, and even if he didn't show it she knew Thomasyn was going through the same thumping inside his head. She could only imagine what Jon was going through.

They gathered up their things and moved toward the path. Fletch waved at the villagers, but they focused at gathering up the bodies. He looked crestfallen to Bethany as he turned back to the road and his walk with the Spears.

Bethany wondered what drove a villager to be the way Dayton had been. The need to control, to have power over others. Yes, the Spears had control and power over others, but it was thrust upon them with little explanation of why it was desirable. She always cringed at the thought of making a person do what she wanted, or needed, them to do. The art of convincing others was not one of her strong points.

Yes, she would have to work on that. Thomasyn had it down. He was a born leader. Jon had some of it as well, but lately he seemed to be slipping more from reality than she had originally believed. Looking over to Jon, Bethany could not fathom the outburst he had at the confrontation. How fragile his mind must be. Why was he like this now? Yes, he had always been a silent, brooding type. He was always interested in his stomach more than the world around him. But why was he breaking?

Master Chail would know. He always knew what to do or say. For some reason Bethany hesitated in her decision to tell their trainer that Jon was still broken. She didn't want to see any disappointment in his eyes, or hear the lamentations of regret he would utter. No amount of time would heal him if he knew something had happened to one of his charges. She remembered the time he wept for a Spear in Flight when an accident caused the loss of an eye. No, Master Chail will not be told right away. She'd first talk to Tess about Jon.

The path was before them and Fletch turned to the left, following it south. The group of Spears followed him, trusting he knew the fastest way out of the forest and to a more familiar area of the Realm.

"The Slovarian hills, they're close by here," Fletch said. His voice was light with pleasure, as if leaving the village had lifted a great burden from his shoulders.

"You lived in the village all your life?" Bethany asked.

"Mostly. I was twelve when I ran away. My ma found me two weeks later and gave me a thrashing. I was half starved from being away for so long and was looking for anything to eat. She said once I was fed I shot up a foot in a year. Imagine!" He laughed.

"We grew up fast as well. But none of us ran away." Bethany watched Fletch. He balanced himself on the balls of his feet. A hunter's walk. At least he didn't twist his step to confuse a tracker. It meant he was only a hunter. Walking like a soldier was not something a person did lightly, or forgot once they mastered it. The hiding of one's footfalls was second nature to the Spears, who were trained in it from a very young age.

"We usually tell stories when we travel with others. Do you have any stories you can tell us?" Thomasyn asked.

"Yes, a story," Jon said. "Tell us about something we don't know, or haven't heard yet."

"But you're Spears," Fletch said. "You've seen more in the last few years than an old man would remember."

Bethany cocked her head at the man. He could have been eighteen, maybe twenty at the most. Tall, slender, but well defined. He was not an old man. Why would he make such a comment? She paid very close attention to his footfalls. They were light, and very little trail was left even when he walked on the sandy ground.

"Can you tell us a story?" she asked.

"I may have one you haven't heard," Fletch said. "But it's probably very simple compared to anything you could tell."

He fell into step beside them, his eyes staring into the distance.

"Many years ago, the elfin people lived in peace with the people of the Realm. They shared their philosophy on life and laws. Many say we owe our way of life to them." Fletch hesitated. "They say the world was a different place back then, after the great hibernation. The land was in pain and all the races came forth to help heal it.

"The Elves, being close to nature, used their magic to bring the different races of this great land together. They say even the Hobs had a place at the table of the council, their voice being one of passion and heart. But the queen desired more of a say in the ruling of the people, and wanted to be above ground, even though they ruled the dark places."

Bethany found differences to any other version she had heard. Now, with someone telling them about others in a way of respect, she envisioned swords clashing against a peaceful people. She thought of her experience with the council so long ago, and belief in the words started to form.

"So the council explained all would be addressed, for everyone had a place in the world. The queen was not happy, for she knew it would take decades, even centuries before her

227

people would be allowed to have the sun on their faces once again. Her voice cried out for equality, but none heard her.

"And with that came the first revolt of the Hobs, and many were slain by the elves, dwarves and humans. The queen was driven to the underworld once again.

"But they say the humans bore witness to the love the elves had for nature and they learned the truth of the Five Gods. The humans at first would not hear of it, wanting to believe that only one God could create the world. They rejected the teachings of the elves and revolted from the council."

Fletch grew silent once again. Jon cast a puzzled glance at him.

"The humans cast out the elves from their holdings, routing them out of the forests, from the glens and from the coasts. With armies in dwarf-made armor they drew up their strength and slaughtered the elves.

"Almost extinct, the elves promised to return one day and reclaim what was theirs. Not to take everything, but to take back what they had been driven from. They wanted the forests back, they wanted their coastal cities back, and they wanted to be back in their capital city once again."

"Where was their capital city?" Jon said, looking at Fletch with curiosity.

"They say it was near Capital. And even now Capital has part of the elfin people's old home inside it. The training grounds for the Spears was part of the old elven city, did you know that?"

Bethany shook her head, frowning. It was more of a lesson then a story. She didn't understand how this person would know so much about another time so long ago. For the brief respite between his speaking she recalled the teachings of the Speaker of the Spears, and how the elven people had tried to take the Realm from the people. She didn't recall anything about sharing the land with them.

Fletch continued. "So the elven people will return and claim what was taken from them."

"I don't think that's a very good story," Jon said.

"It's a fable more than anything else," Fletch said.

"But if the elves were not from The Realm in the first place, how can they claim it as their own?" Thomasyn asked.

"That is the question, isn't it? How can a people who were not of The Realm claim it for their own? It so happens they were here long before the humans were. They departed when the humans claimed dominance, but left many things behind." Fletch scratched the side of his head. It was the first time his hair had moved to reveal part of his ear.

Bethany noticed scarring on the top of the ear, but said nothing, knowing people suffered in the small villages.

"We need to quicken our pace," Thomasyn said. "Let us know when you tire, Fletch." He started with a slow jog, than increased it. Soon they ran at a good cadence, and Fletch kept up with them.

The forest thinned, and Bethany knew her head would start aching soon if they kept running. They needed to put more distance between the town and themselves. The forest dropped off, leaving fields of short, green grass.

"Clovers," Fletch said. "Breath in deeply." He arched his neck and his nose made a loud noise as air rushed into it.

Bethany did the same, and the aroma of plants in bloom struck her senses. The field was covered with clovers; the plant seemed to be choking the grass and fighting for dominance in the field. Small buds of pink and light purple scattered throughout, and bees were making their way from flowering bud to flowering bud.

"Is there a village nearby?" Thomasyn said.

"Not for several more leagues," Fletch said.

"Wild honey," Jon said. "We could find a bee hive and get wild honey from it."

Bethany laughed inside. Jon was almost himself again, thinking of his stomach once more. Relief flooded through her as Jon's smile lit up his face. Maybe he was not as broken as she thought. Maybe he only needed to be removed from the village to find himself once again.

The sound of bees grew loud as the sun sank low in the sky. With the day almost over, they decided to camp for the night at the edge of the forest. Tents were raised quickly, and Jon was the first to have his up. He made his way into the forest and gathered fallen wood. By the time all of them had their tents up, Jon had a small fire going.

"How are we going to find the bee hive?" he asked.

"You'll get stung," Thomasyn said.

"We harvest honey all the time at the village," Fletch said. "If the bees don't know you're there, it's easy to get honey." He stood and went over to the trees. Reaching up the man pulled down leaves and a few sticks. He made a bundle and placed some of the coals from the fire in the middle of it. Blowing carefully, Fletch made the leaves and sticks smolder. "Use smoke. It makes them leave the hive, and they won't attack you." He held out the smoking mass. "I'd look for trees with open knots in them or up in the branches."

Jon took the bundle and nodded. He stood and scanned the tree line. "It would be easier if we all looked."

They searched for the hive. Bethany thought the bees would be close, but Fletch explained that the beehive could be anywhere. He said bees could fly up to eight miles to find the flowers with the nectar they wanted.

Bethany wanted to make sure someone was with Fletch as he searched. For some reason she didn't trust the man. There was something about the way he walked, and his knowledge that seemed to extend beyond a normal person's that caused her to pause. She couldn't put her finger on it, but something was just not right.

She didn't share her feelings with the others. Was it folly not to warn someone, or prudent to allow others to form their own opinion? But unless he did something wrong, Fletch was still a citizen of the Realm, and she needed to treat him with respect.

As the sun set the group started to make their way back to camp. Bethany saw Fletch in the distant trees and started to make her way toward him. At first in a casual walk, but then, she decided to be cautious. She used the trees to give her cover, and stepped lightly on the ground as she had been taught. If the man noticed her, he did not acknowledge it, but kept nodding with great animation.

Once within a hundred yards, the sound of the conversation could just be heard. She strained but the words were lost. She needed to hear what was being said. Getting closer would be the only way. She stepped quietly behind another tree. Her eyes stayed on the man as she shifted from small cover to small cover. The conversation was clearer but still hushed in secrecy. Who could he be talking to? What was he saying? Why was he so secretive about it?

She was within twenty yards when she noticed another figure not that far from him. It was a man; that she was sure of. He was slim and tall, somewhat like Fletch himself. His skin was pale, almost sickly, as if he didn't see the sun much. Raven black hair adorned his head and his face was so angular that Bethany almost gasped. Ears could be just seen from under the mass of long, thin hair on the man's head, and they were the strangest things she had ever perceived. They looked like a man's ears, but squashed and long, coming to a point at the tip instead of being round.

Confusion stung her, and Bethany thought back as hard as she could. She tried to remember what the Speaker of the Spears had taught them so long ago about the other races. Drawings had been produced, but none of them looked truly like this man did. He had the angular look of the Hobs, but the face of the picture they saw of an elf. The color of his skin wasn't right for that, so she dismissed it. Elves all had fair hair from what the Speaker had said. Fair hair and light of skin. This one was sickly of skin and dark of hair. The pictures also showed common garb of leaves and vines used to hide their modesty, but this one wore leathers and a traveling cloak like a merchant.

She could hear the conversation now, so she listened.

"I need time. They travel slowly," Fletch said.

"And you're sure they haven't discovered you?" The shadow figure spread his arms.

"No, they don't suspect anything, as I told you. We will need to travel for a month. I'll try to get them to believe my wind is improving. It will make them push to run more."

"It was smart, bringing them through this field. You said one of them is broken?"

"Yes, the blond one. His mind is weak and his cares are for himself. He can be turned."

The figure turned his head slightly, as if listening to others behind him but there was no one there. "The council wants this to take place soon. If the Spears can be broken, a wedge shoved between them, we will be able to carry out our plan. Take what is rightfully ours without interference." Again the figure turned his head. "They say the son of the last king has been crowned. He sits on the throne with his siblings biting at his heels. There is much unrest in The Realm now that the gold and jewels have stopped flowing."

"The dwarf king is a fool," Fletch said. "I met with him and planted the seed in his mind about taking his fair share. The cave-in made his mind up for him."

"It was foolish taking such a risk."

"The greater the risk the better the reward," Fletch said. "We have much coming to us if we demand it."

"The moon is setting. Contact once again when it is gibbous. The power of the stones will not be full by then, but we will need more information."

"I serve our people," Fletch said, bowing formally to the figure. He reached down, picked up three small stones and placed them into a pouch at his belt. The figure disappeared.

Bethany pulled her hood up and blended into the tree. She waited.

Fletch walked away from the area, not noticing her. With a slow movement she shifted and watched. Once she was out of view, she emerged from the shadows and went toward the space Fletch had been. Her eyes scanned the ground as she bent, not seeing anything but the remnants of footfalls.

"What did he mean by bending one?" Bethany straightened. Unconsciously she twirled her braid. The realization hit her–Fletch was not human.

-13-

Jon stood on tiptoes, his spear point inches away from the beehive. A small fire smoldered and billowed smoke at the base of the tree, and bees flew, not wanting to make their way through the smoke. A few still swarmed around the hollow of the tree. There were not a lot left, and he was free to cut out some of the honey cones as a treat.

Careful! Don't let them know what you are doing.

He inched forward the spear forward. The tip sliced into the wax. He pushed the spear head in a line.

You have it. One nice piece to take to the others. But there is more. I am the fifth god and can see everything.

The comb was free, but he let it stay in the hive. With a deft move Jon cut a small piece above the large one and speared it. He was able to wiggle it out of the hive and into his eager hands. The blade of his spear was still hot, and the wax had sealed the honey in the comb. He took the small piece and popped it in his mouth. Jon sucked the sweet juice out of the wax and put the tip of the spear back into the smoldering heat.

He produced five small squares of cloth from inside his cloak and laid them on the ground. He took the wax from his mouth and poured water from his skin on it. He rubbed the hard wax against the clean surface of four rags.

The containers ready, Jon pulled his spear from the fire and wiped the end with the last rag. Once clean, the hot end snagged the comb and he pulled it free from the hive. Working quickly, he sliced it into four equal pieces and used the last of the heat to seal them. The cloths made perfect carriers, and he put them in his cloak.

You will have more if you want more.

"No, this is enough," Jon said.

Jon ran back to the camp. Sharing the spoils meant they would be happy, and he needed them to be happy. Bethany was suspicious of him, and he wanted to elude her scrutiny if possible. The longer he kept her at arm's length, the better off he would be.

Clover spread out in front of him. Jon moved into the open area, and skirted the edge of the forest until he was back at the camp. No one was there yet.

He took some of the branches they had collected earlier and built a raised area. Rocks went on next, and he placed the four packages on top of that. Something rustled to his left.

He spun.

Pink eyes stared back at him.

Jon reached into his cloak and drew a throwing knife. The rabbit's nose twitched.

He brought the blade back, ready to throw. The rabbit crouched, prepared to flee. Jon threw.

Jon watched Thomasyn enter the clearing. He carried two pheasants. The smell of honey roasted rabbit filled the air.

"Bethany probably found some berries," Thomasyn said. "She'll be happy about the rabbit and birds. You know which way Fletch went?"

Don't tell him, the voice snickered

Jon shook his head.

Thomasyn dropped the birds as he entered the circle of tents. "I'll clean the birds."

Jon turned the rabbit. Grease sputtered into the fire. "I found the hive."

"Figured you would."

Jon held out one of the packages. "You can eat it, or make the pheasants taste really good."

Thomasyn took out his knife and slit open the first bird. "What's going on?"

He suspects us!

Jon stared into the fire. "I don't know what you're talking about."

"Yes, you do."

Tell him nothing.

"I don't want to talk about it."

With the entrails removed, Thomasyn started to pluck the birds. "Why not?"

Putting more branches on the fire, Jon said, "It's nothing, really."

"Then why not talk about it?"

He won't understand.

Jon picked up a stick and poked at the fire, moving embers around. He said nothing.

With the rabbit done, Jon moved it to a flat rock on a pile of wood. He handed the stick to Thomasyn.

"You're really not going to talk about it?"

Jon looked at him. "Why? Because I'm better than you? Didn't get caught and almost killed? You're not perfect. The golden boy, captured by simple villagers and almost killed, only to be rescued by the one in his shadow. Me!" He stood and pointed at Thomasyn. "You're the big, great fighter. Why do they think that? I killed more Hobs then you did at the battle. Saved more lives than you did. I even saved someone when we were on our Wooder training."

Thomasyn finished skinning the one bird and broke its back. He took some small twigs and splayed open the bird.

He will not admit to it!

"Nothing to say?" Jon asked. "Truth is hard to argue with."

Putting the bird on the fire, Thomasyn said, "Why would I say anything?"

"To defend yourself."

"But you're speaking the truth. What do I have to defend against?"

Infuriated, Jon kicked at a log. He turned, ready to erupt at his friend when his eye spotted Fletch approaching. To the side and behind him, Bethany emerged from the forest.

"I searched but didn't find any hive," Fletch called. "But from what I smell, I think you did."

Do not let anger overwhelm you!

Jon glared at Thomasyn, and no matter how hard he tried, the anger still welled inside. He wanted to lash out, but with immense self-control he lowered his fist and turned. A smile lit his face as he capped the volcano inside him.

Fletch came closer to the fire, his hands extended. "I love the heat of a fire. It gets into your bones."

Thomasyn picked up the second bird and started to clean it. "The pheasant will be ready soon. I think the rabbit is done."

Jon looked at the carcass suspended over the fire. The small bones on the limbs black from the heat. He pulled it off the fire and extended it out to Fletch. The man nodded, and using a small cloth from his pocket to hold the hot flesh, he cut a wing from the body.

"A Wooder taught me the honey trick," Jon said. He put the bird back over the fire, picked up the rabbit and tore off a leg. He then laid the rabbit to the side of the fire.

Bethany came into the camp and looked sideways at Fletch. She stepped toward the fire and sat down between Jon and Thomasyn.

Jon noticed the hand signal from Bethany. Trouble. He didn't know what it meant, for there was nothing around. His eyes scanned the darkening field before them. Nothing stirred, and he dismissed the warning.

"Pheasant?" Thomasyn asked Bethany.

"Yes," she said, reaching out for the bird.

There it was again. Jon noticed it this time with the definite nod toward Fletch. How could that man be trouble?

Another sign. Why was she telling them "enemy"?

Fletch stood, walked toward his tent, stopped and turned to face the three. He had a smile on his face.

"Enemy?" he said. "What gave it away?"

Bethany stood and faced the man. "In the woods."

Fletch nodded. "What did you see?"

She glanced toward her friends before turning to him. "Enough."

He shook his head and stepped back. The fire light barely reached his face, and one hand reached up and pulled an amulet from under his shirt. It was a large round bauble, and the reflection of the fire danced in its surface. He lifted the chain over his head.

Features melded and formed. The angular face squeezed together, making it thinner and longer. His eyes enlarged and took on a strange, alien look. He was thinner, as well. Not emaciated, but wiry. Long fingers placed the jewelry into a small pocket at his side.

"You're an elf!" Jon said.

"How observant," Fletch said.

Bethany spun to a defensive stance. Her left hand held a short spear and her right drew the sword from its scabbard.

"There will be no need for that," Fletch said, his hand reaching to his shoulder with his palm held out flat.

Jon was on his feet as well, his skinning knife clasped in his hand. "What are you doing in the Realm?"

Fletch smiled. "My group came to the Realm to see if you Spears were as dangerous as before. But all I see are children. Your ranks have shrunk. All our scouts tell us of how weak the Realm is. We want to take back that which was ours. What you humans stole it from us."

"We stole nothing from you," Bethany said. "Your people have tried to steal the land from us for years. What makes you think we'll let you?"

"You have no choice."

Bethany glared at him. She knew the story of the elves and how they marched on the Realm. The Spears would have lost had they not closed the distance quickly and used close combat tactics to defeat the invading army. She scanned Fletch's body and did not see any weapons, but the clothing he wore was loose.

Jon stepped forward and waved his knife. "You elves don't know when to quit. We beat you once; we'll beat you again."

Fletch laughed. "And what about the courtesy of the Spears? You said we would eat, and you would share food between the four of us."

She swallowed. Bethany's eyes met Thomasyn's, and he nodded. It was obvious what Fletch expected. How could Thomasyn promise so much to the elf?

"I did," Thomasyn said. "It was in the town. I promised that we would share food and our protection would be his."

Bethany turned her attention fully on Fletch. Her eyes searched his face. "Are you one of your word?"

"Only when I give it." Fletch spread his hands out to his sides, palms up.

It was hard for her to decide whether to trust the elf or not. She needed more information than what she had, but taking a chance was something she knew she would have to do. It was a leap of faith she had to take. She took a deep breath.

"So if you have faith—"

"I have faith," Fletch said.

"What is your faith?" Bethany asked.

"We now believe in the one God. He is the creator. It is his will that made the heaven and earth that we are all in. His is the will that brings the sun over the horizon. His is the will that makes the crops grow." Fletch brought the two fingers of each hand to his forehead as he bowed forward. "We never break our word if we swear on our faith."

Bethany nodded. She did not believe in the same faith that the elf did, but honor would not let him destroy his word. She counted on him being an elf of his word. "Will you swear to your God that you will not harm us?"

Fletch smiled. It was unnerving to Bethany as she watched it light his face. The elf was not very handsome. It was the closeness of his eyes that threw her. She did not sign to Thomasyn, for she realized that Fletch could understand their hand signals.

Fletch sighed, "I give you my word."

Thomasyn stepped forward. "Then we can eat."

The rabbit was eaten along with the birds. The honey flavored the food and made the meal that much more enjoyable.

Not much was said. Bethany did not want him to understand what she was thinking. Not yet. Both Jon and Thomasyn would have to be made aware of what she planned.

"So," Bethany said. "All the town folk are elves?"

Fletch laughed. "No, not all of them. We found the town and took it over. It was only a few huts when we arrived."

Jon glared at the elf. "So what happened to the humans? And was Dayton and elf as well?"

"Dayton? An elf? No, he was convenient. The humans are still there. We don't kill if we don't have to."

Thomasyn tossed a bone into the fire. "But you did kill."

"Only when we needed to." Fletch pulled a blade of grass out of the ground and used it to clean his teeth. "I do want to meet your king."

Bethany's jaw dropped and eyes widened. "Our king? Why would you want to meet with him?"

Fletch finished cleaning his teeth and smiled at Bethany. "If we can come to an agreement we can live together, can we not?"

Jon snorted. He tilted his head as if listening to someone. "I think elves cannot be trusted."

Tossing the grass into the fire, Fletch looked directly at Thomasyn. "I know your type. You're the leader. Sit back and watch what happens. Take everything in and make a decision. What do you think?"

Thomasyn sat back and stared into the fire. Bethany watched him. His eyebrows dropped down. He was thinking, and he would come up with a solution. Did the elf really think he would see the king just because he wanted to? Her eyes drew down Fletch's neck. She started to think of that day in the Town of Lands when they woke up together in the field.

Bethany shook her head. It was not right to think of those things. Thomasyn was her Clutch mate. A fellow Spear. Someone she fought beside, not bedded. The realization hit her. It was approaching that time of month. Her time.

She pinched herself in order to center her mind.

"I think," Thomasyn said, "that meeting the king would be a good idea. First you would have to meet with Master Chail. He may need more reassurance than us."

Her mouth resembled a cavern. "Thomasyn, I thin—"

"No," Thomasyn said. "We have to get the elf to Master Chail."

"We're going home?" Jon asked. "For sure this time? No stopping anywhere, straight to Capital?"

"Yes, Jon," Thomasyn said. "We're going back to Capital."

Jon could hardly believe his ears. It was finally going to happen. Home. He wanted desperately to go home. Sleep in his own cot. Have a meal from the mess hall and practice in the training field.

Are we going back home?

Jon stood and walked away from the fire. He did not want the others to hear him, not yet. The voice was one of the gods, and the others did not hear it for they were not worthy. The voice told him this from the first time it spoke to him in the dwarves home, so he believed it.

Once out of ear shot he said, "Yes. Home."

Are you sure that's what you want?

"Yes."

Master Chail may not understand what is happening. He may not believe you are talking with a god. He may just think you're not right in the head just like others think when we talk to them.

"You've talked to others?"

Yes.

"How many others?"

There was a long pause before the voice sounded again. *Many years ago we talked to a Spear just like you. He was betrayed by those around him.*

"How long ago?"

Many generations ago. One day I will tell you about it. For now, we must keep silent.

"Until when?"

Until I tell you.

Thomasyn studied the elf's every movement. Even when Jon stomped off, Thomasyn kept watching. It was what he did best. Bethany and Jon investigated, asked questions. He kept tabs on what they found, a mental checklist.

The answers given by the elf added up. There was no inconsistency. He just wanted to talk to the king. And when Jon left, it gave Thomasyn the best time to jump in and discover more information about what the elf wanted to do. So far, all he wanted was peace.

"Since we have at least one more month worth of travel, we will need to sleep," Thomasyn said. "Will you be able to keep up with us if we run?"

"Yes, I can run for the whole day," Fletch said.

"But camp at night, right?" Bethany asked.

"Yes, camp at night," Thomasyn said. "I don't think we have to push as hard as you did getting back to Capital last year."

"Good."

Thomasyn remembered the blister scars on her feet. He did not want to have all of them injured from such an exertion.

His thoughts went to the actual time left to reach Capital. Just under four weeks. Wake, run, sleep. If they ran each day all day they could be back in Capital by the twenty-fourth day. But his thoughts did not stay on the subject. They wandered to Bethany, and how good looking she was.

He shook his head. How could he allow himself to fall into this? He knew they did not have sex that day in the Town of Lands. He smiled, remembering of how fun it was letting her think they had for a few seconds. But did he go too far? Only time would tell.

"I'm going to sleep."

And with that, Thomasyn went to his tent.

-14-

Fletch smiled as he breathed in the night air. He only needed three hours of sleep, and now he lay on his back gazing at the night sky. Different colored stars winked at him from the heavens. Once, years ago, he had tried to count them, but the task was past even his intellect. Happiness kept the smile on his face, now that the spell he had used to disguise his features was dropped.

The spell of disguise had not only affected his appearance, but masked his words as well. He was glad it was no longer needed, for using it made him feel as if he watched someone else move his body and say words from his mouth that only resembled what he thought.

Yes, being free of the spell allowed him to escape the fog that muddled his thoughts. Finally, his intelligence could roam the full expanse of his mind. He moved the tent flap and pulled the rest of his body out into the night air.

Small puffs of breath floated as he walked toward the fire. He threw a few pieces of wood on it and watched them catch. His hand felt for the three stones. They still rested in the pouch. Maybe he could call upon the magic now that his mind was free of the spells.

He strode away from the camp and into the forest. His eyes adjusted. Trees showed their life with pulses of light running up and down the trunks. Wild life scurried through the leaves. He could see them all. Their life force, a green glow that outlined the shape of each animal, moved through the forest as they lived their lives.

Fletch stopped and placed the three stones on the ground. His eyes scanned for something to sacrifice to bind the spell but found nothing that would have the energy he needed. The only thing he could do was bleed himself for the power needed.

He pulled his knife out. A quick slash. His palm bled, and he dripped the blood onto the stones. Fletch took out a small cloth and bound his hand to stop the bleeding.

"Tal a Pakal'na," he chanted.

Power congregated around the stones, glowing first orange and then blue. Lines of energy erupted from the stones and collided in the center of the triangle they formed on the ground.

The lines diffused, and a figure formed. Soon it solidified and familiar shape of his controller back home. The other elf looked surprised.

"You contact again, on the same night—your guise! Why are you—"

"I was found." Fletch was not upset. His plan originally entailed him revealing his true self to the king. He could have killed the boy and taken his place. The invasion could have been masked with a quick takeover of the Realm.

"I knew you were careless."

"The girl child found me," Fletch said. "She is more intelligent than we would have thought. But I need to talk to you about the other one, the boy whose mind is broken."

"And who is he, really?"

Fletch smiled. "He is the one."

"The one?"

"Yes, the one. He is the best candidate for our needs."

"But he's a Spear."

"He's broken. We can use him." Fletch listened to the world around him and heard the footfalls of someone trying to be quiet. He raised his voice slightly. "He is the better fighter."

"A good fighter?" the phantom asked.

"Yes. He is the best out of the three. Fast and smart." Fletch recognized the footfalls that approached him. Bethany was very quiet, and did not breathe heavy when moving. No one could hear Thomasyn. He was stealth. It could only be Jon. The plan formed in his head immediately. He could do something that would cripple the morale of the Realm. He could make a Spear leave willingly.

It would not be easy. No, far from it. Each Spear, trained from early childhood, was indoctrinated into the life. It was a form of twisting the mind. It made them believe nothing else mattered. They wanted for nothing, and still did not take everything that was offered to them.

But Jon was broken. He had seen it with his own eyes. The man child continually talked to a voice in his head. He was quick to anger and recover.

"High praise."

Fletch nodded. "I want to see if he will join us. If not as a fighter, as a leader of our armies."

"You believe this highly in him?"

"My spirit tells me," Fletch said. "It is his soul that I see. The strength he has yet to show. His skill is beyond the others. You did not see how he fought. He mastered his opponent who was stronger than him by far." Fletch looked at his hand. The blood dripped from it. The wound would not stop bleeding. The use of magic drained him, took the life from him. He needed to finish this communication, but with Jon close by he also needed to be heard. If he went to Jon, the Spear could just think he was flattering him. But to have him overhear praise, that was something different than the constant nattering the others constantly subjected him to.

Fletch decided to drive home his plan before his strength was spent. "I would like the authority to offer something. To give the one I have chosen something to bring him to us."

The figure hesitated. "Are you sure?"

"Yes, I am sure. The other two, though good, are not of the same mettle as this one. He figured out how to use the strength of the brute against him. He is fast of mind and body. A true fighter, and I believe he could train our troops on the tactics needed to take back our home. The home that was taken from us." He motioned with his hand to the figure, telling him not to question what he was about to say. "The Spear is honorable. We could show him the secret tomes that show Capital was ours until man took it away from us. He would judge with honesty and see the validity of our claim. We could have our home back after all these years."

The figure nodded. "Then offer him what he wants. He could be the trainer of our armies and have the honor to allow us to have our home back again."

"I must break the spell. Look for my next report at the full moon." Fletch clenched his fist. The pressure stemmed the bleeding. The figure bowed and dissipated like smoke does in a light wind. "I must now speak to Jon."

"I am here," Jon said.

Fletch spun. His eyes opened to show surprise that he did not feel. "Jon!"

"Yes," he said, moving from the shadows. "Is it true?"

Fletch bent to pick up one of the stones. "I don't know what you are talking about."

"Don't be a fool," Jon said. "I heard what was said to the…ghost."

"It was no ghost," Fletch said. He kept the smile from his face, knowing the boy could be the biggest prize for his people. It would not take long for him to capture this child.

"Then what was it?" Jon asked.

"My king."

"Your king?"

Fletch allowed himself to smile. "Yes, my king. He is the one who makes the decisions. It is his word that I carry."

"And what is the word that you carry for your king?"

Fletch turned and picked up the last two stones and placed them into his pouch. He took a deep breath, wondering if what he was about to say would sink in for the young boy. He should take the chance; it would be a giant step. Could he succeed? If he won, that would be a victory worth talking about. It would be a victory that will have the king in debt to him.

His thoughts went to home, where he had not been for a number of years. Fletch imagined his wife's reaction when he returned ahead of schedule. Linetta, the child he left when she was but a new born, would be close to a young woman, not much older than Bethany. He wanted to see his family. He looked at Jon, and saw the question still hanging there between them. Something had to be said.

"The word is, you are needed," he said.

Jon's eyebrow arched upward.

A beam of light trespassed into the tent and caused Thomasyn to blink. He had overslept, and Bethany would tease him if she was up before him. He wondered how much of the day had passed.

His hands moved the blanket and pulled on clothes. He shivered. The air showed his breath. Dew would be ice outside and maybe, if they were lucky, the fire would still have embers.

"Thomasyn," Bethany called. "Quick. We have a problem."

"Get Jon to start a fire if you're having a hard time." He shook his head. Why did she think he was the only one who could start a fire?

Bethany's voice rang with a little more urgency. "Thomasyn! You need to get out here. Now!"

With an exasperated huff, Thomasyn pushed the flap aside and walked out into the bright mid-morning day. Dew crackled on the clover under his feet. He slipped but caught himself before he went down.

Bethany stood by the small fire pit, but the fire did not smolder for some reason. She only stared at the fire pit.

"What?" he asked, but as the word left his mouth he realized the truth. Only two tents remained in their camp.

Bethany turned to him, a tear threatening at the corner of her eye. "Jon and Fletch are gone."

Douglas Owen is a Canadian born writer of Science Fiction, Fantasy, and Fiction novels. He was born in Scarborough, Ontario and has since moved North to Stouffville.

Doug's writing career started with elaborate back stories for characters in role playing games and expended to what is now called Flash Fiction. He never thought much about extending his talent until later in life.

Douglas now creates works of fiction from flash stories, short stories, and full novels. His most surprising success is his young adult series, Spear, which is celebrated by readers of all ages. His short stories have enticed many and his flash fiction is a delight to his writers group.

With many projects on the go, Doug still finds time to run his writing seminar called "The First Draft" for aspiring writers in the GTA. He has also worked with young adults and coached them into creating amazing works of fiction, stories, and songs.

More information on Doug's upcoming events and upcoming releases please visit his website or Facebook page.

http://www.daowen.ca

https://www.facebook.com/pages/Douglas-Owen

Made in the USA
Charleston, SC
19 November 2014